VINDICATE

BETH YARNALL

VINDICATE

1

CORA

I got my driver's license on my sixteenth birthday so I could visit my brother in prison. California Institute for Men in Chino, California, sounds like one of those super-snooty colleges you have to be rich to get into or else be the next generation in a long line of alumni. But this is no college. Chino Men's, as it's referred to, is one of the most violent prisons in the state.

That's where they sent my brother to serve out his life sentence.

Five and a half years later, I've made the nearly two-hour trip from San Diego to Chino and back close to a hundred times. Four hours of driving to spend an hour—or more, if I'm lucky—with my brother. If I've gotten too late a start and visiting hours are over before my number is called or if Beau's visitation has been revoked because he's done something stupid, I don't get to see him at all.

I don't count those times.

"Seventy-three," one of the corrections officers intones.

I stand and give my number to the guard, like I'm in a deli about to order lunch or something.

"Name," he says.

"Cora Hollis."

"Inmate."

"Beau Hollis."

"Relationship."

"Sister." You'd think he'd recognize me by now. I've been here so many times. But every time he acts like it's my first visit and puts me through the same drill.

I've already been through the metal detector, searched, and patted down so thoroughly I'm questioning my sexuality. Another guard comes over to lead me to a room full of lockers where I stow my cellphone and car keys. Then I finally get to follow him to the visiting room, where Beau is already waiting for me.

Sometimes it takes me a moment to recognize him. He looks so unlike my brother. This bullshit prison has stolen more than years from Beau's life. It's robbed him of his dignity and anything resembling happiness.

I want to give him a hug, but that's not allowed. Instead, I drop into my seat opposite him. "I put twenty extra dollars in your commissary account this month."

Beau looks away, picking at the side of his thumb with his index finger. Even as a kid he always did this whenever he was agitated or annoyed. "I don't need it."

"I thought—"

His narrowed gaze swings back to me. It's his mean big-brother look, the one he always tries to intimidate me with. It didn't work when we were kids and it doesn't work now.

"I don't need a present," he says. "You need the money more."

"Yeah, well, I can't take it back out, so you're stuck with it. Happy birthday."

"Some fucking birthday."

"I'd have brought some pointy hats and balloons, but they wouldn't fit up my ass."

"Watch your fucking mouth." He's barely two years older than me, but he's always taken the job of big brother seriously. Even after all he's been through.

"You're a fantastic example," I tell him.

I mean it as a joke, but it falls flat as Beau's ever-roaming gaze takes in the room around us. Since being incarcerated, my once fun-loving prankster of a brother has turned into a suspicious, twitchy, hypervigilant, hardened prisoner. I don't dare comment on the fading bruise under his left eye or his freshly sheared hair. He always looked like he needed a haircut even after an appointment with the barber. But that was before.

Before he was arrested, then convicted for the brutal rape, sodomy, and murder of his ex-girlfriend Cassandra. Before our family was torn apart and life as we knew it changed forever. Before I watched, helpless, as my brother turned into someone I hardly recognize anymore.

"Yeah, I'm not exactly winning Best Big Brother of the Year this year or any year, am I?"

I hate it when he puts himself down. "You're at the top, as far as I'm concerned."

He makes a rude noise, but doesn't comment.

"Did you get my card?" I ask.

"I got it. Thanks. How's school going?"

"I'm taking a really great online class this summer." I never got around to telling him that I quit school last year to work and save money for a possible appeal of his case. Or that the job I took is in a law office, where I have ample access to the law library and case reviews.

"It's not on something stupid like criminal law or how to be a private investigator, is it?"

I shift in my seat.

"Aww, shit, Cora. You promised you'd give up on the stupid idea that you could get me out of here. Why are you wasting your time? I'm a lost cause. Everyone knows it. Take those beauty classes like you always wanted. Face the fact that you can't do what Mom's and Dad's lawyers and the public defender couldn't. I'm done. You're not. You still have a life."

"I don't believe that, Beau, and neither should you. Those charges were bullshit then and they're bullshit now. You didn't kill her. There's no way I'll ever believe it and I'm never going to stop looking for a way to get you out of here."

"Doesn't really matter if I did it or not. I'm convicted, aren't I?"

"I wasn't going to tell you this because I knew what you'd say, but I think I might have a new lead."

He holds up a hand. "Stop it. Stop it, right now."

I ignore him and continue. "I think I found a witness who could—"

"Damn it, Cora! I told you to stop."

His outburst has a couple of the guards coming off the wall where they've been leaning and looking at him hard. Beau waves them back and takes a deep breath, scrubbing his hands over his face.

"My life is ruined," he finally says. I hate it when he talks like this. I refuse to believe that he'll never get out of here. I refuse to believe that the criminal justice system that failed him won't ever redeem itself by righting its wrong and setting him free.

"Your life isn't," he continues. "I don't want any more of this to touch you. For fuck's sake, let it go." He leans across the table at me. His look and tone turn threatening. "Let it go." Then he gets up from the table and heads for the door that will take him back to his cell, ending our visit.

"Happy birthday!" I call after him. "I love you!"

He doesn't respond or acknowledge me in any way. His mind is already back on the cell block. I've screwed up this visit and his birthday. I have to find a way to make it up to him, but I know nothing short of getting him out of this hellhole will make it right.

As I stand to leave, I wonder why I bother with these visits. He never seems to enjoy them, is never glad to see me. If anything, he appears to be annoyed and inconvenienced by my visits. He's given up on himself just as our mother, then our father, gave up on him. Maybe, I think, as I burst out of the prison and into the blazing mid-afternoon sun, I keep up the visits to give us both something we haven't had in a long, long time—hope.

But hope is a dangerous thing to court when there's nothing to support it. Sometimes it almost feels as if I'm tipping headfirst into a kind of vicious insanity where I keep doing the same things over and over, expecting different results. It's no way to live, but it's my life. And it's Beau's until I can figure out a way to get him out of here.

I climb into my car and curse its lack of air-conditioning. I have the money to fix it, but it's not my money—it's Beau's. So I roll down the windows and crank up the radio over the sound of the wind and head for home.

Some NPR talking head begins the hour with one of those feel-good stories that people like to repost over and over on social media. About how there really is good in the world and good in people. But with the prison behind me, and a long, hot drive ahead of me, I'm finding it hard to believe there's anything good or just here or anywhere else in the world.

Something the host says has me cranking up the sound on my crappy radio as high as it will go.

"—your work with The Freedom Project led to the release of Maurice Battle after he spent nearly forty years in prison for a crime he didn't commit."

I jerk the wheel and skid to a stop on the shoulder. A cloud of dust comes up around the car and into my rolled-down windows. I cough, scrambling for the notebook I always keep in my bag, as the man being interviewed answers.

"Our agency takes on one pro bono case per year. We devoted as much time, energy, and effort toward this case as we do all of our cases. We're thrilled that our work led to the exoneration of Mr. Battle."

"What agency?" I scream at the radio, my pen poised to write it down.

They talk a little bit more about the case and the evidence the agency found that made all the difference, and I feel like I was meant to hear this story. That my fight with my brother was part of a grander scheme that put me in my car at the exact moment when the information I needed to help Beau would be handed to me.

The story is winding down and I still don't know who this magician is who freed a wrongfully convicted man. A truck honks at me just as the host is thanking his guest and I catch only the last part of his sentence before they cut to the next segment.

"—Nash Security and Investigation."

"What city? Where?" I yell at the radio as the commercial starts. Something about getting lower insurance rates that I couldn't give two shits about.

Nash Security and Investigation. I'm thankful to have that much, at least, as I grab my cellphone to test my

Google-fu and see if I can figure out where in the U.S. this Nash agency is. But I'm in the middle of the godforsaken California desert and there's no service.

I stuff my phone into my bag and pull back out onto the freeway, thinking about what I just learned. I never look for signs or believe in fate or angels or anything I can't touch, taste, see, smell, or hear, but I can't ignore the feeling deep in the pit of my stomach that I'm onto something big here. That finally there might be someone who can help me help Beau.

2

LEO

The phone hasn't stopped ringing since my dad was interviewed on NPR. Mostly it's a lot of people wanting to get out of traffic tickets, child support, and probation. An occasional sob story gets thrown in the mix now and then, and I can see dad wanting to help, but the fact is he can't pay Savannah, Al, Jerry, himself, and me if every case he takes on we do for free.

Not that I get paid much. I'm supposed to be learning the business from the ground up so I can take over when Dad retires. This means coffee runs, filing, trash duty, and the occasional fast-food pickup. Only dad hasn't taken the hint that I'm not going to law school just so I can stake out cheating spouses and fraudulent disability claims.

When my dad starting doing Freedom Project cases four years ago I didn't think about how or why people got convicted. And then I noticed that the bulk of wrongful convictions were because of official misconduct—police, prosecutors, and other officials abusing their authority just to clear a case. I know I could do more working for the district attorney's office than I could ever do working on only one case a year here at Nash Security and Investigation. Unfortunately, this means that Dad's dream of his son taking over the business like he did from his father just isn't going to happen.

But right now it's the start of the summer and I don't have fuck all to do for the next couple months except be the office gofer and save my measly paychecks for the coming school year. Only one more year of school and then I'll be applying for jobs that will take me out of San Diego and out of the running for the new head of Nash Security and Investigation.

Savannah has the radio on because she's hoping to catch a rerun of Dad's interview. I've already heard it and the recording of it that Dad played for Mom, so I've got my earbuds in, listening to Jay-Z uh, uh, uh his way through a song while trying to figure out if I should file The Viking Group's file under T for The or V for Viking. The door opens. I know this because of the draft that comes in and the sunlight beam that runs along the carpet next to where I'm standing.

The door is open longer than necessary for just one person to walk in, and that's what makes me turn around. My first thought about the chick coming through the door, hefting one of those tax boxes with the lids, is that she's got to be in the wrong place. She doesn't look like a delivery girl and she's definitely not someone Dad would hire. But she is, without a doubt, absolutely, the most bangable girl I've seen in a long time. Too long.

I adjust my stance by the file cabinet for a better view without seeming obvious about it and jerk on the cords of my earbuds so they pop out of my ears. I want to hear what this girl has to say and what her explanation is about the box.

"Can I help you?" Savannah asks the girl.

Savannah's a couple years older than me and I made the mistake last summer of sleeping with her a few times. She wants a repeat this summer, but I've kept my options open. And now, seeing the chick with the box, I'm glad I did.

"I'm here to see Ed Nash," the girl says, as she flips her blue-and-black streaked hair out of her eyes.

It's the same blue, I notice, as her eyes. Which is weird because the blue is not an ordinary blue and I don't normally notice a girl's eyes. Tits and ass, yes. Legs, maybe. Eyes, no. And now I'm letting my lecherous gaze wander from those startling blue eyes to the rest of her, which is just as extraordinary.

"What's your name?" Savannah asks.

"Cora Hollis."

Cora catches me staring as Savannah lowers her head to look at Dad's appointment book. Cora's gaze takes the same slow route down, then up my body as mine had done hers. When she finishes I'm half hard and trying not to grin at her smirk. She liked what she saw every bit as much as I liked what I saw. I close the drawer of the file cabinet and lean against it.

"I don't have you on the books," Savannah says, her tone set to bitch.

"I don't have an appointment," Cora replies, her attention off me and on Savannah. "Do I need an appointment?"

"What's this about?"

"I was hoping Mr. Nash would take a look at my brother's case—"

Savannah puts up a hand, interrupting. "You need an appointment to see Mr. Nash to hire him for a case." Savannah clicks around on her computer and I can see over her shoulder that she's jumped ahead a few weeks on my dad's appointment book, past lots of open spots. "His next available appointment is July twenty-third at two o'clock."

Such bullshit. Savannah must have caught the once-over Cora gave me.

Cora drops the box on the edge of Savannah's desk like it's heavy. The way it thunks against the faux-wood laminate, it sounds heavy. "My brother can't wait a month. I'm here now." Cora smacks the flat of her hand on the top of the box. "And I've brought all of my files. Is Mr. Nash here or not?"

I can see this is going to get ugly, so I slip into Dad's office. He's scrolling through a report on his computer.

"Dad?"

"Yeah?" he answers, without turning around.

"Savannah's trying to scare off a client."

He turns and blinks up at me over his reading glasses. "Did I forget about an appointment?"

"No. This girl doesn't have an appointment, but shouldn't you at least talk to her? Could be an interesting case."

My father chews this over for a moment. He loves interesting cases, but he loves interesting paying cases more, and I have a feeling that Cora Hollis is going to be the former, not the later.

"You want to sit in on it with me? See how it's done?"

Up until now I've managed to find an excuse to be anywhere but where I might learn how anything in this office is done. I shrug a shoulder, trying to hide how glad I am that I get to find out what Cora's deal is. "Sure."

He tosses aside his glasses and runs a hand over the three hairs he combs back to hide his bald spot. "Show her in, then."

I arrive back at the reception area just in time. Cora's leaning across her box, pointing a finger in Savannah's face.

Savannah hates that shit more than she hates being stood up, which I did to her last night. This is why she's been such a bitch all day and giving Cora a hard time for no reason.

I finally understand the phrase "Don't shit where you eat."

"Mr. Nash has time for you now," I say, moving to pick up Cora's box.

She jerks it away before I can get a hand on it. "Thanks," she says. "I've got it."

"Are you sure? It looks heavy." I can feel Savannah glaring at me like a hot laser on the side of my face.

"I just carried it up a flight of stairs," Cora says. "I think I can manage another few feet."

I gesture for her to precede me. As she passes I get a whiff of something spicy. My thoughts immediately go into the gutter and my gaze fixes on her ass as I follow her into Dad's office. I've got to find out what this chick's story is. Does she have a boyfriend? Does she live close by? Can I get her number?

As I close the door to Dad's office, I catch Savannah flipping me off. Shit. She caught me checking out Cora. I really screwed up with Savannah. She's nice and all, but I'm not looking to hook up permanently, which was all she talked about when I wasn't drilling her into the mattress. I'm such an asshole sometimes I can't believe any chick would want to have anything to do with me half the time.

I've got to find a way to fix things with Savannah. Or this summer is going to be a living hell.

"Cora Hollis," I begin the introductions. "This is Ed Nash. And I'm Leo. Leo Nash. Dad, Cora Hollis."

Dad comes around his desk to try and take Cora's box for her, but she won't let him. I like her independence. I like a whole hell of a lot about her.

She sets the box next to one of the chairs and holds her hand out to my dad. "Thank you for seeing me without an appointment."

"My pleasure. Please, have a seat."

She takes the one closest to the door, next to where she put her box, and I take the one on the other side. I can look at her now without seeming like a big giant creep. It's like my senses have gone supersonic where she's concerned. I take in everything about her. Like her nails, which are long and painted that same vivid blue—Cora blue—all except for her pinkies. Those she's chewed to nubs. She dresses like she couldn't care less what people think of her. I respect that. There's something about her that's lost, but she acts as though she knows exactly where she's going. And she doesn't seem to give a shit about me, which makes me like her even more.

"What can I do for you, Ms. Hollis?" Dad asks.

"I understand your agency does pro bono work for The Freedom Project," Cora begins. "My brother, Beau, was falsely convicted of the rape and murder of his ex-girlfriend five and a half years ago. He's serving a life sentence without the possibility of parole."

"I'm sorry," Dad says, and I want to kick him under the desk, "but we've already taken on our one case for the year. If you come back in December—"

She pops out of her seat, her hands out in front of her, pleading. She's suddenly vibrating with anger, frustration, desperation, or maybe a mixture of all three. I can't stop staring at her. She rivets me. She's like one of those warrior women, going into battle. I imagine her with a shield and a cape that flaps out behind her.

"Every day my brother sits in prison is another day he could be killed." Her voice cracks on the last word. "He's survived two thousand seventeen such days already, including today. I've spent every single one of those days working to get him free." She folds her hands over her heart. "Please reconsider. I'll pay you what I can. I have some money. I'll even help with legwork or whatever." She gestures to the box on the floor, the one I've been curious about from the moment I saw her with it. "I've brought all my work with me. Please. I need your help."

She doesn't look like she wants or needs anyone's help, but here she is, standing in the middle of my dad's office, demanding it. I switch my attention to Dad, who seems just as struck by her intensity as I am. I can see him wavering. But he can't afford to take on another charity case.

"He's only twenty-three," she says. "Maurice Battle sat in prison, convicted for a crime he didn't commit, for thirty-nine years. He was nineteen when he went in and fifty-eight when he finally came out. I don't want that for my brother. Please."

"I could help." Both of their heads swivel in my direction. I didn't realize I'd opened my mouth, but now that the words are out I'm not sorry I said them. "With your guidance," I add lamely.

Dad considers me for a moment. I can see the wheels turning in his head. He's thinking that this might be the way he gets me to finally agree to take over the agency. He looks at Cora, who's staring at me like I just ruined her moment, like she can't believe what a dumbass I am. I can't blame her. I am a dumbass. This is a stupid idea. I've just put the noose around my own neck. But I don't really care about me right now.

I look up into her face, into those electric-blue eyes, and I want to be her hero. I want to go through that box with her, follow leads, and do other investigative-type stuff. I want to find the clue that will set her brother free.

"That could work," Dad says. "I can offer Leo to you for the summer free of charge or you can come back in December and apply for our help then. What do you think, Ms. Hollis?"

"Does he have any experience other than filing?"

Ouch. But she's not wrong. I have shit for experience, but I've been hanging around the agency since I was in diapers. Something had to have rubbed off, right?

"He's in training," Dad hedges, and I want to thank him, but that would give everything away. "I have another appointment in"—he checks his watch—"twenty minutes and I need to finish making notes for my report to the client. We could meet tomorrow morning and go over your brother's case. I can help Leo form a game plan. And we'll go from there."

She's glaring at me with those deep, penetrating eyes and I can't tell if she loathes me or if she's trying to resign herself to this strange turn of events. She's won her battle, but it's not the victory she wanted. I'm a pale imitation of my father. She knows it and I know it. What she doesn't know is that I'll work my ass off for her.

Turning back to my dad, she nods once. "Okay. But I have a condition."

She's not exactly in a place to put on conditions. So damn ballsy.

"A condition?" Dad asks.

"We work together. You train me while you train him."

My dad offers her his hand. "Deal."

3

CORA

While I was in Nash's office I calculated that I have just enough money to pay my rent, eat, and put gas in my car—if I'm careful—for about three months. It will take all of my savings, but I can do it. I'm taking a huge risk that:

a)this guy Leo actually has had some training in private investigation.

b)Mr. Nash will teach me enough that if at the end of the summer we haven't been successful, then at least I'll have learned something I can use to help Beau.

c)We find some kind of lead that will eventually go somewhere.

Those are big risks.

And now here I am on a leave of absence from my job and about to put Beau's life in the hands of the owner's kid, who looks like one of those loser skater dudes who make just enough money to cover skate-park fees and buy new trucks for their board once in a while (if they can't get their parents to buy them). I have to make sure his dad is as involved as possible and that he teaches me everything he knows before the summer is over and skater dude goes back to whatever it is he does the rest of the year.

Balancing my box on my hip, I open the door to the office the second I hear the click of the door being unlocked. The box is damn heavy, but it holds everything I collected on Beau's case, including a possible lead on a new witness. I accidentally bump that blond bitch who wouldn't let me in to see Mr. Nash yesterday and she lets out a yelp. I guess she wasn't expecting the door to open or else she wouldn't have still been standing so close to it.

"Sorry," I say, as I close the door behind me. "I didn't know you were there."

And then my gaze tracks to the reason she was so distracted. Leo's standing near the file cabinet again, just the way he was the day before. It's like Groundhog Day and I'm caught up all over again in whatever drama is playing out between Leo and the receptionist. The way she looks at him —a combination of lust and loathing—makes me want to laugh. Except I kind of know how she feels.

Leo doesn't ask me if I need help. Not that I'd take it. I'm very protective of my box. He just stands there like he's posing for a camera or waiting for a bus, his gaze latched on to my chest like he's seeing his first set of tits. I wonder for the millionth time if I'm doing the right thing here or if this is just a colossal waste of time.

"Why are you here?" Blondie asks. Her hostility toward me is completely baseless. Skater dude can leer at me all day, for all I care. I'm here for my brother. End. Of. Story.

Leo peels himself off the file cabinet and swaggers toward me. "We're working together on a case."

Reception lady gives me the once-over, one side of her upper lip lifting like she smells something bad. "A charity case?"

If I wasn't holding this box . . .

"Knock it off, Savannah. She's a client . . . and also kind of a temporary employee."

Savannah's as pretty as her name, even when she's being a bitch toward me. She really needs to get over her whatever with Leo and move on to bigger and better things. Like a guy with a real job, a real haircut, and real aspirations.

"I'm only here to help my brother," I tell Savannah, trying to make it clear that I have no intention of horning in on her territory. "Mr. Nash has agreed to go over his case and train me to be a private investigator."

"Call me Ed." Mr. Nash stands in the doorway of his office with a mug of coffee in his hand.

I didn't notice him. From the way Savannah immediately tries to look busy, I'm guessing she didn't either. Leo looks like he couldn't give a shit. Typical boss's kid who gets everything handed to him.

Mr. Nash (I just can't call him Ed) waves me into the office next door to his. "Come on in and let's get started. Leo . . ." He motions with his head for his son to follow.

We all shuffle into an office with a conference table that's too big for the room. Mr. Nash stands behind a chair and waits for me to put my box down and sit. What a gentleman. His son takes the seat across from me before my butt hits the chair. Since he clearly hasn't learned any manners from his father, I hope to hell he's at least learned something about private investigation.

"Can I offer you some coffee?" Mr. Nash asks me.

"No, thanks. I don't drink coffee."

Leo looks at me like he can't believe I'm for real. Whatever.

Mr. Nash takes his seat. "Tell me about your brother's case."

I reach into my box and pull out the binder where I've recorded the timeline of Cassandra's murder. I have a page devoted to each witness; each of the cops who were involved, from the first responder to the detectives who arrested Beau; the prosecutors; the medical examiner . . . Anyone who was involved in the case is in my binder. I have copies of reports, news articles, blog posts, etc., in my box, but I'll save those for when I come to them.

I start the story, from the last time anyone saw Cassandra alive to Beau's last appeal, pulling out my backup information and the expert reports as I come to them. By the time I've finished, I've nearly covered the table with paper and my box is empty.

As I drop back into my seat, I take a long pull off the bottle of water Leo got for me about halfway through. I'm exhausted yet energized. My brother's story has lit a fire in Mr. Nash's eyes, and Leo—much to my surprise—has not only filled a notebook full of notes, he asked some really intelligent and relevant questions that I could tell also impressed his father. Maybe he's not going to be as useless to me as I thought.

"And your brother?" Leo asks. "Will he talk to us about the case?"

"No. He's . . . resigned to his fate." I'm afraid to tell them that Beau's given up. No, I'm terrified to admit it, because his defeatist attitude could be seen as an admission of guilt.

Mr. Nash flips through my notebook to Cassandra's page. He studies the profile I created on her. It's not as complete as I'd like it to be. None of her friends or relatives were eager to talk to the sister of her accused murderer. I don't blame them, but it's made my work harder and I can't help the tiny seed of resentment I have against them. Even with those omissions, my profile on Cassandra is pretty good. I had to think outside the box since I'd made the mistake of approaching her friends and family as myself instead of pretending I was a journalist or a kid doing a report for school or something. Learning that lesson early helped me create more rounded profiles for the other people connected to the case.

Leo picks up the copy of the coroner's report. It's gruesome. The photos . . . the description of Cassandra's wounds and what was done to her . . . horrific. I looked at it only once. Halfway through the photos I bolted to the bathroom to vomit. I got to know Cassandra pretty well during the time she and Beau dated. I liked her. I liked her a lot. Seeing her like that . . . I still have nightmares. She comes to me in dreams sometimes and she begs me to help her, begs me to make "him" stop hurting her. I wake up screaming, coated in sweat.

"How did you get this?" Leo asks.

"If I told you, I'd have to kill you," I joke.

That report was not easy to get. The San Diego coroner's office has a brilliant firewall. But not as brilliant as my friend Jamie. I had to promise to do her hair for a whole year in order to get that file. She loves the way I cut her hair even though I've never taken a class and don't have a license to do hair. Someday, when my brother's free, I'll go to beauty school. Until then, my little side haircuts and colors help to finance a lot of the work I do on Beau's case.

Leo's eyebrows jump up on his forehead. "You're a hacker?"

"Not me," I hedge. "I've managed to find ways in and around the system to get a lot of this." I make a sweeping gesture, indicating all of the papers spread across the table. "I learned quite a bit about investigating in the last five years."

"Impressive," Mr. Nash finally says.

Up until now he's been quiet, listening and jotting down notes. His compliment makes my cheeks burn and I stare at my hands in my lap. I don't get many compliments. Not because I'm unworthy of them, but because the people who would give them—like my parents or Beau—are too caught up in their own grief and suffering to notice if I've done anything at all.

"How long have you been working on this?" Mr. Nash asks.

"Pretty much since the day my brother was convicted."

"You believe that strongly in his innocence?"

"Yes," I say, my gaze rising to meet his. "He's as innocent as I am. As innocent as you and your son. Beau loved Cassandra. They were getting back together when she was killed. That's why his DNA was found on her body. He didn't do this and I won't give up until he's freed."

"Okay," he says with a nod, and some of the tension runs out of me. I finally have the help I need. I want to jump up and down and go to my brother and shake him into believing in himself again. Beau now has a champion in this middle-aged man with tired eyes, graying hair, and a jelly doughnut stain on his tie.

"You've done a lot of the work for us," Mr. Nash says. "Tell me about this witness that was never interviewed by the police."

I catch Leo watching me. He has this look on his face like he's impressed. And I realize that he hasn't so much as glanced at my tits since I took my notebook out and started turning its pages. Maybe he's not the total-loser asshole I thought he was.

"She was Cassandra's downstairs neighbor at the time of the murder. She's an elderly lady confined to a hospital bed for the past ten years." I open my folder containing the photos I took of Cassandra's apartment building and point to a lower window. "Anyone taking the stairs to Cassandra's apartment would have to walk past her bedroom window. At the very least she can verify that my brother wasn't there. A few years ago she moved and I haven't been able to find her."

"She could be dead. I wonder why the police never questioned her."

"If she is there's no record of a death certificate on file. There's a note in one of the reports that the detectives made a couple of efforts to contact her, but were unsuccessful. She's confined to a bed," I scoff. "Where's she going to go?"

Mr. Nash nods. "Could be lazy police work. After all, they had your brother's DNA and an eyewitness who saw him leaving Cassandra's apartment. Why go out of their way to find another witness? Or there could've been a cover-up."

I lean over and flip through the pages of my notebook until I find the one I created for the eyewitness. "Damien LeFeaux. He's got several arrests for possession and three for dealing. He's a big, fat meth head. He testified in my brother's case and somehow escaped California's three-strikes law. Of course, he's such a freakin' idiot that he got arrested again for possession and is serving twenty years in Donovan. I guess he didn't witness any new crimes to get out of that one."

"I'd like to talk to him," Leo says.

"That might be a job better suited for me," Mr. Nash cuts in. "I have a connection at Donovan. We're going to have to tread very lightly with Mr. LeFeaux." He turns a few more pages. "I'm not joking here, Cora. This is some of the finest, most thorough investigative work I've ever seen. You're organized and resourceful. If you're ever interested in a career in private investigation, I'd hire you in a minute."

I lower my head and nod. My cheeks are on fire, my heart is thumping hard, and I don't know where to look. "I'll keep that in mind."

"Where do we start?" Leo asks.

"We start at the beginning." Mr. Nash flips back to the first page of my notebook. Cassandra's page. I used a photo Beau had taken of her. She's smiling at him and you can see how much she loved him.

"We start with the victim, Cassandra Bethany Williams."

4
LEO

My dad isn't easily impressed. He's certainly never been as enthralled with anything I've ever done as he is with Cora and the work she did on her brother's behalf. I should be jealous or ashamed, but I'm not. Cora is damn impressive. When I think about her—which has been pretty much every waking moment since I laid eyes on her—I imagine what life has been like for her since her brother went to prison. I try to picture myself putting my life on hold to help one of my sisters, but I can't. That realization does shame me. I wouldn't have done what she has. Not many people would.

Glancing over the papers strewn across the table after she unloaded her box, I realize I'm totally fucked. Luckily my dad helped us map out a plan and now it's up to me to captain this investigation. I'm in way over my head. Cora is looking at me like she expects me to either come up with something brilliant or fall on my ass. I will not fail her. I won't. This isn't at all the way I pictured my summer, but now, looking into her take-no-bullshit stare, I can't remember any of the plans I made. I've fallen headfirst into her life, inserting myself into it like I had a right to be there. She challenges me on that every time I dare to meet her gaze.

"Tell me about Cassandra," I say.

She pulls her binder toward her. It's meticulous. I mean that in the most sincere way possible. It's a work of art. She took the tiniest pieces she could find and fashioned them into something that is organized, informative, and flat-out fucking brilliant. I can see the case the way she sees it. She laid it all out for anyone who would care to look. But I don't need her to tell me what's in it. I need her to tell me what's not in it. I need to know what can't be put down on paper— her impressions, her feelings, her, I don't know, . . . intuition.

She opens the binder to the first page—Cassandra's page. For a split second I can see the grief on her face and then in the next blink it's gone and her usual don't-fuck-with-me expression is back.

"What do you want to know?"

"Tell me how she and Beau met. What was their relationship like? What did you think of her?"

"They were both juniors in high school when Beau asked her to prom. It was their first date. They were insepa-rable after that. She was his first serious girlfriend. I don't know if he was hers or not. She came over to our house a lot, so I got to know her pretty well. Some of his friends were real assholes to me, but she wasn't. She treated me like a sister. Even let me borrow her clothes sometimes."

She loves Cassandra. I can hear it in her voice, but I don't think it's an old love. I think it's a love that grew from necessary familiarity through the case and with Cassandra being a victim in this just like her brother.

"Why did she and Beau break up?"

"I'm not really sure." Her gaze slides away to the photo of Cassandra.

"Beau never said?"

"No."

"How long were they broken up?"

"Two months. Maybe a little longer. Cassandra was getting ready to go to UC San Diego. Beau was supposed to go to Santa Barbara. I don't know if they broke up because they thought they had to because of the distance or if it was . . . something else."

She rubs her thumb over Cassandra's hair. She's far away, somewhere in her head. I want to reach across the table and take the hand that can't stop touching the photo of a dead woman. Instead, I stand and move around to her side of the table. She glances at me as though I materialized into the chair next to her by magic. I pull the binder away from her and try to see what she sees when she looks at the photo. All I see is a pretty young woman with brown hair and brown eyes. I have no emotional attachment to this person, but I can tell by the expression on her face that she was happy. And in love.

"Did Beau take this?"

"Yeah." She's uneasy letting me touch her binder. She puts a hand out as if to take it back and then pulls the gesture, tucking a blue strand of hair behind her ear. Earrings stud her ear from bottom to top. That blue again. Cora blue.

I stroke my thumb over the pic just the way she did. I want to know Cassandra. I want to know what it's like to have a chick look at me like Cassandra's looking at Beau. I want Cora to look at me like that just once. That's a stupid, fucked-up, selfish thing to think, but I can hardly think of anything I want more.

"Why do you think they broke up?" I have to know. How could they go from this picture to . . . nothing? Beau must've hated not seeing that look on Cassandra's face anymore. I know I would.

"I think . . ." She stares down at the photo as though she doesn't want to betray a woman who wouldn't even know it if she did. "I think Cassandra met someone else." Not just Cassandra. Cora's admission betrays Beau, too, because it gives him a motive to kill.

"What makes you think that?"

"I overheard part of a conversation Beau had on the phone with her a couple weeks after she stopped coming over. Beau locked himself in his room every day when he was at home, so I knew something was up. Then one day I heard shouting, so I put my ear to his door. I heard Beau ask her how many times and then he asked her why she was just telling him this now. He was very, very angry with her."

Whoa. "What do you think he was talking about?"

"I don't know. That's all I heard."

"Did you ever ask Beau about that conversation?"

"He wouldn't talk about it then or now. He gets mad all over again when I mention it. I didn't find anything that might answer your questions in my investigation. But then my notes on her aren't as complete as they could be."

I nod. We're going to have to find a way to get in with Cassandra's group of friends and family. That isn't going to be easy. We can't come at them with the truth.

Cora takes a long drink of water. I watch her throat move and the way her lips press against the mouth of the water bottle. She drains it and replaces the cap, looking at it like she doesn't know what to do with it. I take it from her and toss it behind us. She gapes at me like I've just committed some horrible crime. I like surprising her. She doesn't seem like someone who's easily shocked.

"I'll get it later," I tell her.

She taps her nails on the table once, twice, and then looks at the bottle.

"I'll get it," I say again.

The expression on her face as she turns back around makes me laugh.

"No, really. I will."

A corner of her lip tugs up. "Uh-huh."

"Are we having our first fight?"

"Something tells me we're going to have lots of fights before the summer's over."

"As long as we make up."

I took it too far. The almost smile fades and she takes in a breath like you do when you're about to deliver bad news.

"It was just a joke," I cut in, before she can say anything.

I don't like the rejection in her eyes. I want the almost-smile back. I want to make it grow into something real that creases her cheeks. But I have a feeling it's been a long time since she's allowed herself to smile with any real happiness. Too damn long. I don't feel sorry for her though. You can't look at her and feel pity. That's not one of the emotions she provokes in me or from the world in general. There's pride there—so much pride—and determination. She's stubborn, but it's the kind of obstinacy that draws you in and makes you want to be a part of whatever she's involved in.

That's exactly why I'm sitting in this chair next to her, silently vowing to be her knight in this battle she's waging. And why I gave up whatever fuck-around things I was going to do this summer to do the one thing I swore I'd never do— become a private investigator, if only temporarily.

"What did Cassandra do after she and Beau broke up?" I

have to get her mind back on the case. That's the only way I'm going to win with her. "Did she have a job?"

"She worked at a clothes store in the mall. But that was years ago. I doubt anyone would still be working there who knew Cassandra."

"We can try."

"Yeah, okay. I guess."

"I think I should talk to Beau. Alone."

"He doesn't talk about Cassandra."

"Not to you, but he might talk to me."

She thinks this over with flickers of hurt flashing across her features like lightning across the sky. It had to have occurred to her that her brother wouldn't want to talk about his love life with his little sister. I sure as hell wouldn't. I don't want my sisters to know anything about sex, especially since the youngest one just got her first boyfriend.

"Maybe," she relents. "But you have to tell me what he says."

"I can't make that promise."

"Why the hell not?"

"He's not going to confide in me if he thinks I'll take everything he says straight to you."

"If you can get him to talk."

"Challenge accepted."

"This isn't a game. This is my brother's life."

And hers too. Both siblings have a lot at stake here. Neither one of them has had a life since Beau's conviction. Even though Beau's the one in prison, Cora built and maintains a wall that blocks her off from the rest of the world. Beau's the convict, but they're both doing time.

"We're going to figure this out," I say, wanting more than anything to touch her. "Trust me."

She doesn't really have a choice, but I feel like I have to

ask for her trust or she won't completely give it. I have to want it and I have to show her I want and deserve it.

She lets out a laugh like she can't believe what she's about to say. I hold my breath because I don't think I'll be able to either.

"Okay." She doesn't add the part about her not having any other choice but to trust me.

I won't forget that.

5

CORA

Leo wants more than my trust. He wants to invade parts of my life where no one's ever been. I've been alone with my notes and my reports and my never-wavering faith in my brother. But now he's here, taking up too much space in the room and asking questions that make me look at my brother's case the way someone who hasn't lived it and breathed it would. I can see the holes. In just a few short hours Leo exposed the cracks in the case that make Beau look guilty.

I know Beau's been hiding something from me and everyone else, including his attorney. It's one of the reasons he doesn't want me investigating his case. I get so angry with him sometimes. He sits across from me at that dirty, scarred table, looks me right in the face, and talks about stupid shit instead of giving up his secrets. It's the talking but not saying anything that frustrates the hell out of me. It's the beatings he'd rather take, the obliteration of our family, and the blithe acceptance of his fate that I can't stand. It jolts me out of a sound sleep. It keeps me awake at night. And it rides my shoulders all day.

And now Leo thinks he can get my brother to open up and fill in those gaps? As if one quick trip out to the prison will clear everything up. I've got five and a half years of prison visits behind me and not a goddamned thing to show for it. But Leo is going to fix all that. Right.

He asks me to trust him and the stupid, messed-up thing is—I do.

He's been flipping the pages of my notebook back and forth for nearly an hour now, taking notes. Every once in a while he asks a question or asks me to find a report for him. So far I've been able to answer every question except why Beau and Cassandra broke up and why—after months apart —he went to her apartment the night before she was murdered.

"Who found Cassandra's body?" Leo asks.

He's been poring over the paperwork on the table for hours and it's making me twitchy. I want to get out there and do something.

"Her neighbor across the hall. They were supposed to go to a yoga class after work." I flip through the binder of copies of the police reports I got from Leo's attorney until I find the right page. "Here." I point to the entry by an Officer Hannigan. "Zelda Marks. She said she knocked on Cassandra's door and got no answer. So she called. Again no answer. Cassandra's car was parked on the street, so she knew Cassandra was home. Zelda used the key Cassandra gave her to feed her cat when she went on vacation and found Cassandra's body in the bedroom tied to the bed." I grab a folder and open it. "Here's the nine-one-one transcript of Zelda's phone call at six-thirty-two p.m."

The transcript doesn't even come close to the agony in the recording. The horror in Zelda's voice of finding her friend's naked, bound body echoed around the courtroom as they played the recording during Beau's trial, while Zelda broke down on the stand, reliving that moment.

"I have a recording of the call." I pull a disc from a sleeve between the pages and hand it to him.

"Hang on." He leaves and comes back in the room with a CD player.

I push back from the table. "Where's the restroom?"

He glances up at me as the disc begins to spin. "Take a right past Savannah's desk. Second door on the left."

"Nine-one-one. What is your emergency?"

I'm out the door before I can hear Zelda's reply. I don't need to hear it. I've got it memorized. Savannah isn't at her desk and I let out a sigh of relief. Maybe she went to lunch.

No such luck. I run into her as I round the corner, bouncing off her and back a step.

"Watch where you're going." She knocks my arm with her purse as she passes.

I whorl around and follow her. This is going to be a long, tedious three months if I have to constantly put up with Savannah's bullshit jealousy.

I plant a palm on her desk as she drops her purse into the bottom drawer. "I don't know what I did to piss you off, but if you bump me like that again you're going to find yourself on your ass."

She rises to her full height, which is half a foot taller than me. She doesn't scare me. I've been up against worst bullies than her. Having a convicted murderer for a brother opened me up to anyone who wanted to take a shot. I know how to throw a punch and how to take one.

"I don't like you."

"Like I give a shit."

She crosses her arms over her chest and the advantage shifts to me. I can hit her before she can free a hand to block it.

"Whatever you think is going on or going to go on between Leo and me—isn't," I say. "He's all yours. The only thing I want from him is his father's help."

She makes a rude noise and echoes my earlier statement. "Like I give a shit."

"Look, I'm not going anywhere, so unless you plan on quitting this job in the next five minutes, we're stuck with each other for the summer. It's up to you how you want that to go down."

Her gaze flickers to the doorway of the conference room. I follow her line of sight. Leo is leaning against the door frame, his hands tucked into his front pockets, looking way too satisfied with himself. He thinks we're fighting over him. What an ass. I head for the bathroom and away from his smug face.

I close myself in the restroom. Savannah and Leo's voices come through the thin wall. She's giving him an earful about broken promises and how he just fucked her because he was bored. Ouch. No wonder Savannah's carrying a grudge the size of Nebraska toward me. She's got it bad for Leo. I can totally see why. He's hot. Not my type at all, but hot just the same. The two of them make an impressive couple.

I finish my business and wash my hands, but the two of them are still going at it. Leo is apologizing and she's having none of it. He tries to placate her by telling her he's not good enough for her. He's got that right. She deserves way better than him. He tells her that it was fun, but it was just a fling. Oh, jeez, this guy's such an idiot. That's just what every girl wants to hear—she didn't mean anything, she was an itch he scratched and nothing more.

Savannah is crying. I can hear it in her voice. The way it wobbles rips at me. Why is she wasting her tears on this guy? She can do way better. I can't walk back out there with all of that going on and I can't stay in here. She'll probably want to wash her face or something.

I crack open the door and glance up and down the hall. My options are limited. There's only one other door. I take it and find myself on a balcony overlooking the back parking lot. An orange cat winds its way around the dumpsters, sticking to the shadows. It reminds me of Oliver and the way he hugged the walls, trying to maintain as much distance from me as possible for the first few months after he came to live with me. Since then we've reached a wary kind of peace. I don't try to pet him and he eats the food I give him and doesn't shit where he's not supposed to.

After five and a half years of living together we aren't any closer than the day I found him hiding in the shrubbery outside of Cassandra's building. I still don't know why he let me pick him up and put him in my car. I don't like cats and he doesn't seem to like me. We have an unspoken pact— other than when I have to cram him in his carrier for vet visits, I don't touch him and he doesn't try to sit on my lap or rub up against me in any way. I have no idea why he doesn't run away. Maybe he realizes his situation. I don't know.

"There you are." Leo joins me on the little balcony, stuffing his hands into his pockets. He stands shoulder to shoulder with me and we watch the cat eat something off a paper wrapper. "Savannah and me . . ." he begins.

"I really don't care."

"No. I know. It's just that . . ." He kicks the metal balcony railing, making it vibrate. "I'm sorry you had to hear that."

"Me too."

"I'm not really like that."

"It doesn't matter to me what you are or aren't like."

I try to go around him, back through the door, but he puts a hand on my arm to stop me, then pulls it at my glare.

"What I'm trying to say is . . ." He lets out a frustrated sound. "Things'll be cool now between you and Savannah."

"Okay."

"I'm sorry."

"What for?"

He shrugs a shoulder. "All that happened last summer with me and Savannah. It's ancient history, you know?"

"Apparently not."

"It definitely is now. Okay?"

"Sure. Whatever." What does he expect me to say? What does he want from me? "Can we go back inside?"

He opens the door and holds it for me to pass through first. I look for the orange cat one last time, but he's gone. I think of Oliver and our understanding. Maybe Leo and I can work out the same kind of unspoken deal for the summer, where we coexist in the same space without getting attached, where we get what we need from each other and then go our separate ways. But as I brush past him, I realize that his confession and apology have made it a little harder to breathe around him. He takes up so much space—both physically and figuratively—that it's hard to be comfortable around him.

I'm learning that despite appearances there is something more to him than a pretty face and an I-couldn't-give-a-fuck attitude. He does, actually, give a fuck. More than he'd want known. And if he knew how badly he failed at hiding it sometimes, he'd only respond by doubling his efforts to cover it up. I wonder how many people know that about him, how many look past the clothes, body language, and arrogant facial expressions to see what lies beneath it all. And if they did, would they see what I was beginning to see?

6

LEO

I follow Cora back to the conference room past Savannah's now empty desk. She took off for lunch after I got her calmed down. After I practically begged her to leave Cora alone and took everything she threw at me. I had it coming. I never should've touched her, no matter how many times she "accidentally" brushed her tits over my arm or leaned over so I could see down her top. I knew better. But at the time I was just so knocked out that she even wanted me, especially after my girlfriend of six months had dumped me right before summer started.

Thank God Dad wasn't here to hear Savannah and me go at it. As far as I know he doesn't have a clue about what happened between us. But Cora does and now it's stressing me out that she thinks I'm an even bigger douche bag than she originally thought. She wouldn't look at me out there on the balcony, while I stammered out my lame-assed explanation and apology. I don't know why I felt like I needed to apologize to Cora. Maybe because Savannah sucked her into our drama just to get back at me and screw me over with Cora before I could even manage to get anything started.

Cora sits in the chair she was in before and starts going through her bag. She's still not looking at me.

"Are you hungry?" I ask. "There's a pretty good sandwich place down the street."

"Nope." She pulls a sandwich from a brown paper bag, takes a bite, and chews.

"I'll run down there by myself, then. Want anything?"

"Can you make it quick? I want to finish going over this with you so we can finally get started."

"Sure."

She pulls out her phone and jabs in a text as she munches on another bite of sandwich. I'm ignored. I run down to the shop and get back in record time. I'm hardly breathing heavy, thanks to the deep breaths I took before returning to the conference room. She's on the phone with someone. I slide into my chair and go through the motions of tucking in to my sandwich.

She tilts her head back and laughs. It's the most beautiful sight I've ever seen, but inside I'm dying. Who is she talking to? What did they say to her to get her to smile like that? It creases her face and reaches her eyes. For a split second she looks at me with that smile and I pause mid-bite, my mouth hanging open above my sandwich. Then she turns away and mumbles something into the phone. Her low, sexy chuckle at whatever the asshole she's talking to says in return makes the bite I just took taste like shit and I fight to swallow it.

I toss the sandwich aside and watch as she strolls the edge of the room, twisting a piece of blue hair around her finger as she talks. More throaty laughter. I imagine making her laugh like that as we roll around in bed. She'd be insane between the sheets. I just know it. The thought of her naked with me gives me a boner that could pound rocks. I want her. I want her in a way that I've never wanted anything or anyone ever. Before her I thought I knew what it was to get a hard-on for a chick where you just can't get her out of your head, where all other girls go away for you and it's just her. That was nothing compared to the way my hands shake and I have to fist them to keep her from seeing. I know where she is in the room at all times, like my body is a big, giant homing beacon set to her frequency. I can feel her and yet I only ever touched her that one time out on the balcony.

She punches the end button on her phone and pockets it.

"Was that your boyfriend?" I ask, trying for casual, but I'm unable to keep the jealousy out of my voice that's burning a fire through me.

"No."

Just that one word. No explanation. Was that No, I wasn't talking to my boyfriend or No, I don't have a boyfriend to talk to? I can't tell. Nothing in her answer or her movements gives me a fucking clue which it is as she takes her seat again.

"You listened to the nine-one-one call," she prompts me.

"Yeah. Right." I pull my notebook toward me and try to come up with something to ask her. Something intelligent. But all that comes out is, "What happened next?"

She searches through her stack of folders until she finds the one she wants. "According to the police report, the first detective to respond was Paul Winfro. He assessed the scene and called it in. A supervisor arrived, then crime-scene techs, the coroner, and so on."

"What time was that?"

"I told you, about six, just after Cassandra would've gotten off work. The neighbor and the yoga class?" Her impatience with me kicks up a dozen levels.

"Right."

"If you've got somewhere else you'd rather be, don't let me stop you from taking off. Your dad gave me the password to the Wi-Fi here and the login and passwords for the websites the agency uses for searches. There's lots I can do without you if you're bored."

"I'm not bored."

She makes a sound like she doesn't believe me.

"I'm not," I insist. "Tell me about what happened next."

I listen and take notes like I'm in class and there's going to be a test. I ask good questions. By the time she's done walking me through it I almost feel as though I know Cassandra. My dad said to start with the victim, but there was no one and nothing in Cassandra's life that should've led to her murder. She was an ordinary eighteen year old. Who would want to kill her in the horrible way she died and why? I have to talk to Beau. I feel like I can get something from him that Cora couldn't.

It's nearly dark out by the time we're finished. Dad's talking to Savannah about tomorrow's appointments and Cora and I have a solid plan to start working on in the morning. I help her pack her folders and binders into her box. When we're all done, she puts the lid on and I carry it to the storage cabinet and lock it up. By the time I get back, she's got her bag on her shoulder.

"I'll see you tomorrow," she says, and starts to leave, then turns back.

It's the first time I've seen her nervous. My curiosity kicks into high gear.

"I don't have a boyfriend," she blurts out, then bolts for the door. She's gone before my brain can restart to stop her.

I lean against the door frame, a dumb-ass smile on my face, and that's how Dad finds me.

He glances from me to the door, then back again. "No. Absolutely not. She's a client."

"Isn't she more of an employee?"

"In my office."

I follow him down the hall, feeling like that time I was sixteen and I accidentally backed his truck into a pole.

He closes the door after me. "Sit down. You and I need to get something straight." He waits for me to take a seat. "I thought it was fairly obvious, but after what happened last summer between you and Savannah, I feel like I need to set some boundaries here."

Shit. He knows about Savannah and me.

"I remember what it's like to be your age." This is going to be one of his long talks, when I'm expected to sit here and listen without comment, then totally change my behavior forever. "Pretty girls turned my head too, but you have to have some common sense. This is a place of business, not a pickup joint. I didn't say anything about you and Savannah, figuring it would work itself out one way or the other. But it hasn't. I regret not putting a stop to that. And now you're looking at Cora that same way and I won't have it. That girl's been through enough."

"I—"

"I'm not finished. I'm serious here, Leo. Leave her be. You have no idea what she's been through. Her family—"

"You investigated her?"

"We investigate all of our clients. You should know that. We have to be sure they are who they say they are and that they're hiring us for the reasons they give us. We don't want to inadvertently help an abuser find their victim or help them break the law."

I should know that, but I didn't. "What did you find out about her?"

"All you need to know is that we're working on a very real case. Cora is who she says she is and the circumstances are exactly as she described them."

I expected that. "Yeah, but what did you mean that she's been through enough? Don't you think I should know what you know if I'm going to work with her?"

He considers this, staring at me for a beat, then two, before he speaks. "During the trial her parents separated, then divorced shortly after that. At sixteen, Cora fought to become an emancipated minor and won. She got a job, moved out on her own, and has been living as an adult ever since. She tested out of high school two years before graduation. She's been completely on her own for more than five years. She's not . . . How can I put this? She's not the kind of person who screws around. She's serious. Her brother's case has been her life. Every job, every community college course she's taken, has been in relation to what she can do to help her brother.

"I'm telling you this so that you can understand where she's coming from and take it into consideration. I need you one hundred percent on the job and not trying to get into her pants. She needs you one hundred percent. This isn't a hobby to her, a way to kill a summer. This is her life. Do you understand what I'm trying to tell you?"

"Yeah, that you think all I want to do is sleep with her. Thanks, Dad."

"I see the way you look at her. And I know she's the only reason you volunteered to help with her brother's case."

"Yesterday, yeah. But today? Today I want to be the one who helps her find a way to free her brother."

"That's not all you want."

"No, it's not, but it's what I mostly want."

"Why?"

"Why what?"

"Why do you mostly want to help her free her brother if it's not to eventually sleep with her?"

The way Cora looked when she practically stormed into Dad's office and demanded our help, the way she stroked Cassandra's photo, the way she talked about her brother, and her box full of papers that's been her life fill my head until I can't think of anything else. She deserves—more than anyone else I've ever met—to get what she wants. She's worked damn hard for it. I respect the hell out of her. I genuinely like her. All of these things roll around in my brain, but looking at my dad, I can't seem to form any of the words to tell him exactly what I'm thinking.

All that comes out is a pathetic "She needs me to."

Surprise flashes across his face first, followed by the barest trace of a smile that he somehow manages to make look stern. "Okay, then."

"Okay." I stand to leave, but Dad's not done.

"Fix things with Savannah."

"I already did." Mostly. As best as I could for the moment.

"Then I guess I'll see you at home later."

"See ya."

I head out to my car and climb in. The summer sun turned the interior into an oven, but I'm not really feeling it. I'm still back in the conference room doorway at the moment that Cora told me she doesn't have a boyfriend. Her words loop over and around like a roller coaster, making my stomach whoosh, and I can't help the stupid grin that splits my face. Because maybe, just maybe, Cora might like me too, or at the very least she's beginning to. I rub the back of my hand across my mouth, but I can't wipe away the smile or the hope.

7

CORA

N*o.*

That's it. That's Beau's one-word response to me asking him if he'll meet with Leo. I check the envelope again, hoping there's more, but there isn't. Why is he being so damn stubborn? I laid everything out for him on my last visit—how Mr. Nash helped to free Maurice Battle, how we're looking for the missing downstairs neighbor, and how Mr. Nash was able to make an appointment to see Damien LeFeaux, the man who claimed to have seen Beau leaving Cassandra's apartment at the time of her murder. That in itself was a seemingly insurmountable feat, but Mr. Nash pulled it off. I came real close to hugging him for it. Beau was supposed to think it over and get back to me. He got back to me, all right.

There's no guarantee that LeFeaux will talk. He doesn't have any incentive to cooperate with us. As Mr. Nash explained it, LeFeaux has a strong motive not to talk and avoid perjury charges. His visit could be a total waste of time. Or it could be the break we need.

It's been nearly three weeks since I started working with

Leo and his dad. Most of what we've done is going over old ground and trying to line up witness interviews. So far, the only person willing to talk to us is one of Cassandra's old coworkers who now manages the store where she worked. That's on today's agenda and I can hardly contain my excitement. So much so that I arrive at the agency before it opens.

I park myself on the stairs and thumb through my emails. Nothing new and exciting. Pulling out my notebook, I start a letter to Beau. I'm going to be relentless in my campaign to get him to talk to Leo. I hate to say it, but Leo was right. Beau will never talk to me about Cassandra, and he might not talk to Leo either, but we have to try. Who knows what goes through Beau's stubborn head. If it was me I'd do everything possible to get myself free. But not Beau. He'd rather sit in prison and rot like some kind of martyr.

Savannah comes up the steps. I was so engrossed in my letter that I didn't hear her pull up. We've developed an uneasy kind of peace between us. She's still pissed as hell at Leo, but she doesn't take it out on me. Much.

I stand and wait for her to unlock the door. She doesn't hold the door open for me. Okay. So today I'm invisible. That I can live with. It's better than biting back smart-assed comebacks to her snide remarks. She flips on all the lights and goes to the little kitchenette to start coffee. Mr. Nash really likes his coffee.

I head for the small office space Mr. Nash gave Leo and me. It's papered with Beau's case. Nearly every space on the walls is covered with photos and copies of reports in a timeline from the night before Cassandra was killed to Beau's conviction. We even have a small whiteboard where we write down tasks to accomplish every day.

Today I'm investigating private in-home nursing-home options. Cassandra's bed-bound downstairs neighbor, Edith

Wheeler, is still missing in action. How could an eighty-four-year-old invalid simply disappear? The last time she filed taxes was about seven years ago and her Social Security checks go to a P.O. Box in Montana. We haven't been able to find any relatives for her in that area who might be cashing her checks, and the post office won't give us the name on the box. Mr. Nash suspects Social Security fraud and he even went so far as to file a report on it. As far as we can tell, no one at the Social Security Administration or post office has opened an investigation on it. Another dead end for now.

Mr. Nash doesn't have an extra computer for me, so I drag my laptop out of my bag and fire it up. He gave me some pointers on how to search for people, and once you get into the databases it's pretty easy to find just about anyone. Anyone except Edith Wheeler. Leo joked that she was probably a CIA operative with a secret identity or something, total black ops. Short of taking a trip to Montana to stake out the P.O. Box, we're pretty short on leads for old Edith.

I'm sifting through old Craigslist ads from around the time when Edith disappeared when a hand holding a cup of take-out tea slides into my line of sight. Ever since Leo found out I drink tea instead of coffee he brings me a cup every morning from the same place he goes to get his coffee fix. I told him a thousand times that I don't want him to get me tea. What I didn't tell him is that I can't afford to pay him back for it. He just shrugged and told me not to worry about it. He was going there anyway. I finally gave up telling him to stop.

"Thank you," I say, with a twinge of embarrassment. I'm not used to people doing nice things for me.

"You're welcome."

He slides into his seat behind his desk, which faces mine. It was his idea to set them up like this. He said it was so we could communicate more efficiently. I think it was so he could watch me. That's what I told myself. I'm ashamed to admit that he's caught me staring more times than I've caught him.

I pop the lid off my tea. It's exactly the way I make it—with milk and sugar. Closing my eyes, I wrap my hands around the cup and inhale. I love the way Earl Grey smells. It reminds me of my English grandma, who used to fix Yankee tea minus the tea—hot water, milk, and sugar—for Beau and me when we were kids. She made a pot of Earl Grey everyday for herself and the scent permeated her house. I take a sip and a brief jog back in time to when our family was together and things were normal. Happier times. Much happier times.

I open my eyes to find Leo watching me.

"What?"

"Nothing." He pretends to get busy turning his own laptop on.

"Hmm."

"Did you start on that search?"

"Yeah, I'm tackling Craigslist first."

"I'll take the PennySaver after I check for updates on the Wheeler family tree on that ancestry website."

We've already eliminated the obvious listings in newspapers and Internet searches. Someone somewhere stashed this old woman and we just have to find out who and where.

We work for the next few hours with no luck. A mysterious relative hasn't suddenly popped up who could be harboring Edith, and the other listing websites were a total bust. I finished up my letter to Beau earlier, so I stick a stamp on it and set it in the outgoing mailbox on Savannah's credenza. She's busy clicking away on her computer or else she's in the running for an acting award, because it's like I really am invisible.

Leo comes up behind me and opens the door.

"Where are you going?" Savannah asks him.

"Cora and I have an appointment." He's using his patient voice, but he's not very good at it.

She crosses her arms. "Uh-huh."

"Tell my dad we'll be back in a few hours."

"More like five minutes," she mumbles under her breath.

I bite my lip to keep from laughing.

"Excuse me?" he asks her. He had to have heard her.

"I said you two have fun."

He waits until we're outside to lose it. "When is she going to stop being such a bitch and get over it?"

"You're getting off easy, Five-Minute Man. If you did to me what you did to her you wouldn't be walking so good."

He makes a face at my nickname. "She's never going to get over me breaking things off with her, is she?"

"She will. When she meets someone else. I put her on the email list of about twenty different dating websites. Hopefully she'll move on soon."

He stares at me across the roof of his car, a slow, wicked smile creeping across his face. "You're an evil genius."

"Only if it works."

We climb in the car and he pulls out onto the street toward Horton Plaza, a big downtown shopping mall. We're meeting Mindy Sumrow at Forever 21, where she worked with Cassandra. I'm hoping she can tell us more about Cassandra's life during the time she and Beau were broken up. Five years ago she was less than helpful when I tried to talk to her. I try not to count on her being more forthcoming this time around.

We park in the parking structure attached to the mall and locate the Forever 21 on the mall map. It's on level one. So are we. As we walk I notice the feminine stares Leo gets and how women continue to blatantly check him out front to back. I know he's hot—I'm focused, not dead—but I don't think of him in that context. We've developed kind of an asexual friendship of sorts. We're together all day everyday, we get along well, but I wouldn't say there is any chemistry between us. One of the chicks we pass lets out a low whistle as she checks him out from behind. I drop back a little to see what all the fuss is about and I get it. I totally get it.

Leo turns to look at me with a question on his face, probably wondering why I slowed down.

"You have a nice ass," I tell him.

He stumbles over his feet and comes to a halt, staring at me with an odd look on his face.

I shrug. "I never noticed before."

"You were checking out my ass?"

"Yeah."

He looks away, then back. He's fighting a smile. "And you liked what you saw?"

"What's not to like?"

"What else do you like about me?"

"You have nice hair."

He shoves his hands in the front pockets of his jeans, rocking a little. "Anything else?" He's enjoying this.

I lift my shoulders. "You're pretty easy to look at, overall."

He continues to stare at me with that strange expression that if I had to guess was a mixture of joy, confusion, pride, disbelief, and . . . longing? We're stopped in the middle of the walkway, forcing people to move around us like water around pebbles in a stream. He takes a step closer to me and I can see that his eyes are brown, but not an ordinary kind of brown. They're a kind of bronze with a dark brown, almost black, ring around the outside. Funny, I never noticed that before. He eases a little closer and I don't move, caught in the tractor beam of his gaze.

He reaches out and captures the first two fingers of my left hand. "You're pretty easy to look at, overall, too." His voice is a husky whisper that only I can hear. "Very easy."

His compliment does strange things to me. I flush, a full-body rush of heat followed by tingling in the palms of my hands and feet and . . . other places. I can't feel anything else except his thumb stroking my fingers and the thick, hard thump of my heart.

Someone bumps my shoulder, pulling my fingers from Leo's, and the spell is broken. Looking away, I clear my throat and start out again for the Forever 21. Leo follows slowly at first and then quickens his stride to catch up to me. If he says anything right now I might just punch him in the face. Thankfully, he keeps his mouth shut.

We enter the store and I spot Mindy right away. She's got the kind of curly hair that explodes out around her pretty square face. She's the same age as Cassandra would be and I can't help but feel a twinge of resentment toward her. The old question of why Cassandra and not someone else swirls and I try to not pin too much hope on what Mindy might say and how it could help Beau.

Leo waits to catch her eye until she's finished with her customer. She does a double take, then saunters over toward us. Over toward Leo, really. I doubt if she's noticed me yet.

"Hi, Mindy?" he says. "I'm Leo and this is Cora."

She glances at me for the briefest second. "You didn't say you'd be bringing her."

Great. She's not going to talk with me here. "I think I'll go get a smoothie," I say.

Leo looks down at me with a crease between his brows. We'd discussed this possibility. It would now be on him to pull what he can from Mindy.

"I'll catch up with you later," he says, running his worried gaze over me.

I give him a jaunty wave to let him know that it's okay, even though it's not. I'm dying to know what Mindy has to say. Glancing back at them as I exit the store, I can tell that Leo already has her wrapped in his charm. Having just been the recipient of that charm, I know how she's feeling.

It's the second time today that I have uncharitable thoughts toward Mindy.

8

LEO

Mindy leads me to her office at the back of the store and closes the door. It's no bigger than a closet. She clears some stuff off a chair so I can sit down. I can hardly concentrate on what she's saying—something about her office being a mess—let alone what I'm supposed to say. My head is full of Cora. She doesn't even know she does it when she twists me up in knots. It's like she doesn't even have to try. Just her being her is enough to knock me back a step.

Like this morning with the tea. It's the same every time. She takes the lid off, grips it in both hands, closes her eyes, and inhales. I don't know what she thinks of when she smells that tea, but the look on her face . . . I can't breathe. It's indescribable. All I know is that look has me bringing her tea every morning just to witness it. I discovered what Earl Grey does to her by accident. We stopped at my favorite coffee place one afternoon when I was dragging ass so I could get a double-shot pick-me-up. While we waited Cora opened the tester tins of tea on the shelf behind us and started smelling them. When she came to the Earl Grey she got that look.

I stood there and watched her, fascinated by her reaction. She held the tin, taking periodic sniffs of it until they called my name, then she reluctantly replaced the lid and put it back on the shelf. That was when I started adding Earl Grey to my morning order.

And then just now, out there in the mall, when she checked out my ass. Until that moment I was beginning to think that she'd parked me permanently in the friend zone. She liked my ass. And my hair. And the way I looked overall. It took a tremendous amount of restraint not to grab her and kiss her the way I've wanted to from practically the first moment I saw her. For the barest of seconds she looked like she might want to be kissed and then some asshole bumped her and she shook it off, becoming determined Cora again.

I don't know what I did to suddenly earn her notice, but now that I have it I feel like a junkie looking for his next fix. I want it again. No, I need it again.

"I don't know how I can help you," Mindy says, drawing me back to the here and now. "I told the police everything I know. Besides, I'm not looking to help free Cassandra's murderer. He can rot in jail forever, for all I care."

"I understand that. You want someone to pay for what was done to her."

"Yes, exactly."

"But what if it's the wrong someone? You seem like an honest person, the kind of person who wouldn't want an innocent man to pay for a crime he didn't commit. It happens, you know. I work for Nash Security and Investigation. We recently helped to overturn the conviction of a man who sat in prison for thirty-nine years, paying for a crime he didn't commit. Can you imagine that?" She shakes her head.

"Me either. That's why I'm here. Cassandra's killer is still out there and we're trying to find him. Anything you can tell me —no matter how trivial or insignificant—will help."

My scare tactic worked. Mindy looks horrified at the possibility that Cassandra's killer is still out there.

"I'll tell you whatever I can."

"Thank you." I gentle my voice. "It must've been difficult to lose your friend. Tell me what she was like."

Mindy launches into her stories about Cassandra and I add them to the others that Cora told me. The more I learn about Cassandra, the more I like her. Sure, people tend to talk nice about the dead even if they weren't such nice people, but I have a feeling that Cassandra genuinely was one of the nice ones.

"Did you ever hang out with Cassandra outside of work?" I ask.

"A couple times."

"Did she mention a new boyfriend?"

"No, no new boyfriend. She broke up with that Beau a few months before she was . . . killed, and I don't know of anyone new."

"Did she ever talk about Beau with you? Do you know why they broke up?"

"Yeah. She talked about him all the time, but I got the feeling there were some real problems toward the end. She cried a lot and then just sort of got into a funk. We didn't go out after work anymore."

"Did she miss any work or have to leave early or come in late?"

"A couple of times. Hey, that's right." She snapped her fingers. "That's when she first brought up some trouble she'd been having."

"What trouble?"

"She complained a couple of times about some weird stuff happening around her apartment complex—vandalism, things missing—that sort of thing. Nothing sinister. Probably just kids. But I wondered if maybe it wasn't Beau who was doing it just to get a rise out of her. It was just little things, annoying things. Like as if he was trying to get her attention or something."

"Do you know if she ever called the police?"

"Probably." She shrugged. "I don't know. I would've. A couple of the things she mentioned were just so weird."

"Like what?"

"Someone took her cat, then suddenly he reappeared a couple of days later in a box on her doorstep with a bow around his neck. She was just so happy to have him back I don't think she thought about someone taking the cat just to mess with her. That's kind of a sick thing to do, don't you think?"

"Are you sure it wasn't a neighbor returning her cat?"

"Could've been, I suppose, but why not just ring the doorbell? And why the bow?"

I made a mental note to check to see if Cassandra had filed a police report or if there was any record of her making calls to the police.

"Can you think of anything else you might not have told the police?"

"Oh, I told them about the weird stuff."

"You did?"

"Yeah. They didn't seem to think as much of it as you do."

"Huh. Well, thanks for your time, Mindy." I gave her one of the blank agency cards that I'd written my name on. "If you think of anything else, give me a call." I opened the door, needing to get out of that claustrophobic office before the walls really did close in on me.

Looking down at it, she flicked the card with a finger. "Did your agency really free a wrongfully convicted man?"

"Yes."

"Do you really think that Beau was wrongfully convicted?"

"Absolutely."

"I have to tell you. I met him a couple of times—you know, before they broke up? I couldn't see him snapping like that and doing what they say happened to her. He loved her. That was as plain as anything. Even after the breakup I don't think he was the type to hurt anybody, especially Cassandra."

I nodded.

"If I called you, would you let me know what happens? If it wasn't Beau, I'd like to know who the bastard was who killed her."

"Sure. And like I said, if you can think of anything else, let me know. Thanks."

I head up to the third floor, where the food court is, and spot Cora right away. Even without the blue hair she would be hard to miss. She's just sitting there, people-watching. Her look is so far away and lost I wonder what she could be thinking. I'd give my left nut to know what she's thinking. I don't know anyone harder to read than Cora. The FBI could do a study on her and train their agents on how to mask their thoughts. I'd hate to play poker with her.

I approach her from the side and her head immediately swings in my direction. Sliding in the chair opposite her, I notice that she's been biting her left pinkie nail. That habit is the only outward sign that Cora is as flawed as the rest of us. I want to take her hand and tell her everything will be okay, that I'll fix what's wrong for her. But I'm not entirely sure what would happen if I did, so I don't.

Cora straightens in her chair and braces her elbows on the table, leaning forward. "Well? What did she say?"

"She said that weird things had been happening to Cassandra before her murder. Vandalism and things coming up missing, including her cat, which was later returned. Did you know about any of that?"

She sits back in her chair, contemplating. "No."

"Mindy wasn't sure if Cassandra had called the police or not, but if she did there would be a record, right?"

"Yeah."

"She didn't think Cassandra was seeing anyone new and she had some nice things to say about Beau."

"You're surprised?"

"No. Of course not."

"Yes, you are." She comes forward in her seat at me and I can tell I somehow hit a sore spot with her. "Why wouldn't Mindy or anyone else have anything nice to say about my brother?"

"I didn't mean it that way, okay? I guess I was surprised that she didn't seem to hate him for what she thinks he did to her friend. Most people want to believe the worst in others. Mindy doesn't when she has a good reason to. That's all."

She eyes me for a moment before settling back in her seat. "Sorry. I'm not really pissed at you."

"Who are you pissed at?"

"Beau."

This throws me off guard. Her brother's so high up on a pedestal for her it's hard for me to imagine her getting mad at him. "Why?"

"He refuses to meet with you. Stupid, stubborn jackass."

"What if I wrote to him?"

"I don't know."

"Couldn't hurt. We wouldn't be any worse off than we are now."

"I suppose." She taps her nails on the tabletop . . . all except the pinkie that she's chewed down to a nub. "You'd do that?"

She has to ask? I'd do just about anything for her. "Yeah."

"Okay."

"You want a smoothie? My treat."

"No, thanks. I want to go to Cassandra's apartment." She stands and pushes her chair in, so I do the same. "It's up for lease again."

I'm taken aback by this news. "You keep track of that?"

"I keep track of a lot of things, but yeah, I set up a Google alert for it. They're having an open house today. Right now. You can drop me off at my car if you don't want to go."

"No, I'll go." I'm curious to know what she thinks she's going to discover. "How many times have you been there since the murder?"

"I drive by there almost every day, but I've only been inside eight times."

Again she catches me off guard. I don't know what to say when she makes admissions like this. Her life has been poles apart from mine. It's moments like this when the differences between us seem impossible, and I'm over-whelmed by the challenge. I wonder if she even has any room in her life for someone like me or if what I bring is significant enough to matter for her.

Leo hasn't said much since I confessed my obsession to him. I know how strange it is to drive by a dead woman's apartment every day and to find any opportunity to get inside. I know it's weird. I wouldn't have told him about it if he hadn't asked. He's the only person who ever has. Maybe that's why I blurted it out, forgetting to put the filter on my crazy. He asks questions no one asks. He wants to know about things no one wants to talk about. He understands things I find inexplicable. And he seems to accept things about me that put others off.

I don't know what to do with all of that. It gives me a shaky, edgy feeling I can't control.

As he drives us to Cassandra's I realize that he hasn't asked for directions and he isn't using the GPS on his phone. He's been here before. On his own. Without me. I'm overwhelmed. The car is suddenly too small and he's too close. I didn't expect any of this when I walked into his father's agency that day. I certainly didn't expect to like Leo or to find a partner in him. Or for him to take on Beau's case as though finding the real killer matters, really matters to him.

Leo reaches out and pulls my hand from my mouth, wrapping his hand around mine in my lap. I hadn't realized I was biting my nail again. Fixing my gaze out the window, I don't take my hand out of his like I should. I like how warm and sure and strong it feels. He makes me want to rely on him. He put himself in my path like a tree that took root where it shouldn't, and try as I might, I can't go around him. Maybe I don't want to go around him. Maybe I like him there as much as I like my hand in his and the fact that he knows the way to Cassandra's apartment.

He stops the car across the street from the apartment building and reaches under the steering wheel to turn the car off with his left hand, keeping a hold of mine in his right. The air is thick and ripe and I don't know what is supposed to happen next. He turns toward me. His eyes are darker now than they were earlier. He's watching me that way he does sometimes when he thinks I don't know. Only this time he's not hiding it or looking away suddenly. It's out there. What he wants. Me. And he wants me to see it.

"You knew the way here," I blurt out.

"I came by once and checked it out."

"Why?"

"It's important." He touches a finger to my hair, sweeping it out of my eyes. His movements are slow and purposeful. He doesn't say it, but I feel the words just the same—You're important.

I don't know when this happened or why I'm just now noticing it, but I realize that he's become important. He's a partner in the battle I'm waging to save my brother. Since the day he joined the fight he's been there every step of the way. Sometimes, like now, I can't remember what it was like before he came on board.

"Cora?" He murmurs my name and it floats across my senses, lighting them up.

Leaning across the console toward me, his gaze drops to my mouth. I know what he means to do and I want him to do it. Everything in me leaps and I bow my body toward him. His hand is on my cheek and he's so close his breath whispers across my skin. I can smell the cologne he wears and the after-coffee mint he popped earlier. My lashes flutter closed and my lips part. I want this.

And then his mouth is on mine. Gentle, so gentle. He's agonizingly slow and careful. I can hardly move. His hands are in my hair and the kiss changes. I fist the front of his shirt, bringing him closer. Everything spirals. A whirling of sensations I didn't know existed. He's good at this, so good. I want it to go on forever and ever. But he's already pulling away.

Fear spikes within me. Did I do something wrong?

His hands are still in my hair and he's staring at me like he doesn't know what happened. His breathing is rough and labored as though he just ran a mile and stopped suddenly to kiss me. Mine isn't any smoother, and with my heart pounding so hard it hurts, I pull on his shirt, bringing his mouth back to mine. I want more. His tongue pushes at the seam of my lips and I open for him. He changes the angle and that's when all hell breaks loose inside me. I want him. I want him to not stop. Ever. I want things I don't have any knowledge of and I want them all with him.

What am I doing?

Some sense slips in and I use the hand that pulled him closer to push him away. He lifts his head. His eyes are even darker than they were before and his gaze flickers between my eyes and my mouth. If I yanked him back toward me he'd keep on kissing me. I know this, I want it, and yet I push him away.

He traces a finger along my bottom lip. "Cora, Cora, Cora," he chants breathlessly.

I run my fingers around the edge of his face. I feel like I'm just now seeing him. We keep touching each other, little discovering touches. He leans in and smells me, nuzzling his nose along my jawline to my ear. My hands are in his hair, sifting through strands that are softer than I thought they'd be. I breathe him in like he did me and he makes a noise at the back of his throat that tests the limits I just set for myself.

"Cora." He sounds agonized.

I know how he feels. I ache in places I didn't know could be so electric and sensitive and alive. All of my senses are on alert for what he'll say or do next.

"We have to stop."

I'm confused. Why?

"God, not here." He catches my face in his hands, stopping me from licking the spot just below his ear. He gives me a quick kiss. "If you keep that up we're going to give the neighbors a show and what I have planned for you is very, very private."

"You have plans for me?"

Putting his forehead to mine, he makes a frustrated noise. "You have no idea."

This cheers me immensely.

He pulls away and looks down at me in surprise. "That is the most amazing smile I've ever seen."

I shut it down and try to duck my head, but he's got ahold of me and I can't move.

"No, don't hide it. I like it," he says.

I glance past him to Cassandra's apartment building. Reality creeps in. Gripping his wrists, I pull on his hands so he'll release me. We're sitting out front of Cassandra's apartment, making out. That's wrong on every level. I'm supposed to be helping Beau, not indulging in my own curiosities.

My gaze goes to the building across the street. If I close my eyes I can still see the police cars with the lights flashing sitting out front. Police tape marks off the area, while crime-scene techs and police officers walk in and out of her apartment. The coroner's van is parked close by, waiting to take Cassandra's body in for examination and autopsy. The scene is eerie and macabre, made worse by the image of Beau rushing toward the apartment, screaming Cassandra's name. I try to grab him by the waist to hold him back, but he slips past me. He's crying. That was the only time I'd ever seen my brother cry.

I shake my head, trying to dislodge the memory, but the emotions of that night are as raw now as they were then. What am I doing here with Leo, while my brother sits in prison?

Leo releases me and sits back in his seat. The moment that never should've been between us is gone. His mouth—which I now know is soft and skilled—is pressed into a frown as he turns to see what stole my attention from him. I climb out of the car. I don't wait for him. The apartment pulls me in, drawing me across the street. 1-2-3-4-5-6-7-8-9-10-11-12 steps to the second floor. The door on the right is open, so I walk through it.

A small living room/kitchen/dining room, then a short hall. The bathroom is on the right, the bedroom straight ahead. Her bed was on the far wall. With the window open she would've had a nice breeze while she slept. But she's not sleeping. Her eyes are wide open. Blood smears her face, neck, and hands. Red mars the pretty floral sheets. Her hands are tied together above her head, the rope woven through the wrought-iron headboard. Each foot is tied to the iron posts of the footboard. She's naked. Her legs are wide open and there's blood there too.

I stand there, imagining all the things that were done to her, the hours it took to accomplish them. After all that, he took the matching pretty floral pillow and pressed it against her face. It took about three minutes for her to black out and another six to eight minutes for her to die. He threw the pillow onto the floor when he was done.

Putting both of his arms around me, Leo hugs me, drawing me in to his chest. "Ssh, stop," he says, and I realize I've been talking this whole time, describing what I know from the reports. "No more." His voice is raw, his arms strong and sure around me.

"I don't understand why he used the pillow."

"Cora."

"All of that violence—the ripping and tearing, the blood —and he uses a pillow. Why didn't he use his hands or the rope he brought? Why the pillow?"

He lays his cheek on my head, bringing me in tighter. "He's a coward. Maybe he didn't want to see her face. Maybe even he has a threshold that can't be crossed."

"Yes. That's it. That's it exactly. Thank you."

"Are you two interested in the apartment?" a chirpy voice asks.

I face away and swipe at tears. Leo continues to hold me, looser now, but he's not letting go.

"We're not sure," he answers.

"Is everything okay in here?" Her question is for me.

"Yes," I lie, plastering on a fake smile.

"Are you sure?" She doesn't look convinced, but she does

look like my cousin Millie—big blond hair and matching boobs.

"Just something in my eye," I say. "I'm fine, really."

Beside me, Leo is a rock. I fist his shirt in the back where the lady can't see. I don't want him to let me go. I'll float away without him anchoring me.

"What's the rent?" Leo plays along.

"Fifteen hundred dollars per month. There's a two-thou-sand-dollar deposit. Half is due on signing and the remaining when you get the keys." She eyes us skeptically. "Are you two USD students?"

"He is," I find myself saying. "I'm in cosmetology school."

"This would be our first apartment together." Leo smiles at her.

"How nice. You make a lovely couple. When would you be looking to move in? The apartment is ready anytime."

"Oh," I say, putting the proper disappointment in my voice. "We wouldn't be ready to move in until next month."

"I see. It wouldn't hurt to fill out some paperwork—"

"I'm not sure it's us. What do you think, Bluebird?"

His nickname startles me for the barest second. "No. I don't think it's us."

"Well, if you change your mind, here's my card." She hands a card to Leo.

He glances at it. "Thanks, Lisa. We'll let you know if we do." Then, to me, "Did you want to look around a little more to be sure?"

"No. I think I got everything I came for."

We head back out to the car and my head is light. My whole body is light. I hold on to my anchor as we make our way down the steps.

"Bluebird?" I ask.

He shrugs. He's embarrassed. How odd. I never thought

of him as someone who gets embarrassed. He always seems so sure of himself.

"I like it. My mom used to call me Cora Belle, but that was a long time ago." I don't tell him that he's the only other person to give me a nickname or how much I really, really like it.

"I could use some coffee," he says on a sigh. "Want some tea?"

"Yeah. I could really use a cup."

LEO

I kissed Cora, then Cora kissed me.

This should be the only thing I'm thinking about besides how and when I can take it further with her, but I'm not. I'm thinking about her hollow voice as she described the murder scene and how her tears absolutely gutted me. I find any reason to touch her, but I haven't tried to kiss her again. I can't.

I voluntarily took the seat next to her in the roller coaster of her life. I can take the twists and turns with her, holding her hand. I can repeat over and over for her that the ride will end soon even as it cranks up to the top of yet another hill. But she's been on it long enough to see through the platitudes. She knows it won't be over anytime soon and my presence beside her doesn't make the ride any easier to take.

I don't know where that leaves us other than to keep doing what we're doing. Because short of finding the real killer, there is nothing I can do or say to take any of this away from Cora or make it better for her. So that's what I'm going to try to do. I hope the letter I sent to Beau will make a difference. Cora wouldn't like what I wrote. I basically called Beau out. He should know enough about his sister to know that she won't give up until he's freed. By putting her off he's just prolonging her pain. What I didn't say is that I will never have a chance with Cora as long as her brother sits in prison.

This is a truth that tears me up. It's a near physical ache for something I don't have a chance of ever having. If she didn't like me—okay. I could live with that. Possibly. But she does like me. Maybe not as much as I like her. Aaargh. Definitely not as much as I like her. Freeing Beau is her life. There is no room for me or anyone else in that life. I thought there could be for the barest of seconds. I saw a flash of it in her smile in the car the other day when we kissed until she remembered she isn't supposed to smile.

She isn't supposed to have a life her brother can't.

I don't know how to get around that or if I should even try. Time she would spend with me on a date is time she's not working to free Beau. There's no way for me or anyone else to compete with that. It's just there, always between us. The grief radiates out of her, bleeding into the air around her. I breathe it in and it coats my skin until I can't separate myself from her or it. I've absorbed so much of it now I wonder if I'll ever be rid of it or even if I want to be.

So I plod along beside her, giving her what I can and working my ass off to find a clue that will end this nightmare for her.

A week later I finally have something that might help, if only for a moment. Beau has agreed to meet with me. I debate whether or not I should tell Cora before or after I meet with him . . . but for only a second.

No matter how early I wake up, Cora always manages to get to the office before me. I set her tea next to her and take my seat across from her. She goes through her usual routine with it. I've come to depend on moments like this with her. They're as necessary to me as breathing.

It's Saturday, so we're the only ones in the office. Dad gave Cora a key a week ago, after Savannah complained about Cora sitting on the steps, waiting for her to open up. It's quiet except for the hum of the fax machine spitting something out. I'm supposed to run my daily Internet search for Edith Wheeler, the downstairs neighbor, to see if she suddenly pops up out of nowhere. Instead, I'm waiting for the perfect moment to tell Cora about Beau.

She glances up from her cup. "What?" She knows something's going on.

"I'm going out to the prison today to visit Beau. Do you want to go with me?"

She freezes, staring at me like she can't process what I just said. Everything stills in me, waiting for her reaction.

"He agreed to talk to you?" Anger is not the emotion I expected. "How in the hell did you get him to agree to that?"

I should know better by now than to try to predict Cora. "I guess I wrote a persuasive enough argument."

She narrows her eyes at me. "What did you say to him?"

I should come clean, but I can't. What I said to Beau is between him and me. "I told him that you're just going to keep bugging him until he relents. He relented. Why aren't you happy about this?"

"Why should I be happy about it?"

"You were mad at him when he wouldn't cooperate. Now he is and you're still mad?"

"Yes. No. I don't know. I guess I'm mad that he gave in so easily to you when he's been so damn stubborn with me."

"But this is a good thing."

"Maybe. Just because he agreed to see you doesn't mean he'll talk to you."

"Leave it to me. Do you want to ride out there with me or not?"

Her gaze shifts to her computer screen, then back to me. I can tell she's debating how her time would be best served —riding in a car or working on finding Edith Wheeler.

"I'll go with you." She checks the time on her phone. "We should leave within the next twenty minutes."

The drive is long and boring, but I'm holding Cora's hand and she's letting me. So there's that. I have in mind what I want to say to Beau and the things I want to ask him. I'm not sure how it will go. I'm pissed as hell at him on Cora's behalf. It's an irrational anger, I know. And while Cora shoulders some of the responsibility for putting Beau's life before her own, I put the bulk of it on Beau's head. He hasn't cooperated at all. My line of thought is that Cora might have been able to free him before now if he'd only fucking participated.

It's strange to never have met someone who I know so much about. Beau and I have Cora in common, but not much else. His life took a turn I can't fathom. I'm not sure what to say about that when I see him. What do you say?

Cora gave me the drill on prison security, so before I know it I'm through screening and walking into the visitors' room of the prison. It takes me a minute to spot Beau. He doesn't look like any of the pictures Cora showed me. He's bigger, bulkier. His hair is short and he scowls as if he'll hit anyone who dares to look in his direction, let alone talk to him. I see now what has Cora so frightened and why she stormed into my dad's office that day the way she did. The prison is a cancer and Beau's riddled with it. She's not just fighting for the brother she knew, she's fighting for his life.

I take my seat opposite him and sit still for his inspection. I don't flinch at his stare. I take him head-on.

"You have balls," he says.

"Yep. Two."

"What do you want?"

"I want you to stop jerking Cora around."

He puts an arm on the table and leans in. "What the fuck is it to you?"

I mirror his posture. "Why don't you give her what she wants?"

"I told her a thousand times to forget about me and get on with her life."

"And how has that worked out for you so far?"

He makes a rude noise.

"You should know Cora better than anyone," I press. "She's not ever going to give up. So stop fucking jerking her around and tell her what she wants to know."

"What's the point?"

"Have you seen her files on your case?" I forge on, despite his stony silence. "I have. She has a whole damn box full of them. For the past five and a half years she's done nothing with her life except fight for you. What have you done for her?"

"What am I supposed to do from here?" He sweeps his arms out wide. If I thought Cora carried around too much anger, it's nothing compared to the rage that pumps off Beau. I can taste it at the back of my throat and feel it pushing at my skin.

"You're a coward."

Cold blue eyes that are nothing like Cora's stare back at me. And yet the resemblance is there. Like a faded photo over a faded photo, there's a washed-out sameness that bends my sympathy toward him. But I can't show him that. I have to match his attitude, blank stare for blank stare.

"What do you want to know?" he finally says.

I don't dare let out the breath I've been holding and go right for the jugular. "Why did you and Cassandra break up?"

There's more fury-filled silence and then he leans in again. "That has nothing to do with what happened to her."

"You don't know that. There could be something in there. Or not. But I have to think that your reluctance to talk about it could be the thing the real killer is counting on."

"I broke up with her."

"Why?"

He does that thing with his hand that Cora does when she's agitated—tapping the tips of his fingers on the table-top, pinkie to index finger, pinkie to index finger, like a wave. "I'm going to say this so Cora will finally let it go, but you have to promise me you won't tell her or anyone."

I agree. I warned Cora that I might not be able to tell her everything Beau tells me.

"She got pregnant." The shift in Beau is subtle and filled with pain. "We talked about keeping it, but in the end . . . I went with her to her appointment."

"Why did you break up with her?"

"She had a hard time dealing with it. I tried to help." Resting his elbows on the table, he scrubs his hands over his face. "Her parents are very religious. That's how she was raised. The guilt ate at her and she took it out on me. We argued. A lot. I didn't know how to fix things for her. Then she told me she met someone else and, I don't know, I sort of lost it. I told her I never wanted to see her again." He lowers his hands. "But that wasn't true."

"Was she seeing someone else?"

"Yeah. A few times."

"Do you know who it was?"

"Ask her friend Maisy."

"You don't know his name?"

"Would you want to know the name of the guy your girl was cheating on you with?"

"Only so I could find him and punch him in the face."

He cracks half a smile. "It was tempting. But then I'd have a name and a face to imagine her with."

I change the subject. "The two of you were getting back together."

"She called me one night and we talked. She apologized. I apologized." He bows his head. "She cried."

Cora's tear-streaked face flashes in my mind and I feel for him. I hate it when chicks cry. I especially hated seeing Cora do it.

"What else did you talk about?" I ask.

"She told me about the strange things that were happening around her apartment."

"Do you know if she ever called the police?"

"I told her she should call the cops. She said she would. We talked a few more times over the next couple of weeks. Things got . . . better. She invited me over to her apartment."

"The night before she was killed."

"Yeah."

"You had sex with her."

He doesn't answer. He doesn't have to. It was his DNA on and inside her body that hung him at trial.

"I loved her." His softly spoken words echo inside me, reverberating in time with my heartbeat.

It takes a moment before I can find my voice again. "Thank you."

I start to rise, but he reaches a hand out. "Is there really a new lead, like Cora said? A witness?" He pulls his hand back when I resume my seat.

"The downstairs neighbor, but we're having a hard time finding her."

"Mrs. Wheeler?"

"That's the one."

He rubs at his jaw. "She had a cousin who used to come and take care of her. Joni. No, Jodi something. Aagh. What was her last name?"

"Jodi Samuels. She's dead. Can you think of anyone else who might know where she is?"

His harsh laugh has heads turning. "Just my fucking luck. Are you sure Mrs. Wheeler isn't dead too?"

"There's no death certificate and someone keeps cashing her Social Security checks."

He's quiet so long I start to shift in my seat. And then, "Zelda would know. Have you talked to her?"

"Cora tried—"

"But she wouldn't talk to the sister of Cassandra's murderer."

"Something like that. I'm planning on taking a shot at her on my own. She doesn't know who I am or that I'm working with Cora. I can come at her from a different angle —a law student investigating a local case, maybe."

He studies me as though he's trying to get a read on me. "You and Cora?"

Me and Cora. There are no words for me and Cora. "Not really," I answer truthfully.

"Huh." He does that quiet thing again where it's like he's trying to do a mind meld with me or something. "It's because of me, isn't it?"

"It's because of a lot of things, but yeah, mostly you."

He takes a moment to process this. "Ask me anything

you want. I'll answer. You can call. I get phone privileges once a week, so you don't have to drive out." He stands. "Don't let her get away with that shit. I'd give up the rest of my days for just one more day with Cassandra."

He disappears through a door before I can form a response.

I walk out of the prison into the sunshine to find Cora leaning against my car. Her head is bent over her phone. I walk straight up to her, lift her chin with a finger, and kiss her. She doesn't react at first, and then she's melting into me. This is the first time I've kissed her with her body up against mine. She feels so damn good. I move closer, pressing her between the car and me. She's not very experienced, but I don't care. I like it. She's a very fast learner. Kissing her has been all I've wanted to do for weeks, and now that I am, I'm imagining so much more. I want to take her clothes off and lie down next to her. I want to explore her body and make it mine. I want so many things with her.

I break the kiss and look down at her, rubbing my knuckles across her cheek. She's so damn beautiful. I get lost sometimes looking at her.

She wraps her arms around my waist. "What was that for?"

"Would you go out with me tonight?"

"Did Beau tell you something? Do you have a new lead on Edith Wheeler? What did he—"

I press a finger to her lips, cutting her off. "I'm asking you out on a date."

"What? Why?"

The fact that she has to ask makes me wonder if she's ever been on a date. "Because I want to pick you up at your place, take you out for dinner, and kiss you good night."

"I was thinking of talking to a friend of Beau's tonight who knew Cassandra pretty well—"

I silence her again. "Tomorrow. Tonight you're going out with me."

"What the hell went on in there? What did Beau say? Did he—"

"I'll tell you over dinner." I walk over to the other side of the car and open her door. "Wear something pretty."

She climbs in and glares up at me. "I don't know what the hell happened in there or what Beau said to you, and I'm pretty sure I don't want to know."

I close the door and get in on my side. It's a long ride back and a long time to dodge Cora's questions. I turn up the radio and take her hand.

"Just enjoy the ride," I tell her.

Beau's whispered declaration of love for Cassandra haunts me. Somewhere out in the middle of the nowhere desert I decide I'm not ever going to give up on Cora.

Something pretty. I don't own anything pretty. I own useful and comfortable, and that's about it.

Leo makes me leave the office earlier than I want to. He's going to pick me up in an hour and a half. I don't know how it got this far or why I haven't stopped it before now. I shouldn't be going on this date. I shouldn't want to be pretty for Leo and I shouldn't like him as much as I seem to. That last thought has me wondering again—how in the hell did this happen?

The other day I caught myself staring at him instead of at the computer screen. What's the matter with me? He's somehow wormed his way in through the cracks in my defenses. And the thing is I never saw it coming. There was nothing overt or forthright about his approach. He stole in like a thief and dismantled all of my defenses against him. I don't protest at all when he takes my hand or hands me something I was just about to look for. I answer when he calls. I let him kiss me.

I pull up to my friend Jamie's house and park. She still lives with her mother in the house she grew up in. Someone else lives in the house I grew up in. Some new family, pressing new memories into the walls and pushing my family's out. Dad moving out during Beau's trial was the beginning of the end. A few months later I came home from school to find a For Sale sign in our front yard. I never told Beau they sold the house. I didn't have the heart to.

Jamie answers the door, chewing a wad of gum as big as her tongue. I don't know what it is with her and gum. It's some kind of oral fixation I don't want to know the roots of. People say we look alike, but personality-wise we're opposite in every way. Somehow we work. I don't question it. I just roll with it.

"I've got just the thing." She yanks me into the house and tows me down the hall to her room. It's a mess—clothes everywhere. She pulls a couple dresses out of her closet and holds one up to me. "I like you in black, but not this one." She tosses it on the bed and holds up another one. "This could work." She hangs it on the door of the closet. "So tell me about him." She does some more rifling through the racks.

"His name is Leo."

Her head pops out. "Leo Nash?"

How did she . . . ? "You know him?"

She snorts. "My brother played baseball with him. Girl, you bagged yourself a big fish if you're going out with Leo Nash."

"What do you mean?"

"I mean he got drafted by the Pirates right out of high school, but he took the full ride scholarship to UCLA instead. Now I hear he's in law school, top of his class. He's already gotten a couple of job offers and he doesn't graduate for another year. Plus he's hot. Seriously hot. How did you meet him? Oh, right, his dad's agency. Wow. Okay. This"—

she shoves the dress she set aside back into the closet—"isn't going to work. We need something special, sexy. Oh! I know just the thing."

She digs around some more and comes up with a garment bag. "I've been saving this for a special occasion, but I think it will be perfect for you. Oh, man, are you going to knock him on his ass when he sees you in this."

She pulls the garment bag away and I can't believe how beautiful the dress is. I've never worn anything like it. I've never seen anything like it. I finger the fabric. The ivory Ultrasuede is buttery soft and surprisingly light.

She shoves it at me. "Try it on."

I pull my T-shirt off and shuck my jeans. She helps me pull the dress over my head and zips up the back.

"Look at yourself." She pushes me toward the stand-up mirror in the corner.

I turn from one side to the other, examining my appearance. The way it nips in at the waist makes it look incredibly tiny. There's just enough cleavage that I'm not going to have to worry about bending over.

"I was going to wear that when I lost ten pounds." She pinches her waist. "That was five pounds ago. It's perfect on you."

"I can't." I finger the price tag hanging under my arm. "This is new."

"Shut up. Yes, you can. Oh! I've got the perfect shoes." She dives into the bottom of her closet. After a few moments she comes up with a shoebox and lifts the lid. "These."

Cobalt-blue leather slides sit nestled in white tissue paper. "No. I couldn't."

"Yes. Yes." She takes them out of the box and shoves one into each of my hands. "Put them on right now. Do it."

I slip them on and stare at my reflection. I've never worn anything so fancy and nice.

She bundles my hair at the top of my head with her hand. "You have to wear your hair up. Damn. You have no idea how pretty you are, Cora. He's going to just die when he sees you."

"It's the dress. And the shoes. Are you sure, Jamie? What if I spill spaghetti sauce on it or something?"

"Don't order spaghetti."

"I can't."

"Wear it and the shoes, and we're even. But you have to tell me everything that happens on your date. Ooooo," she squeals. "I'm so excited for you."

She doesn't say it, but she knows this is my first date. Ever. I wasn't nervous before she told me all that stuff about Leo. He was just Leo then, but now he's like this unattainable, way-out-of-my-reach guy. I can't do this. I'm going to call and cancel. No, I'll text him, then turn my phone off so I can't see his response and he can't talk me into changing my mind.

"Don't you dare cancel on him, Cora."

I swear it's like she can read my mind. "This is such a bad idea."

"He obviously doesn't think so, and neither do I. Go. Have fun. And then call me and tell me if he's a good kisser or not."

Heat creeps up my neck to my face.

"Oh, my God. You've already kissed him. Well?" She nudges my arm with her elbow. "How was it?"

I can't speak. I don't have words for how very much it was to kiss Leo Nash.

"That good. Damn. Good for you. It's about time you got out."

Jamie and I have been friends since the third grade. She's the only one I have left from my life before. All of my other friends dropped me one by one until I looked around one day just after Beau's conviction and realized they were all gone. And the odd thing was I didn't miss them. I wasn't the same person they'd befriended. I was someone new and unrecognizable. I didn't understand the things they talked about. My life had taken a million-mile trip to places they never could've imagined.

"I don't know," I tell her. Because I don't. I don't know what the hell I'm doing dressing up. I don't know how to act on a date and I don't know what to do with all of the new information I have on Leo.

"Go. You deserve this. And I want you to know right now that if you don't go out on this date I will never speak to you again." She's not serious.

"Why did you have to tell me all that stuff about him?"

"That's what's freaking you out?"

"Kind of." Yes.

"He asked you out because he likes you. That says more about him than anything I could say." She takes me by the shoulders and turns me toward her. "Go out. Have a good time. Get your lipstick smudged by a hot guy. You deserve this more than anyone else I know. Beau would be so pissed if he knew that you've turned your life into a shrine to him."

"I have not."

She glares at me.

"It's not a shrine," I insist.

"Go on this date and prove it."

"I don't like you."

"I've had a crush on Leo Nash since the eighth grade, so right now I'm not liking you very much either." She smiles. "Wear this dress and those shoes and knock him on his ass."

"Fine."

I take the shoes, the dress, and the earrings she pressed into my hand before sending me home. I spend more time putting my makeup on and doing my hair than I ever have in my life. Normally I'm pretty minimalistic, but tonight I add a smoky eye shadow that makes the blue of my eyes pop and a shimmery lipstick that makes my lips look fuller than they are. Even with the extra time I took, I'm ready fifteen minutes early.

As I stare at my reflection, hardly recognizing myself, I wonder what Leo is going to think. And then I wonder why I care so much. And then I think about Beau and it takes everything in me not to rip everything off, scrub my face, and pretend I'm not home when Leo rings the doorbell. This feels all wrong. I can't believe I let Leo bulldoze me into agreeing to this date. Twisting my hands, I pace back and forth in my small apartment. Oliver sits a few feet away, his tail curled around his feet, watching me with his accusing green eyes.

I can't do this. I pull my cellphone out of my purse to text Leo when the doorbell rings. Oliver continues to stare at me. The bell rings again.

I'm sorry, I silently tell Oliver. His gaze bores into me and I'm trapped by the condemnation in his eyes.

Leo knocks and I jump. "Cora?"

"I can't leave him out there," I tell the cat.

No response. His glare tracks me as I go to the door and open it.

Leo's hand is raised as though he was going to knock again. His jaw goes slack and now I have two sets of eyes staring at me from opposite sides. I don't know what to do. I'm caught between what I should do and what I want to do.

"Wow," Leo finally says. His gaze is everywhere, taking

me in, from my freshly painted toenails to the soft bun at the top of my head. He offers me a small bouquet of white roses. "These are for you."

"Thank you." I love the smell of roses. I wonder how he knew that.

He's the most dressed up I've ever seen him, in a button-down shirt and nice slacks. His hair is combed back from his cleanly shaven face and I can't believe how handsome he is.

We stand there in awkward silence, taking in each other's appearance. I have no reference for what I'm supposed to do here. What is the protocol? Should I let him in? I should let him in.

Opening the door wider, I wave him inside. "Come in."

Leo's gaze stays glued to me until he passes. He stops abruptly just inside the door. "You have a cat."

I close the door. "That's Oliver. He's not really my cat. He just lives here."

"Cora." His voice is soft with shock. "Is that Cassandra's cat?"

"I found him outside her apartment a few days . . . after. No one wanted him, I guess."

Leo leans against the door, looking at me like he just can't believe me. I don't know where to look or what to do. Somewhere behind me I know Oliver is staring at me the same way Leo is.

Leo reaches for one of my hands, untwisting it from the bouquet that I'm practically crushing. "You took him in."

"It's more like he lets me feed him."

He puts a hand to my cheek and leans in to kiss me. He smells good. So good. I close my eyes and kiss him back.

"I don't know how you do it," he says, as he ends the kiss. "But you constantly surprise me."

I can't tell from his tone if that's a good thing or a bad thing.

"That dress." He steps back and studies me again, with that same kind of glazed look in his eyes. "Wow."

"I should put these in some water." I untangle myself from him, needing some distance. I wonder if I'll ever get used to compliments.

Oliver flicks his tail and walks away. He's not happy with me. I'm going to pay for this later, probably with a regurgitated furball on my pillow.

Leo takes a short stroll around my apartment. Such as it is. I was lucky to find this converted garage. It's small, but it suits my purposes. I take care of the main house when the owners go out of town. In exchange, I pay next to nothing in rent. He stops to examine a photo of Beau and me that was taken just before Cassandra was killed. It's my favorite pic of the two of us. I can see who we used to be before and I can almost remember how it felt.

I don't have a vase, so I put the flowers in a blue jar I got at a garage sale and set them on my little dining table. They look pretty. I finger a petal. These are the first flowers I've ever gotten from a guy. How sad that is.

"Are you ready?"

No, I'm not ready. I still think this is a really bad idea on every level. But there's so much expectation in Leo's face I feel like I can't let him down. Smoothing the front of my dress, I decide that I'll see how tonight goes. It's just one night. I can give him one night.

"Sure."

He walks me to his car and holds open the door for me. His hands are a little shaky and I wonder if he's anywhere near as nervous as me. That's not possible. He's probably been on hundreds of dates. I don't hold that or his prior relationship with Savannah against him. He doesn't owe me anything. It's not like we're a couple, anyway. We're . . . I don't know what we are. Whatever it is, it's just for tonight. Tomorrow we'll go back to the way things were.

Even as I tell myself this, I don't believe it. I can't imagine going back, and the truth is I don't want to.

12

LEO

H o-ly. Shit.

I'm trying really hard to act cool, but Cora in that dress is killing me. When she opened the door I thought my head was going to explode. She did something with her hair—piling it on top of her head—making everything about her softer somehow. And her eyes, that intense, drop-me-to-my-knees blue, pinned me where I stood. I thought she was pretty before, but I was wrong. She is absolutely without a doubt the most beautiful girl I've ever seen.

And she's going out with me.

I don't know what I was expecting when I asked her out on this date. All I know is that she is so far out of my league and she doesn't even know it. I steal another glance at her. I've been sneaking looks at her all night. I'm not the only one. Every guy we pass gives her the once-over, making me want to punch him in the face. If I'm not holding her hand, I touch her back or her shoulder to signal that she's mine.

Except she isn't, really. We're on this date, attempting to have a good time, but I can tell her mind isn't entirely on what's happening at our small table in the corner of the restaurant. I figure she'll break sometime before the waiter comes to take our order and ask me what happened with Beau. What her brother is going through is as much a part of her as the blue of her eyes. I have to accept that. He's the other person at the table with us. The invisible uninvited guest. Everything she does is a means to the end of freeing her brother. Even this date we're on is part of it. I don't kid myself that she agreed to go out with me because she wanted to. I'm holding information she wants.

She lays her menu down and I know this is it. She's going to ask me about Beau. We can't have anything that's just ours.

She takes a quick sip of water. "I hear you play baseball."

I stare at her for a moment. What?

"You used to play with my friend Jamie Osborne's brother Matt."

"Yeah."

She fiddles with her water glass. "What position do you play?"

"Pitcher. Or I did. I don't play anymore."

"Oh."

"How do you know Jamie?"

"We've been friends a long time. Since elementary school."

"So you know Matt."

"He tried to make me eat a bug once." She has a hint of a smile, so I know this is a good memory. "I got him back by putting snails in his bed."

"That sounds like him. Good for you for getting him back."

"Do you ever miss it? Playing baseball?"

"Sometimes. I'm too busy now with law school. It was fun while it lasted."

"What kind of law do you want to practice?"

At every turn she catches me off guard. This is such a normal, first-date kind of conversation I'm having trouble believing I'm having it with Cora.

"I want to work for the district attorney's office here in San Diego."

"You want to put people like Beau in prison?" Her tone takes a dangerous turn.

"I want to put guilty people in prison."

"How can you be sure they're one hundred percent guilty? I'm sure the DA who prosecuted my brother thought she was doing the right thing. Especially when she asked the judge for the death penalty."

I'm in deep shit here, with no way out. I should've seen this coming. "I won't be like that."

"Why a prosecutor and not a public defender? The system could use a hell of a lot more good public defenders. I know Beau could've used one." She holds up an angry finger. "Just one."

"I can't undo what was done to your brother, but I can make sure that every case I prosecute is a good one."

She sits back in her seat and glares at me. She hates me now, I can see it. I'm lumped in with the asshole who sent her brother to prison. I have to find a way to convince her I'm not the enemy. I can do more good on the prosecutor's side than the defender's side. I know this. I have to make her know this.

"Cora, you should know me well enough by now to know that I will be better than the DA who sent your brother to prison."

"You say that now and maybe you mean it, but when

you've got a hundred and fifty cases that you're expected to close with a conviction or a plea deal, you cut corners to do it. Did you know that close to seventy-five percent of all wrongful convictions are due to official misconduct, including prosecutors?"

"That's not going to be me. Someone has to put away the bad guys, Cora, and I want to be one of the people who do that. They can't be allowed loose in our society to perpetrate again and again."

"And you're fine with a few innocent people getting put away in the process?"

"Of course not."

"It happens."

"And dolphins get caught in fishing nets. But that didn't stop you from ordering fish for dinner."

Her mouth drops open and she glares at me like she can't believe what a complete and total asshole I am. My whole body goes hot. I can't believe that just came out of my stupid fucking mouth either. I've just equated her brother to so much debris that inadvertently gets swept up in the greater good of the justice system's net. I thought Cora would be the one to ruin our date. But no, it's me. I've fucked this up so badly I don't see any way of recovering it.

And they haven't even brought us our salads yet.

She snaps her jaw shut with a click I can hear across the table. Her lips flatten and the blue of her eyes is barely visible. I've seen myriad emotions on Cora. By far this is the scariest I've ever seen her. It's worse even than her tears, and at the same time she's so goddamn beautiful, glaring at me across the candlelit table, that I'm struck again by how fucking lucky I am to be in the same room with her, let alone out on this date.

"So," she says, "basically your justice-system philosophy

equates to: You can't bake a cake without breaking a few eggs?"

"It's not that simple and you know it. There is no black and white here. Our justice system is the greatest in the world and I have to believe that the vast majority of the people working in it are good and genuinely interested in seeing justice served. Otherwise what's the point of it all?"

"A part of me knows you're right, but the other part of me knows firsthand that our justice system is not just. It's as flawed as the mortals running it. And when you involve people in everything from religion to our court system you invite greed, revenge, laziness, and ambition. People are self-ish. They'll put their own goals and desires before others in a hot minute."

"Maybe I have more faith in humanity than you do."

"You definitely do, because I don't have any at all."

The waiter appears at the table with our salads and slides them in front of us. "Freshly ground pepper?"

"No, thank you."

"Yes, please."

We can't even agree on fucking pepper.

"Can I get anything else for you?"

We both shake our heads.

"Your dinners will be out shortly."

The waiter is gone and so is the energy at our table. I'm not going to convince her to see my side and there's no way I'll ever see hers. We chew in silence, the clinking and clanking of our silverware unusually loud in the void. There are so many fundamental differences between us it's a miracle we can stand to be in the same room with each other.

Cora sets her fork down and wipes her mouth. "What did Beau tell you?"

"He broke up with Cassandra because she was seeing someone else."

"Did he know who?"

"No, but he said her friend Maisy might. I'm going to see if I can talk to her, maybe use the law-student-studying-a-local-case angle. I'm also going to try to take a run at Zelda to see if she might know where Mrs. Wheeler is."

"What else did he say?"

"He said he gets phone privileges once a week and that if I have any more questions for him I should call instead of driving out there."

"What did you say to him to get him to cooperate?" she asks.

"What do you mean?"

"You know exactly what I mean. What did you say?"

"He didn't want to answer my questions at first. I reminded him how stubborn and relentless you've been on his behalf and that it didn't matter what he said. You'll never give up on him, so he may as well help out."

"That's not all you said."

"No, but that's between him and me."

She eyes me like she's trying to decide if she's going to kick me in the nuts or punch me in the face.

"I got him to cooperate," I say. "I thought you'd be ecstatic about that."

"I am."

"So that's your ecstatic face?"

"No, this is my pissed-off-at-my-brother face mixed with my frustrated-with-you face."

I laugh. She never does or says what I expect her to.

The waiter arrives with our dinners, sets them in front of us, does the usual can-I-get-you-anything-else thing, and leaves.

Cora stares down at her plate.

"Something wrong?"

"Fish doesn't sound as good as it did when I ordered it."

"Want to switch for my chicken?"

"Actually . . . yes."

I swap our plates.

She looks so relieved. "Thank you."

"I figured it's the least I could do since I don't seem to have a problem with breaking eggs and dolphin casualties."

She pauses with a bite of chicken inches from her mouth. "I wasn't exactly being fair with you earlier. I do know that you won't be like the prosecutors who go after convictions no matter the cost."

"Thank you. Besides complimenting my ass, that's the nicest thing you've ever said to me."

She covers her mouth and laughs, deep-throated and sexy. This is the first time I've ever made her laugh. And only the second time I've ever seen her do it. I have got to get her to do it more often. Whatever it takes. She's someone who should be laughing all the time. In the photo I saw of her and her brother at her place I could tell she once was someone who laughed freely and openly. I bet she never covered her mouth or somehow managed to look guilty doing it back then.

"You're so gorgeous," I fumble out.

She stops laughing, a bewildered expression replacing her joy. She looks down at her plate. "Thank you."

She's embarrassed. I've embarrassed Cora Hollis. I didn't think it was possible, like not even remotely. She's even blushing. This is a side of her I've never seen. I like it. A lot.

"So, cosmetology school?" I ask her.

"What?"

"You told that realtor you were in cosmetology school."

"Oh, yeah." She shrugs. "I had to tell her something."

"Is that something you want to do?"

"Maybe someday."

"Have you looked into it?"

"No. Even if I had the time, I don't have the money."

"Do you do your own hair?"

She nods. "And some of my friends' hair too."

"You must be very good if they're willing to let you work on them without going to school."

One of her shoulders goes up. "I haven't melted off anybody's hair yet."

"Would you cut mine?"

"I could."

"I'd pay you. I mean, I pay a lady now. I may as well pay you instead."

She shakes her head. "You don't have to pay me."

"Do your friends pay you?"

"Or we trade."

"So then why won't you take my money?"

"With you it would be more like a trade. You got Beau to agree to talk about Cassandra. I owe you about twenty haircuts for that."

Now I'm the one who's embarrassed. "I didn't do that to get something in return."

"If you want me to cut your hair you're going to have to let me do it for trade."

"How about for dates?"

"Leo . . ." she starts.

I've taken it too far, but hey, it was worth a shot. "Just kidding."

She looks at me for a moment like she's trying to figure out if I really am joking or not. I'm not. Despite how disastrous this date's been, I want to take her out again.

Somehow we manage to finish dinner and dessert without me pissing her off again and now I'm standing on her front porch with her. The moon is huge and low in the sky, hanging over us like a lantern. Cora by Moonlight. That's what I'll call this moment. I lean in for a kiss, but she stops me with a hand on my chest.

"I don't think this is a good idea," she says.

Yes, it is. It's a damn good idea. "Why?"

"Look, I like you—"

"Oh, hell." No good conversation ever starts that way.

"No, I mean it. I do like—"

I silence her with a kiss, backing her up against her front door. I pour everything I have in me into this kiss. I want her to know all the things I can't say before she shuts the door on me, on the possibility of us. She kisses me back and I take advantage, using every ounce of skill I have to get her to change her mind. I want her to want me the way I want her.

Her arms wind around my neck and she brings me closer, threading her hands through my hair. It's all I can do not to push things further than I know she's ready for. I want to touch her. Everywhere. I want her to touch me. Bringing her tight against me, I use my mouth and tongue to say the things I can't. The little sound she makes as she moves against me drives me crazy. If she keeps this up I'm going to break the promise I made to myself to go slowly with her. She's not ready for everything I want to do to her.

I pull back with little nips and kisses along her jaw. She tilts her head, giving me more.

"Go out with me again," I whisper, then bite her earlobe.

She makes a noise that I can't quite make out.

I lick around the shell of her ear. "Cora," I coax. "Go out with me again."

"Yes," she moans.

For a moment I'm struck with the image of her beneath me saying that over and over again. I put one hand on the door behind her, then the other, because if I don't get my hands off her I'm not going to be able to stop.

I give her a hard kiss and push away from her, separating us and unwinding her arms from around my neck.

"Good night, Bluebird." I open her door and guide her inside.

She blinks at me for a moment, then slowly closes the door. I make myself walk back to my car and climb inside. That girl is going to kill me. I force myself to start the car and pull away from the curb. You'll see her tomorrow, I tell myself. And I did get the promise of another date out of her. Even after nearly blowing it with my comments about her brother.

The whole way home, what Cora said about prosecutor misconduct rolls around in my brain. I can't get it out of my head. Somehow I have to prove to her that not all prosecutors are in it to close cases at any cost, including the DA who got the conviction on her brother. If I can somehow get ahold of the DA's case notes and copies of her files, I can show her that Beau's conviction was an unintentional mistake. He truly was a dolphin in the fishnet.

13

CORA

I don't know how Leo does it. From the outside he looks like a total slacker. But somehow he manages to pull things off that I never could. Like getting Beau to open up to him and actually agreeing to talk on the phone. Beau hates talking on the phone. Even before he went to prison he had a thing about telephones. He'd say what he needed to say and then end the call. Sometimes in the middle of the other person's sentence. Used to drive my mom nuts. The only person he ever spent any real time with on the phone was Cassandra.

That fact says everything about their relationship.

I also don't know how Leo managed to get me to agree to go out with him again. Our first date proved how much I suck at it. I can't even carry on a normal conversation without bringing it back to me and especially back to what happened to Beau. I never used to worry about how that little quirk of mine affected my relationships with people. After losing just about everyone in my life after Beau's conviction, there weren't a lot of people left around to offend. And those who stuck accepted my obsession.

What does he see in me? He could have just about anyone. Hell, he had Savannah and probably a dozen girls just like her. What does he want with me and my cargo ship of baggage?

I pace our tiny office, waiting for Leo to get back from talking to Cassandra's friend Maisy. It took us a few days to track her down. To our surprise she agreed to meet with Leo, totally buying his ruse of being a law student researching a high-profile local case. Leo had an appointment with her first thing this morning and texted me an hour ago to tell me he has some news, but he didn't say what. It's killing me not to know.

At some point in the past few weeks I've come to see Leo as a partner in this fight. Before I met him I never would've been comfortable sitting on the sidelines while someone else worked on Beau's behalf. No, that's not true. I can pinpoint exactly when it was that I gave over all my trust to Leo—when he got Beau to agree to his visit.

The outer door opens and I rush out to the reception area, hoping it's Leo at last. I come to a screeching halt at the sight of my mother peeling off her sunglasses.

"Hello. I'm here to see Cora Hollis."

My first reaction is to back away slowly and pretend I'm not here. No such luck. Both my mom and Savannah turn toward me. I have no choice but to paste on a smile.

"There she is," my mother says.

"What are you doing here?" I ask.

"I came to see you, since you don't answer your phone." She says this as though she sees me all the time. I haven't seen her since Mother's Day and I saw her then only out of guilt.

And there's a reason I don't answer my phone when she calls.

Savannah leans back in her chair with a smirk, totally onto what a giant farce my mother's visit is.

"Why don't we take this to the conference room?" I don't want my mom to see Leo's and my office. It's littered with snippets of Beau's case. She'd take one look and launch into some shit about how I don't take her feelings into account and how could both of her children have turned out so badly?

"Mr. Nash has a client coming in fifteen minutes," Savannah says. She's enjoying this way too much.

"We'll be finished by then," I say. "Mom?" I motion for her to follow me down the hall and close the door after us. "What's wrong?"

"For starters, you can tell me why a private detective— one of your coworkers, I assume—called me, wanting to talk about your brother. I'm trying to put that chapter of my life behind me. I don't need my failings shoved in my face all the time. I can only assume this is your doing. Why do you have to constantly find new ways to torment me?"

I take a deep breath. When my mom gets that look of righteous indignation she reminds me so much of Beau that it makes it hard to look at her. He gets most of his features from her, whereas I look my like our dad, except for my eyes —those are all Mom. She used to like it that Beau looked so much like her. Now she does all she can to separate herself from him. Hence the blond highlights and colored contacts. I have good memories of my mom, but they're washed over and scarred from moments like this.

"You assumed wrong. I didn't tell anyone to contact you." Goddamn Leo. Why didn't he check with me first before involving my mother?

"I don't understand you." She looks around the room. "What are you doing here? What happened to that nice job at the law office? And when are you going to stop dying your hair that god-awful color? It's not professional. Men, real men, aren't going to give you a second look, let alone a first one, with that blue hair. You're a beautiful young woman. Why are you trying to turn people off?"

"I don't care what other people think of me."

She props a hand on her hip. "That's obvious."

"I'll tell Leo to leave you alone."

"Who's Leo?"

"You said someone from this agency contacted you."

"His name wasn't Leo."

If it wasn't Leo, then who? "What was his name?"

"I don't remember."

"If it wasn't Leo Nash, was it Ed Nash?"

"It was nobody named Nash."

"Jerry Sullivan? Al Torres?" She shakes her head after each name. I'm stumped. Those are the only guys who work at the agency. "Then it wasn't anyone from this agency. Probably a crank caller and you came down here for nothing."

"No, he said he was with a private detective agency and that he wanted to talk about your brother." Your brother, not Beau or her son, as if his conviction is somehow my fault.

"Which detective agency?"

"I told you, I don't know. I assumed you'd know, since you're the one who won't let anything go."

Yeah, I'm the one who won't let anything go. "If he calls again, get his info and I'll take care of it."

She puts a hand on the doorknob and pauses. "Have you seen your father lately?"

I don't know why my parents split up, because they're always asking about each other as though there's some glimmer of something still left between them. They've always had a strange dynamic I can't begin to understand.

Now that they're divorced, they use me to find out about the other instead of just picking up the phone or taking the time to go see each other. I hate being caught in their whatever it is.

"I saw him on Father's Day."

"How's he managing?"

"Fine. He's managing fine just like you."

"I'm not fine, not that you'd care."

With that, she tosses her hair over her shoulder and leaves. No goodbye. No see you around. She didn't ask about Beau. She never does. Our father never does either. But for our dad it's different. For him Beau is a deep hurt. For mom he's a deep shame. I'm not sure what I am to either of them anymore except a reminder of Beau.

Leo strolls in as my mother huffs out. He gives her a first, then second take. He raises his brows at me. My answer is to go into our office, out of Savannah's earshot.

He closes the door and leans back against it. "That had to be your mother."

"Yup."

"She didn't look very happy." He slides into his chair opposite me.

"She never is." Especially with me. "What did you find out from Maisy?"

"The name of the guy Cassandra was seeing. Dylan Newman."

"No way."

"You know him?"

"He was Beau's best friend. No wonder it was such a secret. Goddamn it. That sucks." I can't tell Beau this. He can never know.

"He apparently had a thing for Cassandra the whole

time she was going out with Beau. He moved in the minute the field was clear. Asshole."

"Yeah, and he stuck by Beau right up until he was convicted. Was in the courtroom nearly every day."

"If Beau and Cassandra got back together, that would've left Dylan the odd man out. Some guys wouldn't take that well."

"What are you saying? That Dylan could've killed her?" I shake my head. "No, I don't see it. He's an asshole for taking up with Cassandra as soon as it looked like she was free, but that doesn't make him a murderer."

"He was obsessed with her, according to Maisy—her word, not mine. That obsession could've turned violent. It also could account for the strange things that were happening to Cassandra."

"But if he's obsessed and he has access to the object of his obsession, why mess with her?"

"To ensure she needs him." He fakes picking up a phone. "Oh, Dylan." He pitches his voice really high like a woman's. "I need you to come over right now. Something strange just happened." He resumes his normal voice. "Could've gone down that way. Some guys have rescue fantasies. In his mind, he could've been ensuring she needs him to save her from the big bad whatever."

"Maybe. Okay, a strong maybe. He was pretty broken up at Cassandra's funeral. But then a lot of people were." Except Beau, because he wasn't there. He was sitting in a jail cell. "He still lives in San Diego. I'll call him and see if he'll meet with us."

"There's something else. After our conversation Saturday night I did some digging. What you said about prosecutor misconduct stuck with me." He pulls a file from his messenger bag. "So I called in a favor and got access to some of the prosecutor's notes and reports on the trial. I wanted to see if there were any inconsistencies."

"And?"

"There was. One."

I bolt upright in my chair. "What is it?"

"Two different DNA samples were discovered on Cassandra's bed."

"What?" I dig through my box until I find the DNA report that was given to Beau's attorney. I flip through it, searching for any mention of this second sample. "There's no mention of it in this report."

"I know."

"What was the sample?"

"A body hair found on Cassandra's bedding with the root intact."

"Why didn't they disclose that to Beau's lawyer?"

"All of the samples were tested and all were a match to the only suspect in the case—Beau. The lone unmatched sample was never compared to any database."

"Why the hell not?"

"They had a witness who placed Beau there at the time of the murder, a preponderance of his DNA on Cassandra's body, his fingerprints all over her apartment, and Beau himself admitting that he had sex with Cassandra shortly before she was killed. There was no reason to run that second sample."

"Except that it could've exonerated Beau."

"It might not have. It could be from her dad, her housekeeper, a friend, coworker, or anyone else in her life. It might not belong to the killer."

"But it might."

"Or it might not."

"There's no way to know that until it's run through the national and local databases."

"I don't want you to get your hopes up. No one's going to run it without a reason to."

"And with a conviction in the case, there's no reason to." I know I sound sarcastic, but I don't care. The unfairness of it kills me. None of this would've happened if they'd run that damn sample.

"Yeah, pretty much."

"So basically we have a smoking gun that can link the killer to the crime, but we have to find the guy before we can match it to him."

"Yup."

"That's so bass-ackwards."

"I know it is. I'm sorry."

I sigh. It's not his fault. The fact that he thought to get that info by himself and discovered the second sample is pretty dang awesome. Not to mention finding out about Dylan Newman and Cassandra.

"I have more news," he says. "Zelda agreed to meet with me."

"What is this magic you have?"

"What do you mean?"

"You get people to do stuff they don't want to do. First Beau, then Mindy, then Maisy, whoever you got that report from, now Zelda." And then there's me.

He taps the tips of his fingers together. "I have my ways."

"If only you could get Savannah to curb the hostility. Your record would be perfect."

"Is she still giving you a hard time?"

"Nothing I can't handle, but it's annoying. Just saying."

"I'll talk to her."

"Don't worry about it. When are you meeting Zelda?"

"Day after tomorrow at four o'clock. Why don't I pick you up for dinner afterward?" He slides that in so coolly.

"Do I have to wear something pretty?"

"If you want to. I'll be in whatever I wear to meet Zelda." Which means shorts or jeans and a T-shirt.

"So it's not a date?"

"It's definitely a date."

"See what I mean about getting people to do what they don't want to do?"

"Oh, you want to go out with me and you know it."

"Not really." Yes. Totally.

14

LEO

"You know, meeting with that Maisy chick was brutal," I tell Cora. "She kept hitting on me. I finally had to tell her I have a girlfriend."

She looks up from the DNA report I got for her, a corner of her lips tugging up. "Poor baby. Girls just throw themselves at you left and right, don't they?"

"Pretty much." Except for the one I really want to throw herself at me.

"You don't look any worse for the wear."

"But I am." I rise and move around our desks to sit down on the edge of hers next to where she's sitting. "I think I need a kiss to make it better."

"Go sit down."

"Come on, Cora. Just a little one."

"The problem with you is you never stop at just one."

"Kisses are like potato chips, you can't have just one."

"I don't like potato chips."

"Come on." I bring her around to look at me with a finger on her chin. "Hey. What's wrong?" Something in her eyes . . .

"Nothing. Get your kiss, then get your ass back to your own desk. I'm working here."

"No. Something's up. What's going on?"

She catches my finger and holds it in hers. A bold move for my little Bluebird. "My mom said something . . . I don't know whether to believe her or not. She can be more than a little dramatic."

"What did she say?"

"She said she got a phone call from a PI who wasn't anyone from here, asking about Beau's case."

"Did she get a name?"

"Of course not. That would be helpful."

"A phone number?"

She shakes her head.

"If he called on her cell or she has caller ID, then we could get the number."

"I didn't think to ask. I'm going to have to ask, aren't I?"

"That would be helpful."

"Ha, ha. But seriously, why would someone call my mom wanting to talk about Beau's case? And why identify them-selves as a PI?"

"Yeah, when they could've used the old law-student-studying-a-local-case ruse. That's worked for me three times now."

"I'm serious. What's going on?"

"I don't know. Could be a reporter."

"Beau's case is old news."

"Get that number from your mom and we'll check it out." I lean in and give her a quick peck on the lips.

She has a thing about not getting caught here in the office. I agree. All I need is my dad coming at me again or Savannah pulling more of her crap. I don't know what I'm going to do about Savannah. I've tried every way I know how to apologize and smooth things over with her, but she just doesn't want to forgive or forget. It pisses me off that she's taking it out on Cora though. That shit is not cool at all.

"We have a meeting with my dad in five minutes," I remind her.

"Yeah, okay." She's nose-deep in that report, comparing it to the one she had.

I go back to my seat and check my email. I put out some feelers that I'm hoping will lead to something new in the case. I don't want to tell Cora about them, because they could come to nothing. Which is pretty much what we've got right now—a whole lot of nothing.

There's a knock at the door, then my dad pokes his head in. "You mind if we start a little early? I've got another meeting."

"Sure," Cora says, packing up her files.

I do the same and we follow my dad to the conference room. He sits down with a mug of steaming coffee and a big grin on his face. Something's up. I close the door and take my seat next to Cora.

Dad starts, "As you know, I've been working on getting in to see your eyewitness, Damien LeFeaux, at Donovan state prison. Well, I've got a meeting with him next Saturday."

"I swear," Cora mumbles, "I don't know what kind of voodoo you Nashes have, but I'm glad to have it on my side."

"How'd you get him to agree?" I ask.

"I promised to give a message to his girlfriend, who won't visit him in prison. I also put a hundred bucks in his commissary account. Half now and half after we meet. He's the easiest and cheapest witness I've ever bought access to."

"I'll pay you back," Cora insists.

"No, this one's on me," Dad says. "I'm dying to know

what Mr. LeFeaux has to say. I have a feeling he'll fold like a lawn chair the minute I put any kind of pressure on him."

"We've made some headway ourselves." I tell him about what we've learned so far and what we've got lined up.

He's impressed. Hell, I'm impressed. I had no idea we'd get so far so soon. Or that I'd be any good at this investigation thing. When I glance at Cora I can tell she's impressed too, and not just with our progress, but with me as well. My throat gets tight and my face heats up. I look at Dad, the wall, the papers in front of me, anything to avoid the look Cora is giving me.

"You two seem to be working well together." Dad glances from me to Cora, looking for her affirmation.

"He's been a bigger help than I thought he'd be."

Ouch. But she's not wrong. I've surprised myself. The biggest shock of all is how much I actually like PI work. Maybe hanging out here during the summer did rub off on me or else it's in my genes. I don't dare let Dad in on any of this. He'd take it and run all the way to retirement if he even got a hint that he could go and leave me in charge.

"Good," Dad says. "And everything else is going okay?"

"There was one weird thing," Cora says. "My mom got a phone call from a man who said he was a private investigator asking about Beau's case. It's not anyone from here."

Dad leans forward in his chair. "Did she get his contact info?"

"No."

"I suggested checking her caller ID to see if we can get a phone number," I supply.

"I'd like to know who this PI is and what he wants. And if he is an actual PI, as he claims." Dad's gaze moves to Cora. "Can you get the number from your mother?"

"I'll see what I can do. She's not always the most helpful person in the world."

I try not to show my surprise. Cora hasn't talked much about her parents at all, and I can tell that her mom's visit upset her. I can also see that the prospect of getting the number out of her mom is about the last thing she wants to do.

Dad nods. "Have your parents ever been contacted by a private investigator before?"

"Not that I know of."

"Did they hire one to help with Beau's trial?"

"Definitely not."

Okaayyy. Sore subject.

Dad rises. "Good work, you two. Keep me in the loop. I'll let you know about my meeting with Mr. LeFeaux." He leaves Cora and me alone.

She closes the file she had open, then just sits there.

"Hey." I take her hand. "Do you want me to talk to your mom?"

"No, that would only make things worse. I'll take care of it."

"Are you all right?"

"You're lucky, you know that? Your dad is a really cool guy. I bet your whole family is cool."

"Not my little sisters. They're annoying."

"You have sisters?"

I can't believe this is the first time we've ever talked about our families. "Two. They're nineteen and sixteen."

"No brothers?"

"Nope. Do you have any other siblings besides Beau?"

"He's it. All I've got. Are your parents still married?"

"Yeah. Yours?" Cora would not be happy to know Dad

investigated her so I don't let on that I already know the answer to my question.

"They separated during Beau's trial. They finalized the divorce about a year after his conviction. I don't see them often."

"Why not?"

"It's awkward. They don't want to talk about Beau and he's all I want to talk about."

"Do they visit him?"

"Never. I'm the only one. His good friend Dylan visited a couple of times. Then I guess he moved on. Everybody's moved on."

I give her hand a squeeze. "Everyone except you."

"Everyone except me." She pulls her hand from mine, gathers her papers together, and rises. "I'm stuck, and now I guess you're stuck with me."

"Beau's lucky to have you and I'm glad to be stuck with you." She gives me a look like she doesn't believe me. "No, really. There's no one I'd rather be stuck with. Wait. That didn't come out right."

Her laugh does something funny to the pit of my stomach. "Thank you." She takes a quick peek at the hallway, then leans down and gives me a kiss.

It's only the second time she's kissed me. She's gone before I can pull her back down for another one.

I head out to follow her and practically run into Savannah. "Oh, hey, sorry."

She bumps my shoulder as she passes me to go into the conference room. "Yeah, right."

This is as good a time as any to talk to her. I close the door. "Look, I know I've been an asshole to you and I'm sorry for it, but when are you going to get over it?"

She slams a folder down on the table. "I am over it."

"You don't look or act like you are."

She shifts her posture, propping a hand on her hip. "Everything isn't always about you, you know. Shittier things have happened to me than hooking up with you. Not many, but a few."

Ouch. "So you're just in a bad mood in general? It has nothing to do with Cora or me?"

She snorts. "Contrary to what you seem to believe, the world does not revolve around you and that little bitch whose pants you're trying to get into. Word of advice? Get some new moves."

"So we're cool?"

"Cool isn't the word I'd use, but rest assured I don't give a shit what you do or don't do." She puts a pen at each person's place. "Or I should say who you do or don't do."

I start to leave, then turn back. "Are you okay? Is there anything I can do?"

She doesn't answer for a moment. It's like she's been put on pause. "Unless you can cure cancer, no." She goes back to laying out the materials for Dad's meeting.

I'm debating what to say or do next when I hear a sniff. Oh, damn. She's crying. She turns to the window and tries to hide that she's swiping at tears. I don't know what to do. I'm shit when it comes to stuff like this. My instinct is to leave and let her be, but it seems my feet don't agree.

I put a hand on her shoulder. "I'm sorry."

She turns in to my chest and lets loose, gripping fists of my shirt and sobbing. Fuuuuuuck. I awkwardly put my arms around her and pat her back. The door opens behind us. I don't even have to turn around to know who it is. Fucking shit, fuck, fuck.

Cora.

The door closes again, harder than normal. Goddamn it. I want to pry Savannah's fingers off me and run after Cora.

Instead, I ask, "Who has cancer?"

"My m-m-mom. Stage four."

I don't know anything about cancer except that the higher the number, the worse it is. "I'm sorry." I don't know what else to say. She's still holding on to me, so I put my arms around her for real and hold her. I am an ass for thinking her bad mood was all about me. "I'm sorry," I say again, for an entirely different reason.

She knocks my chest with her fist. "Stop saying that. You make me sound pitiful."

"You're not pitiful."

She pulls away a little and gives me a wobbly smile. "And you're not a total asshole."

"Thanks." I smile at her. "I think."

"I should get back to work." She steps out of my hold and swipes at her tears, wiping her hands off on her pants.

"Is there anything we can do?" I grab a box of tissues and hand it to her. "Does my dad know?"

She pulls out a wad and blots her face. "No, I haven't really told anybody. When I try to, I just start crying."

"Do you want me to tell him?"

"Yeah, could you? I have to go to the doctor with her next week. I don't want to have to explain. But just him. I don't want everybody in the office looking at me and feeling sorry for me."

"Sure." I back toward the door. "Will do."

"Thanks for, you know . . ." She motions with the tissues.

"Sure. Any time. I really am sorry about your mom."

"I know. Thanks."

I give her a half-wave and go off to find Cora, hoping I'm not totally screwed.

15

CORA

I'm not jealous. I'm not. It's not like there's anything going on between Leo and me. I mean, there is or there was, but it's not like we're exclusive. I don't know what we are exactly. Okay, no. That's bullshit. There is something between us. I just don't know what it is or—more importantly—what it is to Leo. I'm not even sure I know what it is, so how can I expect him to know or to act like he knows? Ugh.

Okay, I am jealous. He had his arms around Savannah. They were in a room with the door closed like they wanted privacy. I don't know what to make of that except that there's still something between them. And if there's still something between them, then there is going to be absolutely nothing between him and me. There. Decision made. Moving on. Except . . .

Leo walks into our office and closes the door. I don't look up. Whatever. I have more important things to do, things I should've been concentrating on instead of wasting time going on dates with someone who clearly doesn't know what or whom he wants. Let me make that decision for him —not me.

"It's not what it looked like in there," he says.

"Okay." I can feel his stare boring into the side of my head.

"Okay?"

I don't answer. I really don't want this drama in my life. I have enough going on with the phone call I just made to my mother and with my brother sitting in prison.

He leans against my desk next to me. "She was . . . I can't tell you what she was, but it wasn't what it looked like."

"Um, o-kaaayyy." This guy really needs to get off my desk and get his ass back to his own. We have work to do.

"Cora."

I don't look up. He can fuck off with his explanations.

He kneels down next to my chair. "Cora, look at me."

Sighing, I slam my pen down and look at him. "What?"

"I didn't mean for that to happen. She was—"

"Yes, I know. You can't tell me what she was, but it wasn't what it looked like. Got it. Can we get back to work now? My mom gave me a phone number for that PI."

"I was comforting her. She's been going through something—"

"Really. I get it. Can we move on?"

"She was crying." He holds out the front of his shirt, which has some wet spots on it. "See?"

"Sure."

"I couldn't just walk out of the room and leave her that way."

"Of course not."

"Cora, look at me." He turns my chair and plants his hands on the arms, trapping me and forcing my gaze back at him. "It wasn't what it looked like."

"Oh, my God, if you say that one more time I'm going to punch you. I've got it already."

He laughs. "God, you're so pretty when you're pissed."

"Then I must be gorgeous right now, because you're annoying the hell out of me."

He leans in for a kiss, but I turn my head. "Hey." Grasping my chin, he brings my face around to his. "You really are mad about Savannah and me. I swear I was just comforting her. She's going through something bad. That's why she's been in such a terrible mood."

"I'm not pissed at you, okay?"

"Then what is it?"

I'm mad at myself for allowing things to get this far—far enough that I care what he does or doesn't do with another chick. I hate that I was actually jealous of that bitch. And I hate that I'm relieved it wasn't what it looked like. But I don't tell him any of that. I have enough crazy going against me that I don't need to advertise my insecurities.

"It's my mom," I say instead. "She drives me insane." And that is the bald truth.

"So we're good?"

"I don't know what the hell we are, but good probably about covers it."

"Yeah, about that." He kisses me, catching me off guard.

I can smell Savannah's perfume on him and it makes me want to gag. I push him away.

"Hey." He strokes my cheek with his thumb, a worried line between his brows. "I thought we were okay."

"You reek of perfume. It's like kissing Savannah."

He tugs on his shirt and takes a whiff. "Yeah, I wouldn't like it if I kissed you and you smelled like another guy. I'll change my shirt. This one's all wet, anyway."

He pulls his shirt off in that way guys do—from the back

of his neck, over his head, and off. My gaze latches on to him like I've never seen a guy without a shirt as he goes to his desk, opens a drawer, and pulls out a new one. I can't stop staring. It's not like I've never seen a shirtless guy. I have a brother, for God's sake. But for some reason Leo without a shirt makes my nipples leap to attention like an arctic breeze just blew through here. Too soon he's tugging on the new shirt and the view is gone. Damn.

I cross my arms over my chest and try to pretend I'm not dying to know what the rest of him looks like. "Are you ready to get back to work now?"

"I don't know. Do I smell better?" He makes me smell him, which is not such a hardship now that he doesn't have Savannah's stench on him.

"You're fine." I pretend I'm totally unaffected by him, but his nearness combined with his scent and the sight I just saw is making that very difficult.

"Are you sure you're okay?"

No. "Yes."

Thankfully, he takes his seat at his desk and doesn't try for another kiss. "What's the number your mom gave you?" He keys it into the website the agency uses for reverse number lookup.

I hold my breath. The more I think about the PI phone call my mom got, the more it makes me jittery. Something isn't right.

"Huh," Leo says.

"What?" I'm up and out of my seat to look over his shoulder at his screen. "Why would a legit PI have a pre-paid cellphone?"

"We use them sometimes when we don't want to be traced, but if he was calling your mom in an official capacity, then there's no reason why he'd have to hide his identity."

"Let's call it. I want to see who answers."

I pull my phone out, but Leo puts his hand over the screen. "If this guy isn't legit, we don't want him knowing we're onto him. Hang on." He leaves, then comes back with a cellphone. "We should use a burner phone. Dad keeps some around for stuff like this." He keys the number into the phone and hits send.

I put my head next to his so I can hear. It rings and rings and then stops ringing. No outgoing message.

"He might've already gotten rid of the phone." Leo stares off for a moment. "I don't like this."

I've got goose bumps for an entirely different reason now. "What does it mean?"

"I don't know. We should talk to my dad."

"He's got that meeting."

Leo sits, tapping the burner phone on his desk. "Do you know if your dad has gotten any calls?"

"If he has, he hasn't told me about them. But then I haven't talked to him in a few weeks."

He looks surprised by this. My relationship with my parents is nothing like the one Leo has with his. There's no way to explain what the past five and a half years has done to my family. Besides the obvious things like Beau's conviction, my parent's divorce, and my emancipation at sixteen, the changes came swift and dramatic like a tsunami, washing some things away entirely, damaging others, and leaving some virtually untouched. There is no rhyme or reason for why things are the way they are between us. They just are. A closer family might've survived virtually intact. Then again, it might've been completely destroyed.

"Can you call him?" He has no idea what he's asking me to do, and I don't have the tools to explain.

"Sure." It has to be done. I know this. But I can't do it in front of Leo. I hitch a thumb over my shoulder. "I'm going to grab a water and some fresh air. I'll let you know what he says."

Sitting back in his chair, he gives me the strangest look —a mixture of confusion and concern and something else . . . hurt, maybe? I don't know and I don't have time to coddle his lack of understanding. Some things he'll just have to deal with and accept. Or not. That's totally up to him and not on me. I won't let it be on me. This is his problem, not mine.

I head out of our office and into the reception area, where Savannah is clickety-clacking away on her computer. She glances up at me for a second, then resumes whatever she's working on. I grab a bottle of water from the mini-fridge and go out onto the balcony. I immediately look for the orange alley cat. The big Tom sits on the fence, surveying the back passageway. He turns his head and our gazes collide. He watches me with ill-disguised boredom, barely blinking in the bright afternoon sun. For some reason he gives me the courage I need to make the call.

It rings three times and then Dad answers. "Hello?"

"Hey, it's me." This is a test. Sober Dad should recognize my voice. Drunk Dad will likely mistake me for just about anyone, including whoever he's banging at the moment.

"Cora?" Halfway to Inebriated Dad. Great.

"How are you doing?"

"Okay. Is something wrong?"

Yes. Everything. "No. I just called to ask if anyone's called you about Beau's case."

"Cora." He makes my name sound ugly, like a curse word. He hates it when anyone says Beau's name.

"Have you gotten a call or not?"

"This is why you called?"

"Yes."

I can hear the liquor sloshing in the bottle and his audible swallows. "No."

"Would you let me know if you do get a call?"

"No."

I control my sigh so that he can't hear it through the line. "So you did get a call?"

"I've got to go. I can't talk about this. You know that."

"I know. I'm not asking you to talk about it. I just need to know if you got a call like the one Mom got or not."

"Your mother got a call?" This is his way of asking about Mom but not really asking about Mom.

"Yes. She came to see me about it today. I thought maybe you might've gotten one too."

"She came to see you?" More sloshing and swallows.

"She asked about you."

He's silent so long I have to check my phone to see if we're still connected. Then finally, "What did you tell her?"

"Just that I saw you on Father's Day. The call upset her."

"How upset was she?"

"The usual. So did you get a call or not?"

"Yes."

"What did they say?"

"Why the fuck should I remember?" Deflecting. I learned a lot about this at my Al-Anon meetings.

"Was it from a private investigator?"

"No, goddamn it. Someone from the DA's office. I gotta go."

"Wait. When did they call?"

"In the morning. I think. Woke me up."

So pretty much sometime when the sun was up.

"Did you get a name or phone number?"

"Why do you always have to put your problems on me? I've got enough of my own. I really gotta go." He hangs up.

The fat orange cat stares at me with the same accusation that was in my father's voice. I take a deep breath and close my eyes, tilting my face toward the sun. My dad wasn't always like this. He was a musician with the most beautiful voice. He could play guitar like no one I'd ever seen. Every once in a while when I'm digging in the used CD bins at Goodwill I'll come across an album he played on as a session musician. Even if I didn't see his name on the jacket I would recognize his playing anywhere.

As far as I know he hasn't picked up a guitar in five and a half years.

16

LEO

The minute Cora walks back into the office I know something's wrong. My instinct is to go to her and hold her, but she's got her don't-fuck-with-me face firmly in place. If I make a move to comfort her I'd likely lose an eye or get my nuts shoved up into my throat. She's a tough one, my Bluebird, but not tough enough for the world she lives in.

She tosses her empty water bottle in the trash and drops into her chair behind her desk. "My dad got a call from someone in the DA's office. No name. No number. And no, I'm not going to ask him to get the number from his phone. It's a landline, so maybe we can pull his records. The call came in the morning/afternoon-ish, sometime on some day. That's all I've got."

"It's likely we'll run into the same issue that we ran into with the number your mom gave us, anyway, so having the number wouldn't make a difference." I say this partly because it will make her feel better and partly because it's abso-fucking-lutely true.

"Why is somebody calling my parents about my brother's old case?"

"I wish I knew."

"And why would they tell my mom they're from a PI's office and my dad they're from the DA's office? What are they trying to get from them?"

"Did either of them tell you what questions were asked?"

"Of course not. Again, that would be helpful. Why should they do anything remotely resembling helpful?"

I don't know what to say to her to make things better. I understand few things about Cora's life up until now. The things I do know about her are tragic and twisted. Every day she fascinates me more and more. How has she survived and thrived in this world that has done nothing but deal out one fuck-you after another to her?

"And these are the first calls either one of them has received about the case?" I ask. The timing . . .

"The only calls they ever got were from reporters. Everything else went through Beau's attorneys."

"Have you told anyone that you're working with us on the case?"

"Only my friend Jamie. My mom obviously knows I'm working here. I gave her and my dad my new work info for emergencies, but I didn't tell them why I'm here."

"Hmm." My suspicious mind circles the possibilities.

"What does 'hmm' mean?"

I'm not sure I should tell her. The likelihood of those calls being unrelated to Cora's sudden involvement with our agency is slim to none. Again, the timing . . . Why now and not a year or more ago? Could the real killer be monitoring her progress on the case? Could we have hit on something or be about to hit on something big?

"You think it might have something to do with me

working here, don't you?" She jackknifes upright. "It's the killer, isn't it? Oh, my God." She's up and pacing, her hands flapping out in front of her like they're on fire. "He's watching me. That's—"

"We don't know that. I'm just spinning possibilities here." I place myself in front of her to get her to stop pacing. "Hey." I take her chin in my hand to get her to look at me. "It's all right. It could be a reporter, looking for a new angle. It could be anything. We don't know for sure who is behind this or why."

"But why now? No one gave two shits about Beau's case except the media at the time of the trial. Why suddenly all this interest? You can't tell me it's not suspicious."

She's right. I can't tell her that because it is so fucking suspicious it has me worried for her. We're talking about a rapist and murderer who managed to cover up his crimes for more than five years. He's clever enough to use a burner phone to call Cora's mom and bold enough to call both her parents.

"It's suspicious. But . . . but it might not mean anything."

"That's bullshit and you know it. Nobody cared about Beau's case all this time and now out of the blue two phone calls? I don't buy it."

Yeah, I didn't think she'd really go for that bullshit. "What do you want to do?"

"I want to find out who that son of a bitch is."

"Only the government can track burner phones. We'd have to know where the phone was purchased to have any hope of surveillance catching him on camera. If he's smart —which I'm betting he is—he's already ditched the phone or phones he used to call your parents." Wow. I just impressed myself there with how much I know about investigatory stuff.

"So it's a dead end."

"Pretty much."

She lets out a frustrated noise and pulls away from me to start her pacing again. "How did he know to call my parents? Is he watching me? How much does he know about the case? How is he getting his information?"

Her questions are good and valid. If only I had answers for her. "We need to bring my dad in on this. He might have some answers." Or create more questions.

She hangs her head out into the hall, then pops back in. "He's still in his meeting."

"Come here." I hold my arms out.

She looks like she needs a hug. Or else I'm projecting. This shit just got real. I'm scared for Cora in a way I've never been scared before. To my surprise, she walks right to me and hugs me hard.

"It's going to be okay," I tell her.

"I know it is, because we're going to track that asshole down and put him in prison where he belongs. Nothing's changed here except that he outed himself. He's exposed himself in a way he never has before and I want to know why. Something we did triggered him to walk out of the shadows. We're going to keep doing what we're doing and draw him out even more."

"That's not a good idea."

"Yes, it is."

"No, it's not." I push on her arms to see her face. "There's more at risk here than freeing Beau. He knows who you are and what you're doing. He knows who your parents are and enough about them to call them. He probably knows the same or more about you. You live alone. Do I have to say it?" I sound desperate, because I am. She wants to taunt a rapist and murderer.

She blinks up at me. I can see that she's not listening to what I'm saying or else she heard me and is rejecting it. Either way, I don't like it.

"That cat didn't protect Cassandra and it can't protect you." I lay it out bluntly. "She's dead and now the man who killed her could be after you. Is this what Beau would want?"

She jerks away from me. "Don't you dare use Beau against me."

"I'll use whatever I have to to get you to listen to me. You're not thinking this through."

"What do you expect me to do? After all this time I finally, finally, have a possible lead on this asshole."

"We're taking this to my dad and whatever he decides is what we'll do. We're out of our league here, Bluebird. Don't you see that?"

"Of course I see it. I'm not an idiot. I'm also not going to tuck tail and run. I'll hear what your dad has to say and then I'll decide how to proceed."

"You're not putting yourself in jeopardy."

"Yes, Dad."

It's my turn to growl in frustration. Half the time I want to kiss her and the other half I want to punch a wall.

I stalk past Cora to the reception area. "When is my dad's meeting going to be over?" I ask Savannah.

"It should wrap up soon. Why?"

"Does he have another appointment after that?"

"No."

"We need to talk to him. Can you make sure he doesn't leave before we get to?"

"Sure."

"Thank you." I stomp back into Cora's and my office. "He'll be finished soon."

We glare across the room at each other, our arms folded across our chests. I'm not sure I can out-stubborn her any more than I can talk her out of doing whatever it is she's planning. Because I know she's planning something. I can see it in her bold blue eyes.

A door down the hall opens and my dad's and a couple other guys' voices drift into our office. His meeting is over. Savannah tells him we want to see him. He comes in to find Cora and me still in our standoff, glaring at each other.

"What's going on here?" he wants to know.

I fill him in on the phone call to Cora's dad, the burner phone, and the conclusions we've come to about the whole thing. I want him to tell Cora . . . Oh, hell. I don't know what I want him to tell Cora. We can't stop looking for the real killer. She has me over a barrel there. She won't ever give up on searching for the real killer and he'll likely do anything not to be found. Catching him solves the problem, but it also leaves Cora exposed.

"He's revealed himself," Cora tells my dad. "He's never done that before. Somehow we drew him out. We have to keep doing what we've been doing and draw him out further. He'll make a mistake, and when he does we'll catch him."

"We're not cops," Dad points out. "We have no jurisdiction to do anything to him. The only thing we can do is keep working the case."

"What if he goes after Cora?" I ask. "She lives alone just like Cassandra did."

Dad contemplates this. "Do you have someone you can stay with or who can stay with you?"

"The only person I could ask is my friend Jamie, and I'm not going to put her in the middle of this."

Dad's attention swings in my direction and his scowl

deepens. He knows what I'm thinking and he knows I won't say it without his being one hundred percent on board. He warned me off Cora and I didn't listen then, but this is so much bigger than my attraction to her—this is her life. I'm aware I have shit for experience. My life until now has left me completely unprepared for what I'm about to volunteer for.

Dad gives a brief nod.

"I can stay with you," I say. "Sleep on the couch."

Cora's gaze lasers in on me with the precision of a military drone. Again I've offered myself to her with absolutely nothing to recommend me. I proved once that I'm not totally useless to her. Maybe I can do it again if she gives me a chance.

I see the struggle in her expression and the moment she comes to a decision. "Okay." It's not quite the enthusiastic victory I wanted, but it's close enough.

"Do we need to have another talk about workplace decorum?" Dad asks.

Cora's eyes widen a fraction and she presses her lips together. She thinks this is funny.

"No."

He gives me the stern dad stare that says he means it. Cora is off-limits. Except I already blasted past and ignored those limits and I'm likely to keep right on doing that. Provided Cora's on board. Her part is yet to be decided. I'm still proving myself, and when I'm not I'm waiting for her to make room in her crowded life. The body is willing, but the mind is not. It's her mind that I'll have to convince that we deserve a chance. She can have more than Beau's case. She can have anything she wants. If only she wanted me.

"Good." Dad looks to Cora for confirmation. "You okay with this?"

My ears pound and my gaze narrows to where all I can see is Cora.

"On the couch," she confirms, for me more than for my dad. She's setting the limits between us and I'm just going to have to honor them.

"On the couch," I vow. I'm surprised at how much I mean it. The usual me would already be trying to find a way around the rules. That won't work with Cora. Nothing about her is usual and neither is whatever it is going on between us.

"Okay, then," Dad says. "Leo, can I talk to you for a moment in my office?"

"Sure." I follow him and take a seat as he closes his office door.

Sitting at his desk, he opens the bottom drawer, pulls out a small case, and hands it to me. I already know what's inside. I've coveted it since I was a kid and he first showed it to me. It's his backup piece from when he was a police officer.

"I want you to take this," he says. "Keep it loaded." He sets a box of ammunition on top of the case. "You don't have a permit to carry, but we can take care of that. For now it's enough that you'll have it at night just in case. I don't want you taking any chances. If anything, and I mean anything, at all happens, I want you calling nine-one-one. Don't be a hero. This gun is a backup plan. Got it?"

"Got it."

"When was the last time you went to the range?"

"A few weeks ago, with Brandon."

I don't own a gun, but my cousin and uncle own an arsenal. We go to the range whenever I come home from school. Coming from a long line of law enforcement officers and former military, it's practically in my DNA for me to love guns. Dad taught me not only to shoot, but to respect firearms. He taught my sisters too. It was the one cool thing about having a dad who's an ex-cop private investigator.

Dad nods. "All right, then. You're all set." He pauses and I know what's coming before he even thought to say it.

"I know," I say. "Respect her limits. I will. I do."

"There's something about her . . . I don't know. It brings out the dad in me, I guess. I don't mean to be hard on you. It's just that she needs . . . protecting."

"I feel the same, except for feeling fatherly toward her."

He chuckles. "Yeah, I got that."

"Thanks for this." I stand. "I'll take good care of it."

"I know you will. Remember—nine-one-one."

"Got it." I stop at the door. "One more thing. Savannah's mom has stage-four cancer. I don't know what kind. She might have to go to some doctor appointments with her. She wanted me to let you know and to keep it between just us."

"Damn. I knew something was up with her, but I thought it had to do with you."

"So did I. Learning the world doesn't revolve around me was quite the wakeup. Anyway, that's what's going on with her."

"Okay. Thanks for telling me."

"Sure."

"And Leo?"

"Yeah?"

"You're a good kid."

I leave with the case in hand and my dad's words echoing in my head. I know I'm lucky. My dad trusts me with more than his favorite gun. He trusts my word and that I'll do my best to make sure that Cora is okay. Now if only I can live up to all that trust.

17

CORA

We stop at Leo's parents' house for him to pack a bag. I'm not excited about having a roommate, especially one who pushes all of my buttons, even the ones I didn't know I had. I'm used to living alone. I've been on my own for a long time now, nearly a quarter of my life. I like being alone. Having him there is going to be awkward and weird, and I'm not sure how long I can be on my best behavior. I'm not hostessy. Jamie is the only person who has ever spent the night at my house and I'm ashamed to admit that most of those mornings I couldn't wait for her to leave.

Leo's parents' house looks a lot like the house I grew up in. The neighborhood with the toys in the yards, the dads out doing whatever dads do in garages, and the occasional dog walker give me an unexpected nostalgic pang. I took it for granted that things would always stay the same and that someday I'd bring my own family back to my childhood home for a visit. I don't imagine a converted garage apartment would have the same effect.

He opens the door and the sound hits me first. A dog

barks. Female voices drift from somewhere at the back of the house and the play-by-play of a baseball game blares at us from the left. Mr. Nash sits in a recliner with a beer in hand. For a moment I tense and then I remember that not everyone drinks to forget until the blackout of oblivion turns him into someone you don't recognize or want to know.

"Hey, Dad."

Mr. Nash raises a hand, his concentration on the game.

"Come and meet my mom," Leo says to me.

I don't remember the last time I met someone's mom.

We move into the kitchen area, where a woman lifts the lid on a pot and gives the contents a stir. Now I know where Leo got his good looks. He's the young male version of his mother. A young woman sits at the counter bar, doing homework. The radio is on, tuned to something classical.

"Hey, Mom. This is Cora."

Both sets of feminine eyes turn in my direction. Mrs. Nash smiles and puts the lid back on the pot.

"Cora, this is my mom, Laura. And that's my youngest and most annoying sister, Anne."

"Leo," Mrs. Nash admonishes. "Don't talk about your sister like that. Nice to meet you, Cora. Will you join us for dinner?"

Anne takes her time looking me over. "Hey," she finally says.

"I don't know," I answer Mrs. Nash, because I really don't know. I don't know how to act or what to say or how to get Anne to stop looking at me like she's memorizing me for a police sketch artist.

Another chick comes into the room, this one a little older than Anne. She skids to a stop when she spots me. "Oooo, Leo brought home a girrrrl." She strings out the last word, making it sound like Leo brought home a giant cockroach or something.

"Cut it out, Mary," Leo growls. "That's my other sister. Feel free to ignore her."

Mary walks right up me. "I love your hair. It totally matches your eyes. How did you get it that color?"

I touch my hair, more than a little self-conscious. "It took me a while to get the color just right. Lots of trial and error."

"You do it yourself? Will you do mine?" Mary separates a section of her hair that falls to one side of her face. "I want a pinkish-red streak right here. I know the exact color I want. Hang on, I'll get it and show you." Off she goes before I can answer her.

"Mary, Cora isn't going to do your hair," Leo calls after her. "I'm sorry," he says to me. "Just ignore her."

"No, it's okay."

He leans in so only I can hear. "Do you mind staying for dinner? I don't know when I'll be back home. Family dinners are kind of a thing with my mom."

"All right."

Mary slides across the wood floor again like an ice skater, coming to a stop inches away from me. "Here." She thrusts an opened lipstick in my face. "This is the color I want my hair. Think you can do it?"

"Leave her alone, Mary."

"Easy," I answer.

"You don't have to do it," Leo says.

"I want to."

Anne's suddenly interested in me. "You're a hairstylist?"

"Not really."

Mrs. Nash pats Anne's hand. "Go tell your father dinner's ready. You two are staying?" she asks Leo and me.

"Yes, thank you."

"Set another place at the table, Leo. Mary, help me put the food on the table."

We all sit down to eat. I'm between Leo and Mrs. Nash. Across from me are the two sisters, who don't stop asking me questions about hair and beauty. Leo tries to shut them down, but I tell him it's okay. I don't have a sister, so I kind of like the back and forth. Plus, they don't know anything about my life or me. They've probably never heard about Beau's case. The Nash family is so normal. I forgot what normal feels like.

Mrs. Nash turns to me. "Ed tells me you and Leo are making good headway on your brother's case."

I glance over at Mr. Nash, who is busy talking to Leo. The girls are arguing about Anne ruining Mary's sweater. It's just Leo's mom and me.

"It's going okay," I answer.

"I remember hearing about the murder on the news. Terrible. How is your brother doing?"

I know she's trying to be polite and making an effort to connect with me over the only thing she knows about me, but damn. I hate it. I hate that there is nothing else to talk about.

"He's okay."

I'm totally aware that I'm not holding up my side of the conversation. There's no way to end her line of questioning without being rude. I don't want to talk about Beau. Not because I'm ashamed. It's because he's not here. It feels like a betrayal to chat about him and his life with a stranger like you'd talk about traffic or the weather.

"It must be rough on your parents. I can't imagine what they're going through."

She means well, I remind myself, even as she drifts past empathy and straight into sympathy.

"And you too," she adds.

I'm an afterthought, a pitiful afterthought. She feels sorry for my family and me. Of all the emotions people have about what happened to Beau, pity is the one I can't stomach.

I slide back in my chair. "Where's the restroom?"

She blinks at me, then points. "Down the hall. Third door on the right."

"Thank you."

I'm out of my chair and halfway down the hall before the tears start. Once closed inside and alone, blessedly alone, I take big gulps of air, trying to calm myself. This is why I don't do social situations. I don't know how to field the inevitable questions and the myriad emotions people want to throw at me as though I'm a universal catchall for whatever opinion they have about the case. They don't care about me. Their only concern is having their viewpoint heard. I'll take a nosy reporter asking questions over people telling me what they think any day.

I stay in the bathroom as long as I dare without drawing attention. When I return to the table, the conversation seems to have turned to something Anne learned in school that day. I resume my seat at the table and paste on a smile, pretending that I'm as normal as everyone else here.

Leo leans toward me. "You okay?"

I nod. His gaze lingers on me as I somehow manage to show the proper response to the story Anne is telling. He takes my hand under the table. I squeeze it hard enough to earn a startled glance. The rest of the meal goes by without incident and I'm starting to relax again when Mrs. Nash asks me another question.

"Do you get to see your brother often?"

The whole table waits for my answer. The girls' faces

reflect identical curiosity. I don't know if it's because of the question or my potential answer.

"As often as I can," I answer.

"It's getting late," Leo says, pushing his chair away from the table. "I should pack so we can get going." He still has ahold of my hand.

I do as he did and stand with him. Everyone's eyes go to our clasped hands. I don't care. It was this tie to Leo that helped me get through what should've been an easy task. Mr. Nash looks like he wants to say something. The girls glance back and forth at each other. Mrs. Nash's smile looks strained, as though she's been holding it too long.

"Thank you for dinner," I tell Mrs. Nash, even though I mostly just picked at it.

"You're welcome." Then, to her husband, "Ed." As though he should do something.

Mr. Nash lays his napkin on the table, saying nothing as we head to Leo's bedroom. This isn't the first time I've encountered someone who can't separate me from Beau's case. I'm a curiosity up to the point where they realize I'm a person who could possibly invade and influence their child's life.

Leo closes the door and puts his arms around me. "I'm sorry about that."

"It's . . . what it is." I push out of his arms and wander around the room.

There are trophies on shelves—baseball trophies. Clothes are scattered across the floor as though they were dropped where he stood. A big TV hangs on the wall with wires coming out of it. Video-game controllers are stacked on top of the dresser under the TV. In the corner is a desk with more trophies and ribbons. It looks and smells like Beau's room used to.

"It'll just take me a sec to pack," Leo says.

I sit on the corner of his unmade bed and watch as he stuffs a gym bag with clean clothes from the dresser and dirty clothes from the floor. He's such a guy. He goes to get more stuff from the bathroom, leaving the door open slightly. Mrs. Nash says something to him, her voice hushed. I don't hear Leo's answer. Mr. Nash replies, his tone soothing, but Mrs. Nash is having none of it. She doesn't like me or who she thinks I am. That's fine. I don't need to be liked. I also don't have to sit here and listen to them argue about Leo staying at my place.

I peek down the hall, but I don't see them. Their voices are louder now. Leo is madder than I've ever heard him. He's defending me. I get a quick rush of happiness over that, but it's instantly doused by what Mr. Nash says. He doesn't want Leo to get involved with me. I've got issues. Issues he doesn't want in his son's life. That's fine too, because involved is more than I want or need right now.

I head out to the front of the house. I've heard enough. The girls are watching TV, so they don't notice me walking out the front door. I'm in my car and backing out of the driveway when Leo comes outside. He runs up to my car and bangs on the window.

"Open the door." He's got his bag over his shoulder.

I roll the window down. "Running away from home?"

He reaches in and unlocks the door. Before I can say or do anything else, he's climbing in. "You were going to leave without me."

I can tell this shocks him. What did he expect?

He closes the door, but I don't drive away. "What are you doing?" I ask.

"Going with you."

"I don't think that's a good idea."

"You heard."

"Don't tell me to ignore them, because I can't. I won't."

"I don't care what they say." He puts his hand on my cheek and leans across the console. "I only care that you're okay."

When he's close like this I forget why things could never work out between us. His scent wraps around me in the small space. I breathe him in and it's like he's a part of me. The stroke of his thumb across my cheek echoes in other parts of my body and I feel myself leaning in to him like a flower seeking the sun. I don't want any of this and yet it's all I want. I want him in and around and on top of me. I want to not be able to tell where he begins and I end. It's a winding, twisting sort of sensation that blankets my senses. I become a solid mass of need. My body wants something that I don't quite understand.

"What do you want from me?" I ask, because I have to know if he understands this any more than I do.

He watches me in the dying summer light. His expression is as serious as I've ever seen it. "Don't you know?"

"No." How in the hell should I know?

"God, Cora." His voice is a sigh that arrows straight through me, fanning out into tiny prickles of pleasure and pain.

His mouth is unexpectedly urgent and hot on mine. He pours every intangible thing between us into this kiss. I grab at him, holding on, a willing receptor for everything he has to show me. The more I know of him the more I want to know. His hands roam free over my body. It's like he's suddenly let loose, pushing past whatever barriers were there before. He grabs my ass and pulls me tight against him. The console digs into my side, but still I try to get closer, needing something only he can give.

He breaks the kiss as abruptly as he started it. "Get us out of here."

I shift into gear and hit the gas as he collapses back into his seat. I'm alive everywhere. My nipples are hard, poking against the lace cups of my bra. I can still feel the brand of his big hand on the right one. The throbbing between my legs makes it difficult to drive. Every movement of my feet on the pedals creates friction and it's all I can do not to shove my hand down my pants and finish what he started. He showed me more than I wanted to know and yet not enough.

He rolls the window down and sticks his head out. He mumbles something that sounds like "I can smell you," but I'm not totally sure what that means or if I heard him right.

I look over at him. He faces away, his hair blowing back in the breeze. His mouth is a flat, grim line. In another glance I can clearly see his erection pressing against his zipper. I want to reach over and touch it. What would it feel like? What would he do if I did?

18

LEO

I want her so badly it scares the shit out of me. If I hadn't stopped, we might be fucking right now, right in front of my parents' house for the whole neighborhood to see. My balls ache and my dick feels like it's going to explode. I don't even know how long I'd last with her. Seconds, maybe. If I was lucky. Just thinking about the sound she made when I touched her breast—like she'd been waiting forever for me to do it—makes it hard to think about anything except being inside her. Right now.

Her ass is firm and lush, making me think of bending her over a bed, a chair, a table, just about any-fucking-where, and driving into her from behind. I force myself to sing "Take Me out to the Ballgame" in my head. It's just about the least sexy thing I can think of at the moment. I'm on the third round and I've got things pretty much under control when she pulls up in front of her garage apartment.

And then my brain leaps ahead to being alone with her in a place with a bed and a chair and a table . . .

"What's going to happen when we go inside?" She sounds expectant yet nervous.

I have to remind myself that she's not that experienced. I don't know how inexperienced she is or if that's what's holding me back. She's so damn beautiful I want to touch her to make sure she's really real. I'm unsure with her in a way I've never been before. My brain is telling me to take things slow while everything else inside me screams to hit it full-throttle.

"What do you want to happen?" My voice comes out calmer and cooler than I feel.

Her gaze drops to my lap. "I want to touch you."

I suck in some spit and start coughing. I'm not fucking calm or cool.

She pounds on my back as I try to wheeze in enough air to breathe again. She catches me off guard at every turn. She can touch any part of me she wants any way she wants. I tell her this and her eyes widen. She gets out of the car without another word and strides up the path to her door. I grab my bag and catch up to her.

She puts out an arm blocking me from moving past her. With a finger she pushes on her front door. It swings open freely. Son of a bitch. The place is a mess.

"Who would do this? Oliver!"

I grab her arm. "Don't go in. They still might be in there."

"Oliver!"

I pull her away from the door and punch 9-1-1 into my cell. "Let's go back to the car."

"The cat. Where's Oliver?"

"We'll find him." My chest is pounding for a whole different reason now. Cora could've been home alone when that asshole broke in.

I give Cora's address to the dispatcher. While we wait for the police, I help her look for the cat. She's frantic to find him and at times I worry she's close to tears. I spot a flash of orange under a bush and creep toward it. "Here, cat." Crouching down, I see that it is the cat. He lets me pick him up.

"Oh, my God. Thank you." She scoops the cat out of my arms and hugs him.

An unmarked cop car comes to a halt behind Cora's.

"You should put him in your car," I tell her. "So he doesn't run off again."

While she takes care of the cat, I go to talk to the officer.

"Someone broke into her apartment," I tell him.

"Did you go in?"

"No."

A patrol cruiser pulls up. The two cops confer and then they head for Cora's apartment, their hands on the butts of their guns. I join Cora at her car and put an arm around her. We watch as the police go in. A few moments later they come back out and head for us.

The big one with black hair speaks first. "Looks like someone was looking for something. Can't tell if anything was stolen or not. You want to come inside and have a look?"

Cora nods and we follow them into the house. It's a god-awful mess. Worse than my bedroom. If someone was looking for something, it's likely they found it. Cora takes in the destruction in silence. I put a hand on her shoulder and give it a little squeeze.

"The TV's still here," the shorter cop says. "Is anything missing?"

She takes a slow tour of the apartment, picking her way over the debris at her feet. Every drawer, closet, and shelf was cleared and everything is on the floor. Most of it's broken, either on purpose or when it hit the tile. She's doing a good job of keeping it together. I wonder how long that will last.

"It's hard to tell one hundred percent," she says. "But I don't think anything's missing."

"Do you have an idea who would do this? An ex-boyfriend?" Big Cop glances at me. "A disgruntled coworker or ex-friend?"

"No."

"We can have a crime-scene crew come over and dust for prints, but if nothing's been stolen there's not much of a case here." Big Cop shrugs. "Just vandalism."

"We'll write a report if you want it for your insurance," Small Cop says.

"No. That's okay," Cora answers.

"You have a place to stay until that lock gets fixed?" Big Cop asks.

"I . . . I don't know. My landlord is out of town."

I put my arm across her shoulders. "She'll be fine. I'll take care of it."

"Here's my card." Small Cop scribbles something on it and hands it to Cora. "That's the case number. The report will be available in a few days. Call us again if you have any more trouble."

"Will do," I say.

Big Cop's gaze roams the room for a moment, then he follows the other officer out.

"I can see if I can rig the door to stay closed." I examine the frame. It's trashed. Someone kicked the door in. Hard.

"There's a shed on the back of the new garage. There'll be some tools in there." She pulls her key ring from her pocket and selects a key. "Here's the key."

She's eerily calm. Neither of us have to say it to know who did this and why.

"Are you okay?"

She nods.

"Why don't you come with me to find those tools?"

"No, I have to clean up."

"Cora." I take her arm, keeping her from bending down to pick something up. "You don't have to do this right now."

"I don't have anywhere else to stay and I can't stay here with it like this."

"We're not staying here tonight."

"Where else am I going to go?" I. Not we.

"We'll get a hotel room or something."

Her laugh is harsh and bitter. "I can't afford a hotel room. I have to pay to get the door fixed. I don't have a job right now, remember?"

"Don't worry about it."

"Don't tell me not to worry about it. Wouldn't you worry about it?"

Yeah, yeah, I would. "I don't mean it like that. Hey, you've got me. Let me help you."

She looks me over, then pulls her arm free. "I've got to get this place cleaned up." She rights a chair, her hands shaky, her lip trembling. "Why don't you go get those tools?"

She wants to get rid of me. It's not going to be that easy. But I let it go for now. "I'll be right back."

I head out to go around to the back of the building. I get two steps out the door and I hear her breath hitch on a sob. It tears through me, stopping me in my tracks. She didn't want me to see her lose it. I want to punch something. Or someone. That asshole who did this to her. What was he looking for? Did he find it or will he be back?

She lets out a low moan and sniffs. My hands curl into fists. I want to go back inside, but I know that's the last thing she wants right now. Some time goes by and then I hear her moving around the apartment. I continue on to the shed and unlock it. There's some wood I can use to temporarily fix the door frame, but the lock is probably shot. She'll need a new one. Tomorrow. Tonight I'll rig it so that no one can get in and I'll take her somewhere. I don't know where. Somewhere safe.

By the time I get back, Cora's cleared some floor space. I get to work on the door, doing my best to temporarily repair what I can. It's full dark when I finish and Cora is sweeping up the broken pieces of her things, which look like confetti scattered across the tile.

"Pack some clothes," I tell her. "We're not staying here tonight."

She looks at me like I've lost my mind.

"My friend Mike's down in Mexico for a couple weeks. I know where the key is to his place. We'll stay there for a few days until all this gets sorted out."

"We can't just break in."

"We're not. I called him when I was in the shed. He's cool with it. Come on. Let's get out of here. I'm sure the cat wants out of the car."

"All right."

She packs more for the cat than she does for herself, and then we're in the car and I'm giving her directions to my friend's place.

"It's on Coronado Island?" She gives me a worried glance.

"Yeah."

"Are you serious?"

"No, I'm making you drive across the bridge for no reason."

"Smartass."

We pull up to the house and she just stares at it. It's a

nice house. Okay, it's more than a nice house. It's a mini-mansion on the beach.

"You have a friend who lives here?" She sounds like she doesn't believe me.

"Yup." I climb out of the car and look for the brick. Ah, there. I push on it and out slides another brick farther down with a dent carved into it just big enough for a key. I retrieve it and show it to her. "See." I unlock the door and flip the lights on, then reset the alarm.

"You're kidding."

"Nope." I take her bag and head down the hall.

She follows with the cat carrier. "Are you sure it's okay to have Oliver here? This doesn't look like a house for pets."

"He has three cats that are being boarded while he's out of town. Relax. He knows about your cat. It's cool," I say again to reassure her. I open a door off the hall. "You can put him in here." It's like a feline Disneyland with a bunch of those tiered, carpeted cat climbers and trails built into the walls. "There's already a litter box." I point to a house-looking thing in the corner. "And automated food and water machines. He'll be fine."

She sets the carrier down and opens the door. The cat steps out carefully, sniffing.

"See," I say. "Come on."

We back out of the room. She follows me down the hall to the spare room, her eyes wide.

I open the bedroom door and give her a moment to soak it in. This side of the house faces the beach. The moon is big and low, reflecting off the water. The rhythmic roar of the waves is a little louder in this room.

"There's only this bedroom and the master," I tell her. "You can have it. I'll sleep on the couch in the living room."

"No." She grabs my arm. "I don't feel like being alone."

"Okay." It feels wrong to be glad about this turn of events.

"Are you sure it's okay for us to stay here?"

"Totally okay."

She goes to the window. "It's so dark out there."

I move in behind her and put my arms around her. "There's a full moon."

"It would be even darker without it."

"Are you afraid of the dark, Bluebird?"

"No, of course not. I'm just not used to looking out the window and not seeing another house or a street."

"There are none of those on the ocean."

"What if I'd been there when he broke in?"

"I think he waited until he knew you wouldn't be home. He was looking for something. But what?"

"I don't know. All of my files are at the agency." She turns in my arms. "What if he breaks in there next?"

"The place is alarmed. Dad would know it the minute he did." Which reminds me . . . "I should call my dad and let him know what happened at your place."

"Tomorrow?"

"Yeah, okay. Are you hungry? I think there might be some—"

Bringing my head down to hers, she cuts me off with a kiss. For a second I'm too shocked to move, and then it's like we picked up where we left off in the car. The full length of her presses against me. Her hands are all over me, under my shirt, over my shirt, on my ass. I struggle to hold back. The last thing she needs is me ripping at her clothes. But she's grinding against me and I forget why I should go slowly. I work a hand into her shirt to unhook her bra.

I'm practically fucking her mouth with mine. She's making these little moaning sounds that drive me insane. I finally work the last hook of her bra and her breasts tumble into my hands. More than a handful. Rolling her nipples between my fingers, I lick my way across her jaw to her ear. She puts a hand on my dick and my eyes nearly roll back into my head.

"I want you," I whisper, and bite her earlobe.

She has both hands on the front of my pants now, working the button. She struggles for a second and I'm about to help her when she finally frees the button and goes for the zipper. She pushes at my pants. I'd help her, but I've got my hands full of her tits. She moves her head to the side, exposing her neck. I take advantage, nipping my way down.

"Oh." Her surprise jolts me out of my haze and I realize she's checking out my dick.

Experimentally, she runs her thumb across the tip. It slides in my pre-cum, which seems to delight her, so she does it again and again. I groan. Her fascination with it is killing me. She wraps both her hands around my dick and gives it a squeeze. I put my hand over hers and show her how to stroke me. She picks up my rhythm. I'm dying. She's torturing me.

I pull on her shirt. She lets go long enough for me to draw it and her bra off at the same time. I shuck my shirt and toss it aside. We're way past going slow. Putting her hands on my chest, she moves them across my shoulders, down my arms, then back again. Her expression is a mixture of fascination and curiosity. I stand still for her. Her hands continue their movement across my pecs and over my abs. I want to touch her, but I don't want her to stop touching me. So I look instead.

I imagined Cora naked so many times. I wasn't even close. She's beautiful. Gorgeous. Perfect in every way. She has her hands on my dick again. It's sweet torture. Bending down, she licks it. She's playing, testing. I lay my hand on her back, encouraging her. I watch as she takes me all the way into her mouth. Moving my hand to her head, I gently coax her, letting her know what I like. She seems to understand, picking up the movement.

"No teeth," I grit out.

She adjusts. For sure I'm dying now. It's like the first time I ever got head, and I can't stop the pressure that's building fast, too fast. If she doesn't stop . . . I lift her chin and her mouth slides off with a pop.

"Did I do something wrong?"

"No," I tell her. "God, no. You did it too right. Come here."

I hold her. Her breasts feel amazing against me. I want to make this good for her. I want to make her as crazy for me as I am for her. I want to hear her scream my name as she digs her heels into my ass. But first I want to make sure this is what she wants.

"Are you sure about this, Bluebird?"

She nods against my chest, her hair tickling. "Are you?"

"Hell, yes."

"Okay, then."

She steps back. While I watch, she takes her jeans off and then she's standing there in nothing but a little scrap of white cotton. I want to touch her, but can hardly move. She hooks her thumbs in her panties and then they're gone too. My heart is beating so hard and fast I can hear it over the sound of the ocean. I shuck my underwear and jeans in record time. Her gaze is everywhere. I stand still for her inspection. My dick is so hard it hurts.

I feel like she needs this, this moment to pause. She could back out at any moment. I don't want to give her a chance to. There's so much to her I feel like it will take me years to learn it all. But if I only get this night, this one moment, with her it would be more than I ever thought I could have. With everything in me I hope she feels the same. I want to be everything she needs me to be, everything she ever imagined.

19

Cora

He's beautiful. If you can call guys that. Everything about him is perfect, at least as far as I know. It's not like I've never seen a naked man before. Well, maybe not one in real life. His penis doesn't feel like I imagined it would. It's soft on the outside and hard on the inside. He let me touch him how I wanted to. I didn't know what I was doing. It was more instinct and an idea of what might please him than any actual knowledge.

He's looking at me like he could pounce on me at any moment. I can't think when he looks at me like that. He's patient, letting me explore his body without grabbing at mine. I don't know where this bravery came from, but I don't feel shy with him. There's something there—I don't know, trust maybe—that makes me feel safe. He stands still for me like a model, letting me experiment with little touches. His body is so different from mine. Leaning forward, I lick his small, flat nipple. His breath catches. I want to touch him all over. I want to lick him all over. I wonder if he'll let me.

"What do you want, Bluebird?"

"I'm not totally sure."

I slide my hands along his sides. His stomach muscles bunch as though I tickled him. Watching the play of his muscles, I do it again, this time moving my hands to his backside. His eyes are hot on mine. It's taking a lot of his control to let me have my way like this. He's given me all the power here. I should reward him. I take his penis in my hand again, stroking up and down like he showed me. A muscle in his jaw tics. He likes this. I explore further, reaching underneath the base of his dick and palm him. His eyes drift closed a little. He likes this too. A lot.

I reach for one of his hands, which are fisted at his sides, and put it on my breast. I liked it when he touched me there. His touch is expert, and with only minimal effort I'm pressing against him, wanting more.

"What do you want?" he asks again, his voice strained.

"I want you to touch me like I'm touching you."

I don't have to ask twice. His hands are suddenly everywhere. The sensations come at me one after the other. His kisses are hot and openmouthed, trailing down my neck and then OH, GOD. He latches on to my nipple and my knees buckle. Sweeping me up, he lays me on the bed, covering my body with his. The weight of him is more than I expected and yet not enough. My back arches under the onslaught of his mouth at my breasts. He's driving me crazy toward something. It's building. I clutch at his head, keeping him right there where I want him.

His chuckle vibrates against me. He bites me, gently sinking his teeth into my flesh. My hips come off the bed. He does it again. His hand is between my legs and I have a moment where I think to push it away. He hits a spot I didn't know existed and then I'm bucking against his hand. He drifts down my body, his gaze burning. Pushing my thighs wider apart, he looks down at me. Before I can stop him he puts his mouth RIGHT THERE and it's like I've been hit with a million volts.

The shock of what he's doing stuns me into submission. I let him lick and suck on me down there. It's good. It's so, so good. I didn't know. He parts my folds, exposing more of me. I lift my head to watch and I can't believe what I'm seeing. I can't believe how damn good it is. I had no idea. He's doing this thing with suction and his tongue, little flicks. It's making me insane. He pinches my nipples softly, then harder.

"Harder," I gasp.

He does it harder. Sensations rush at me, one after another in great waves. His mouth, his hands, his tongue, his . . . OH, MY GOD. Arching back, I cry out suddenly. Shocked, I clap a hand over my mouth.

He moves it away, laughing. "Yell all you want, Bluebird. There's no one but me to hear you, and I like it."

He kisses the inside of my thigh, my stomach, and then the slope of my breast as he makes his way back up to me. Holding me against him, he strokes my back. I'm out of breath and kind of tingly all over. He's so big and warm. I snuggle in to him and let my eyes drift shut. I don't think about how weird it is that I'm lying naked with him or how only weeks ago I wasn't sure I could trust him.

My body gets heavy. My thoughts slow . . .

I wake up sometime later, confused. It takes me a minute of slight panic to realize where I am. The ocean crashes outside in a dependable rhythm. It's dark, darker than I'm used to. Leo's heart beats steadily beneath my cheek. I'm draped across him like a blanket. He's got an arm around me, tucking me in close. Sometime in the night he pulled the covers over us. We're skin to skin. What happened earlier comes back to me and heat creeps into my face. I can't believe what I did. I can't believe what I let him do to me.

But I'm not sorry. I totally get what Jamie's been yammering about for like forever. Orgasms rock. I want another one. Soon. Maybe now. I shift, hoping to wake him up. He pulls me snugger against him and sighs. I slide my hand down his body. His penis feels weird. It's all soft and deflated.

He grabs my wrist, stopping my exploration. "Go back to sleep."

"What if I don't want to?"

"It's late."

"You don't want to?"

"Want to what?"

"We didn't . . . you know."

"We didn't what?" He moves fast. Suddenly he's on top of me. "Tell me what you want, Bluebird, and I'll give it to you."

"I want you to do that thing you did before."

"Which thing? I did a lot of things."

"Where you put your mouth down there." I point between our bodies.

I can feel him grinning in the dark. "Down where? Down here?" He touches my knee.

"Higher."

"Say it. Say the word."

I shake my head.

"Here?" His hand slides up the inside of my thigh.

"Higher."

"I've heard you say a lot of naughty words. You can't say this one?"

"No."

His hand finally finds the right spot. "Here?"

"Yes. There." My voice is all breathy.

He whispers next to my ear: "You want my mouth on your pussy?"

I shiver. "Yes."

"You want me to lick and suck on your pussy?"

That word does strange things to me. Every time he says it I get a jolt. "Yes. Please."

"You want me to make you come again?"

I nod.

"Cora," he growls. "Say the words and I'll make you come so hard you'll think you've died."

"I . . ." I can't say it.

He places kisses along my jaw and then captures my mouth for a long, winding kiss that leaves me breathless. Sliding his fingers through my slickness, he toys with me. He's not really serious. I catch glimpses of the sensation I had earlier, but his fingers skate away before it can really take hold. It's driving me crazy. Reaching between us, I find his half-hard penis and stroke it. He makes a guttural sound that lets me know he likes it. It gets harder and harder. He clamps a hand on my wrist to still my movements.

Heh. Two can play the teasing game.

And then his mouth is on my breast and I can't think.

"What do you want?" The low, sexy rumble of his voice vibrates straight to where his hand is doing wicked things to me.

"I want you to fuck me!"

He stops. Everything. It's the exact opposite of what I want. I slap a hand over my stupid mouth.

He pulls my hand away. His fingers stroke into me exactly where I need it. "Say it again."

I'm fighting against the sensation. He counters by biting my nipple. His strokes are long and deep. I'm close, so close.

"Oh, my God. Fuck me already!"

He throws back the covers, pushes my legs apart, and sucks. My orgasm rips through me. Pushing down on his head, I practically come off the bed, screaming his name. He doesn't let up. His mouth is relentless. Another wave hits, rolling through me like a freight train. I can't breathe. Spots dance in front of my eyes.

And then he's on top of me, grinding against me. Hot liquid splashes onto my stomach. His head drops next to mine and he's having as much trouble catching his breath as I am.

What just happened?

I'm trying to process it all. He's between my legs, on top of me. His weight is comfortable and warm. He kisses my shoulder, the side of my neck, my cheek, and then my mouth, gentle kisses. He drops his head again and sighs, his breath hot against my neck.

"Don't move," he says, disengaging himself from me. "I'll be right back."

A slant of light from the bathroom slashes across the bed and me. I can hear water running. It's cold without him. I want to pull the covers up, but my stomach is covered with his semen.

He returns with a warm washcloth and wipes away the mess. "Sorry."

I lift up on my elbows to watch. "Why did you do that?"

He doesn't look up at me. "It's not . . . Sorry."

"No, I'm okay with it. It's just that why didn't you, you know, go for it?"

"No condom."

"Oh." I get the feeling he's not being totally honest with me. "Is that the only reason?"

"There." He gets up and disposes of the washcloth. Cutting the light, he climbs back into bed, drawing the covers over us. He reaches for me, pulling me up against his side.

We lay quiet in the dark. Something's wrong. I can feel it. Was there something I did or didn't do?

"Leo?"

"Hmm?"

"What did I do wrong?"

His laugh is harsh. "Everything you did was exactly right."

"Then what's wrong?"

"Nothing. Go to sleep."

I don't believe him, but it's clear he's not going to talk about it, at least not tonight. I lay awake for I don't know how long, listening to his breathing, then light snoring. Cycling everything that happened over and over in my brain, I can't come up with a solution. Maybe he'll talk about it tomorrow. I don't know. I don't have any frame of reference here and no one to talk it over with except Jamie. It's too late to call her, and even if I did I'm not sure I could adequately explain what I don't have words for.

All day at the office goes by and it's more of the same. I'm starting to feel like I imagined all of the really good parts of last night. They fade away into insignificance under the overwhelming evidence that something is wrong. I can't even bring myself to ask him anymore because after the two times I did he completely shut down on me. He hasn't even tried to hold my hand or steal a kiss like he normally would. We dance around each other in our small office. We're supposed to have a date tonight after he talks to Zelda. I wonder if that's even going to happen. Past that I wonder where I'm going to sleep tonight because it's very clear that it won't be anywhere near Leo.

19

CORA

He's beautiful. If you can call guys that. Everything about him is perfect, at least as far as I know. It's not like I've never seen a naked man before. Well, maybe not one in real life. His penis doesn't feel like I imagined it would. It's soft on the outside and hard on the inside. He let me touch him how I wanted to. I didn't know what I was doing. It was more instinct and an idea of what might please him than any actual knowledge.

He's looking at me like he could pounce on me at any moment. I can't think when he looks at me like that. He's patient, letting me explore his body without grabbing at mine. I don't know where this bravery came from, but I don't feel shy with him. There's something there—I don't know, trust maybe—that makes me feel safe. He stands still for me like a model, letting me experiment with little touches. His body is so different from mine. Leaning forward, I lick his small, flat nipple. His breath catches. I want to touch him all over. I want to lick him all over. I wonder if he'll let me.

"What do you want, Bluebird?"

"I'm not totally sure."

I slide my hands along his sides. His stomach muscles bunch as though I tickled him. Watching the play of his muscles, I do it again, this time moving my hands to his backside. His eyes are hot on mine. It's taking a lot of his control to let me have my way like this. He's given me all the power here. I should reward him. I take his penis in my hand again, stroking up and down like he showed me. A muscle in his jaw tics. He likes this. I explore further, reaching underneath the base of his dick and palm him. His eyes drift closed a little. He likes this too. A lot.

I reach for one of his hands, which are fisted at his sides, and put it on my breast. I liked it when he touched me there. His touch is expert, and with only minimal effort I'm pressing against him, wanting more.

"What do you want?" he asks again, his voice strained.

"I want you to touch me like I'm touching you."

I don't have to ask twice. His hands are suddenly everywhere. The sensations come at me one after the other. His kisses are hot and openmouthed, trailing down my neck and then OH, GOD. He latches on to my nipple and my knees buckle. Sweeping me up, he lays me on the bed, covering my body with his. The weight of him is more than I expected and yet not enough. My back arches under the onslaught of his mouth at my breasts. He's driving me crazy toward something. It's building. I clutch at his head, keeping him right there where I want him.

His chuckle vibrates against me. He bites me, gently sinking his teeth into my flesh. My hips come off the bed. He does it again. His hand is between my legs and I have a moment where I think to push it away. He hits a spot I didn't know existed and then I'm bucking against his hand. He drifts down my body, his gaze burning. Pushing my thighs wider apart, he looks down at me. Before I can stop him he puts his mouth RIGHT THERE and it's like I've been hit with a million volts.

The shock of what he's doing stuns me into submission. I let him lick and suck on me down there. It's good. It's so, so good. I didn't know. He parts my folds, exposing more of me. I lift my head to watch and I can't believe what I'm seeing. I can't believe how damn good it is. I had no idea. He's doing this thing with suction and his tongue, little flicks. It's making me insane. He pinches my nipples softly, then harder.

"Harder," I gasp.

He does it harder. Sensations rush at me, one after another in great waves. His mouth, his hands, his tongue, his . . . OH, MY GOD. Arching back, I cry out suddenly. Shocked, I clap a hand over my mouth.

He moves it away, laughing. "Yell all you want, Bluebird. There's no one but me to hear you, and I like it."

He kisses the inside of my thigh, my stomach, and then the slope of my breast as he makes his way back up to me. Holding me against him, he strokes my back. I'm out of breath and kind of tingly all over. He's so big and warm. I snuggle in to him and let my eyes drift shut. I don't think about how weird it is that I'm lying naked with him or how only weeks ago I wasn't sure I could trust him.

My body gets heavy. My thoughts slow . . .

I wake up sometime later, confused. It takes me a minute of slight panic to realize where I am. The ocean crashes outside in a dependable rhythm. It's dark, darker than I'm used to. Leo's heart beats steadily beneath my cheek. I'm draped across him like a blanket. He's got an arm around me, tucking me in close. Sometime in the night he pulled the covers over us. We're skin to skin. What happened earlier comes back to me and heat creeps into my face. I can't believe what I did. I can't believe what I let him do to me.

But I'm not sorry. I totally get what Jamie's been yammering about for like forever. Orgasms rock. I want another one. Soon. Maybe now. I shift, hoping to wake him up. He pulls me snugger against him and sighs. I slide my hand down his body. His penis feels weird. It's all soft and deflated.

He grabs my wrist, stopping my exploration. "Go back to sleep."

"What if I don't want to?"

"It's late."

"You don't want to?"

"Want to what?"

"We didn't . . . you know."

"We didn't what?" He moves fast. Suddenly he's on top of me. "Tell me what you want, Bluebird, and I'll give it to you."

"I want you to do that thing you did before."

"Which thing? I did a lot of things."

"Where you put your mouth down there." I point between our bodies.

I can feel him grinning in the dark. "Down where? Down here?" He touches my knee.

"Higher."

"Say it. Say the word."

I shake my head.

"Here?" His hand slides up the inside of my thigh.

"Higher."

"I've heard you say a lot of naughty words. You can't say this one?"

"No."

His hand finally finds the right spot. "Here?"

"Yes. There." My voice is all breathy.

He whispers next to my ear: "You want my mouth on your pussy?"

I shiver. "Yes."

"You want me to lick and suck on your pussy?"

That word does strange things to me. Every time he says it I get a jolt. "Yes. Please."

"You want me to make you come again?"

I nod.

"Cora," he growls. "Say the words and I'll make you come so hard you'll think you've died."

"I . . ." I can't say it.

He places kisses along my jaw and then captures my mouth for a long, winding kiss that leaves me breathless. Sliding his fingers through my slickness, he toys with me. He's not really serious. I catch glimpses of the sensation I had earlier, but his fingers skate away before it can really take hold. It's driving me crazy. Reaching between us, I find his half-hard penis and stroke it. He makes a guttural sound that lets me know he likes it. It gets harder and harder. He clamps a hand on my wrist to still my movements.

Heh. Two can play the teasing game.

And then his mouth is on my breast and I can't think.

"What do you want?" The low, sexy rumble of his voice vibrates straight to where his hand is doing wicked things to me.

"I want you to fuck me!"

He stops. Everything. It's the exact opposite of what I want. I slap a hand over my stupid mouth.

He pulls my hand away. His fingers stroke into me exactly where I need it. "Say it again."

I'm fighting against the sensation. He counters by biting my nipple. His strokes are long and deep. I'm close, so close.

"Oh, my God. Fuck me already!"

He throws back the covers, pushes my legs apart, and sucks. My orgasm rips through me. Pushing down on his head, I practically come off the bed, screaming his name. He doesn't let up. His mouth is relentless. Another wave hits, rolling through me like a freight train. I can't breathe. Spots dance in front of my eyes.

And then he's on top of me, grinding against me. Hot liquid splashes onto my stomach. His head drops next to mine and he's having as much trouble catching his breath as I am.

What just happened?

I'm trying to process it all. He's between my legs, on top of me. His weight is comfortable and warm. He kisses my shoulder, the side of my neck, my cheek, and then my mouth, gentle kisses. He drops his head again and sighs, his breath hot against my neck.

"Don't move," he says, disengaging himself from me. "I'll be right back."

A slant of light from the bathroom slashes across the bed and me. I can hear water running. It's cold without him. I want to pull the covers up, but my stomach is covered with his semen.

He returns with a warm washcloth and wipes away the mess. "Sorry."

I lift up on my elbows to watch. "Why did you do that?"

He doesn't look up at me. "It's not . . . Sorry."

"No, I'm okay with it. It's just that why didn't you, you know, go for it?"

"No condom."

"Oh." I get the feeling he's not being totally honest with me. "Is that the only reason?"

"There." He gets up and disposes of the washcloth. Cutting the light, he climbs back into bed, drawing the covers over us. He reaches for me, pulling me up against his side.

We lay quiet in the dark. Something's wrong. I can feel it. Was there something I did or didn't do?

"Leo?"

"Hmm?"

"What did I do wrong?"

His laugh is harsh. "Everything you did was exactly right."

"Then what's wrong?"

"Nothing. Go to sleep."

I don't believe him, but it's clear he's not going to talk about it, at least not tonight. I lay awake for I don't know how long, listening to his breathing, then light snoring. Cycling everything that happened over and over in my brain, I can't come up with a solution. Maybe he'll talk about it tomorrow. I don't know. I don't have any frame of reference here and no one to talk it over with except Jamie. It's too late to call her, and even if I did I'm not sure I could adequately explain what I don't have words for.

All day at the office goes by and it's more of the same. I'm starting to feel like I imagined all of the really good parts of last night. They fade away into insignificance under the overwhelming evidence that something is wrong. I can't even bring myself to ask him anymore because after the two times I did he completely shut down on me. He hasn't even tried to hold my hand or steal a kiss like he normally would. We dance around each other in our small office. We're supposed to have a date tonight after he talks to Zelda. I wonder if that's even going to happen. Past that I wonder where I'm going to sleep tonight because it's very clear that it won't be anywhere near Leo.

20

LEO

I can't stop thinking about last night and what a monumental mistake it was. Total and complete epic failure. I want to pound my fists against my head and chant stupid, stupid, stupid over and over. What was I thinking? I wasn't. My dick was. Why did I listen to it?

Because Cora was naked and willing and I'm weak. So very, very weak.

I did not think this through at all. I've never taken anyone's virginity. I didn't think about that until last night. I had a box of condoms in my bag next to the gun Dad gave me, but when it came down to it—when Cora shouted that she wanted me to fuck her—I couldn't do it. I came at this all wrong, thinking this would be some summer fun, but this is her life. And the truth is I probably won't be in it in a few months. I'll go back to school and Cora will go back to . . . I don't know what she'll go back to or what will happen between then and now. Hopefully she'll be helping her brother assimilate back into society.

I'm not going to be her first time. That privilege will go to some other guy who had better treat her well and stick around for the long haul, maybe even marry her. Most guys would've jumped at what she offered. I, apparently, am not most guys. I finally get what my dad was trying to tell me, what he's always told me about girls. It's about respect. And I respect Cora too much to add her to my long list of conquests and then leave her. I'm simply not good enough for her. How do I explain this to her when I can hardly wrap my head around it myself? Where do we go from here? Because I have a feeling there's no going back and yet there's no moving forward either.

All day Cora's been casting confused looks my direction. She hasn't asked me what's wrong since we left the house, but she knows something's up. I'm hoping to get out of here in the next five minutes for my meeting with Zelda without Cora bringing it up again. I don't want to hurt her. She's had too much hurt in her life already. I'm not sure I have all the words to explain what happened for me last night when I held her after her first ever orgasm. As she drifted off to sleep I lay awake with the realization that I'm not good enough for her. The weight of that was a physical ache that started in the center of my chest and radiated out until I was a man made of pain.

I was finally asleep when she grabbed my dick, wanting to go for round two. Instead of putting her off I played with her, not thinking for a second that she'd lose it like that. I should know better by now than to hold on to expectations when it comes to Cora. She constantly throws me. Before I knew it I'd gone too far, making her come that second time. I almost thrust all the way into her. If I hadn't slipped up instead of in I would've climaxed inside her instead of on top of her. I was nothing but a thief, selfishly trying to steal what wasn't mine.

"Isn't it time for you to leave to go meet Zelda?" Cora asks.

I was so busy trying to look busy and avoid Cora that I almost forgot about the appointment. "Yeah." I grab my notebook and stand to go.

"I'll be here when you get back." She hasn't looked up from her computer once during this exchange. Her absolute if-you-don't-give-a-fuck-I-don't-give-a-fuck attitude throws me. She's not like other girls. I have to remind myself to stop treating her like she is.

"Okay. See you." I scoot out with everything lingering between us.

I'm almost to the outside door when Savannah's voice stops me. "So you fucked her, huh?"

I whip my head around. "Excuse me?"

"You're escaping like you did something wrong and she's pretty much ignored you all day. I know the signs. I've been on the other side of your love-'em-and-leave-'em antics."

"I don't know what you're talking about." But I do and she's too fucking right.

She lets out a sigh and leans back in her chair. "When are you going to grow some balls?"

I shake my head. "What?"

"You heard me."

"I don't have time for this."

She gets up from her desk and comes around it toward me. "Here's the thing: I like Cora. She thinks I hate her, but I don't. What I hate is you acting like women are just there to get you off and nothing more. You like the chase. The problem is you don't know what to do when it's over. Cora strikes me as someone who doesn't have a whole lot of experience with guys like you.

"Hell, I bet she doesn't have a lot of experience with guys, period. And then you walk into her life all movie-star hair"— she flicks my hair—"and I-fuck-like-a-god stare. And she falls on her back because let's face it, you back up that swagger with real skill. Then, after you get what you want, you're all Peace out. Am I close to what happened since I saw you yesterday?"

I loathe her. I think I honestly hate her. I also hate myself because she's fucking right.

Shaking her head, she takes my silence as confirmation. "When are you going to grow the fuck up?"

"I don't have time for this." I split because, hey, it's apparently what I do best.

I'm halfway down the stairs before it hits me what an asshole I've been. Like truly a big giant fucking asshole. Instead of avoiding my issues with Cora I should've just spelled them out for her. I'm not boyfriend material. Savannah only confirmed what I already knew. I'm not the stick-around type. I'm in it only until I get what I want. Then I lose interest like some kind of ADHD sex addict. I'm surprised I stuck around with Cora long enough to wipe my cum off her stomach. That must be some kind of record for me, some new emotionally mature high I'll never achieve again.

I tear out of the parking lot like my ass is on fire, when, in truth, all of me is burning. I can hardly stand to be in my own skin. It feels like it's going to melt off me and reveal the true me to the world, the one beyond the movie-star hair and I-fuck-like-a-god stare. And who would want me then? What am I if I'm not exactly what people expect?

I'm so in my head that I miss the turn to Zelda's house and have to go back. That's when I notice the car following me. It makes the same illegal U-turn in the middle of the road that I do. I pass Zelda's street on the right and turn left instead. The car follows. We wind our way through the neighborhood. I know these streets. My friend John lived here. Now he's living in New York working as a stockbroker. If I make a left, then a right . . . Aha, there it is.

I circle around the cul-de-sac and stop. The car does the same, only it doesn't stop. It keeps going past me. The windows are tinted too dark to see who's driving. I pull out after it and now the chasee becomes the chaser. There are no plates to run. If I don't keep this guy in sight I'll never find out who he is and what he wants. Although I have a feeling I know—the same guy who broke into Cora's place and called her parents.

I can't let him out of my eyesight.

He goes back the way we came and then out onto the main road. He makes a risky left, cutting off another car, and hits the gas. I have to wait for traffic. By the time it's clear I've lost him. He's nowhere in sight. I circle back, thinking he might have too, but he's gone. I pull into a fast-food restaurant parking lot and pull out my cell to call my dad. What am I going to tell him? A black Mustang with no plates followed me? There's nothing for him to go on. If only I'd gotten a look at the guy. I might have recognized him.

He wanted me to spot him. He was bold enough to out himself making that U-turn. Why? Is it more of the same scare tactics and intimidation? And I almost led him straight to Zelda's house.

Zelda wasn't easy to find. She got married and changed her name. The house is in her husband's mother's maiden name. It's almost like she didn't want to be found. So why did she agree to meet with me?

I retrace my route, watching carefully for another tail. There isn't one, as far as I can tell. I feel safe enough to go to Zelda's house. She's a piece of the puzzle we desperately need. I pull up in front of the house and stare. It's empty. I can tell by the For Sale sign out front, the lockbox on the door handle, and the lack of window coverings. Zelda struck me as someone who would insist on fussy curtains. I don't know why. We had only one brief phone conversation. It's just an impression I got.

I climb out of the car and go up the walk. The porch is littered with business cards and flyers. A peek in the window confirms my suspicions. Gone. Zelda is gone. I pull out my cell, hit redial on her number, and immediately get a message that the phone's been disconnected. Son of a bitch! How am I going to tell Cora that our one good lead on Mrs. Wheeler skipped town?

I start to go back to my car, but the twitch of the curtains on the house across the street catches my eye. Nosey neighbors are a PI's best friend, I can hear my dad say. I hope to hell he's right about that.

I cross the street and knock on the door. Inside I can hear the thunk thunk of a cane on a wood floor. Pasting on my most sincere smile, I stand still for what I'm sure is an inspection through the peephole. After a few moments, the lock turns, then the knob, and I come face-to-face with a little old lady who reminds me of my own gran.

"Hello," I say. "I'm looking for your neighbor." I point across the street. "Zelda Marks Ramirez. Do you happen to know where she's moved to?"

"No one's lived in that house for a couple weeks."

Damn. "You wouldn't have a phone number or address for her, would you?"

She squints up at me. "What do you want with it?"

"I'm a law student studying a trial she was a witness in—the Cassandra Williams murder. Do you remember it?"

"Oh, my, yes. My nephew's son went to school with that

poor young woman. Zelda never said anything about being a witness though."

"She was Cassandra's across-the-hall neighbor. She found her body."

"Oh, dear." She shakes her head sadly. "Poor thing."

"I was supposed to have an appointment today with Zelda, but I guess we got our wires crossed."

"Well, I'm not surprised. Zelda's had, shall we say, a lot on her plate lately with the passing of her husband and being evicted from her mother-in-law's house." She gestures across the street. "And there it sits, empty. It would've cost that woman nothing to let her daughter-in-law stay there while she gets things sorted. But Gert isn't the type of person to do a kindness for another. A Sunday Christian if I ever met one."

"I didn't know Zelda's husband died."

"Oh, yes. A car accident. Died instantly."

"I'm sorry to hear it. Did Zelda give you her new phone number or address?"

"As a matter of fact she did. What did you say your name was?"

"Leo. Leo Nash. I'm studying law at UCLA. I'm home for the summer. I grew up just a few blocks from here." I point toward the back of her house. "Over on Pastora Street. My professor assigned us this project over the summer. I was hoping to interview Zelda. The project really wouldn't be complete without her input."

"Yes, yes. I can see that, especially with her finding the body and all. That's just so terrible. That girl has been through so much. Finding her neighbor, her husband dying, then her witch of a mother-in-law turning her out into the street. Just terrible. You stay there. I'll be right back." She closes the door and shuffles away.

I look back across the street. That would explain why her phone no longer works and maybe why she didn't show up for our appointment. I hope this neighbor comes through for me with a valid address or a work or cell number.

The old lady returns with a pad of paper. "She wrote her info down here for me just in case. I've been collecting her mail, but she hasn't been by in while to pick it up. I was just about to give her a call."

I take a pic of the tablet with my cellphone. "Thanks. I really appreciate your help. I'll let her know to contact you. What was your name again?"

"Dorothy Kuczynsky. But you can call me Dot."

"Thanks, Dot." I start down her steps toward my car. "Have a nice day."

"You too. I hope you get a good grade on your project."

I turn and give her a wink. "Me too."

21

CORA

While Leo's out talking with Zelda, I'm meeting with Dylan Newman about his relationship with Cassandra. I'm glad I've got something to keep my mind off the shit with Leo. I feel so stupid. I thought we had . . . I don't know exactly what I thought we had going. The one thing I do know is that I wanted it. I wanted Leo. And I really wanted to have sex with Leo. But he's made it incredibly clear that isn't what he wanted, like maybe I pressured him into what happened last night. Was it all in my head? Did I read more into his dates and kisses than he intended? Was I too fast for him?

I shake my head in the empty office. No. There is no way I read him wrong. He was as into me as I was him right up until he . . . Oh, my God. That's it. I get it. I get why Savannah's been so pissed at him. He used her, then dumped her, and now he used and is dumping me. He got what he wanted even though technically I'm still a virgin. This has to be some kind of record. Wow. I feel really stupid for not seeing this sooner. I mean, the signs were right there out in the reception area all along. If only I paid attention.

Whatever.

I'm going to take from this what I can and move on. Lesson learned. Orgasms achieved. Virginity intact. And I'm closer than I ever was before to finding out who really killed Cassandra and freeing Beau. That's going to be the big take-away here. If I get anything from my time here, it's that.

"Knock, knock." Dylan stands awkwardly in the door-way, looking a lot like he did when he hung out with Beau. He might even be wearing the same clothes.

"Hey." I get up from my desk and give him a hug. "How are you?"

"I'm okay. You look good." He starts to rub my head like he used to when I was a kid, then pulls the gesture. "How's Beau?"

He gets points for asking about my brother, but loses them and more for not already knowing the answer to that question.

"He's hanging in. Why don't we go into the conference room, where there's more space?"

"Sure."

He follows me out into reception. I catch Savannah chewing on the end of her pen and blatantly checking Dylan out. I motion for Dylan to go into the conference room ahead of me. Savannah mouths He's cute, go for it. I ignore her, close the door, and take a seat next to Dylan.

"So what's this all about?" he asks.

"Well, you know I've been looking into Cassandra's murder."

He nods slowly. I can tell this is a subject he doesn't want to talk about.

"Why didn't you ever tell me that you went out with Cassandra?"

His leg jiggles under the table and he doesn't look at me. "Where'd you hear that?"

"Come off it. We've known each other too long."

"Does Beau know?"

"No. And I plan on keeping it that way, but I need you to tell me everything you know about what was going on with Cassandra around the time she was killed."

"I don't know how I can help you."

"You wouldn't be helping me. You'd be helping Beau."

Staring at the table, he bobs his head like a child learning his punishment. "Okay. What do you want to know?"

"For starters, how did you and Cassandra start going out?"

"Beau told me they broke up."

"Did he tell you why they broke up?"

He glances up. There's angry defensiveness in his gaze and posture. "No."

"You didn't ask?"

"I did, but he wouldn't tell me. I didn't push."

"So Beau told you they broke up. Then what?"

"I called Cassandra. She invited me over."

"Wow. You didn't waste any time."

He bolts up in his seat. "Look, I know what I did was shitty. I don't need you to tell me what an asshole I was."

"Fine. As long as you get it."

"Is this why you called me? So you can make sure I learned my lesson?"

"No." I sigh and sit back. "I'm sorry. I guess I'm still in shock finding out about you and Cassandra. I'm still trying to process it."

To his credit, he bows his head. "I'm not proud of it."

"I heard she was having some difficulties. Know anything about that?"

"What do you mean?"

"Strange things happening around her apartment. I heard she had to call the police."

"There was an incident of vandalism, an incident with her cat, and some things missing. Probably kids. I'm the one who called the police. She didn't want to, but I figured a woman living alone was an easy target. It was better for her to document it in case they caught them."

"You called the police?"

"Yeah. An officer showed up and talked to Cassandra for a while. I had to leave for work, so I wasn't there. She said the officer was nice. He gave her his card and told her to call him if she had any more trouble."

"Did she call him again?"

"Once or twice, I think. Maybe. Things between us sort of ended right after that." His leg pistons under the table, making his whole body shake.

"And how did you feel about that?"

He picks at an invisible spot on the table with the side of his thumbnail. "What do you mean?"

"Did you mess with her after she broke up with you so she'd keep calling you?"

His gaze jerks to mine. "What? No. Of course not."

"Not even a little?"

"No."

I want to believe him, but Leo's words combined with the vibes I'm getting off Dylan make me wonder if he's telling the truth or not.

His gaze drops to his tightly clenched hands on the table. "I didn't hurt her. I could never . . ."

"Rape her repeatedly and kill her?"

"No. God, no. I loved her." He turns to me, his eyes filled with tears. "I was in love with her when Beau asked her out. Did he ever tell you that?"

"Beau wouldn't do that to a friend."

"He did do it. Why do you think I jumped at the chance to be with Cassandra the minute they were over? She was supposed to be mine."

"You told Beau you were in love with Cassandra?"

"He knew I liked her."

"Yeah, but did you tell him you were in love with her? Specifically."

"No." He drops his head into his hands. "I never told Beau about my feelings. I don't know why I said that."

I let out the breath I've been holding. I knew Beau wouldn't do something like that to a friend. I feel sorry for Dylan.

"Can you think of anything else that would help me find out who killed Cassandra?"

"No. I wish I could."

"Okay. Thanks for coming." I start to stand.

"I miss him."

Dylan's words catch me off guard. I'm not sure what to say other than to lay into him for not taking the time to visit Beau.

"I tried to see him a couple of times. In the beginning. He left as soon as he saw me sitting at the table. He never answered a single letter. I miss him. Isn't that stupid after everything?"

Again, he surprises me. I had no idea he's been trying to stay in contact. "No. I don't think it's stupid at all." I say quietly. "I miss him too."

He drops his hands and stands. "Get him out of there.

Find out who really killed Cassandra and get him out of that damn place."

"I'm doing everything I can. If you think of anything else, please let me know."

"I will."

I walk him out to reception and give him a hard hug. It's the closest I've come in five and a half years to hugging my brother. The door opens as we pull apart. Leo stands in the doorway, glancing between Dylan and me. I never got to tell him about Dylan's visit.

Behind me, Savannah sing-songs, "Uh-oh."

Dylan kisses me on the cheek. "I'll call you."

"Please do. Thanks for coming. I appreciate it," I tell him.

Dylan squeezes past Leo, who is gaping at me like he can't believe what he just saw. I turn on my heels and head for our office. Let him think what he wants. I don't care. I have work to do.

For some reason Cassandra's calls to the police never appeared in any of the documents. I need to find out who the officer was who gave Cassandra his card. He might have vital information. I start a new search, guesstimating on the timing of that call. The page pops up just as the office door opens, then slams shut, rattling the pictures on the walls.

"Who in the hell was that?"

M y head is going to explode. Literally shatter into tiny fucking bits, splattering the walls and everything in the room. Less than twenty-four hours after getting naked with me and Cora's already in the arms of some other guy. I debate for half a second about going after the asshole and punching the shit out of him for touching her. Then Cora strolls off like nothing and closes the door to our office, shutting me out. No. Fuck, no.

I go after her. Before I reach the door Savannah gets in a jab: "You snooze, you lose. Idiot."

I ignore her and the fact that she's totally right and storm into our office, slamming the door after me. I've got to know. "Who in the hell was that?"

"Hmmm?" Cora doesn't look up from her computer screen. She jabs at the keys, the clicking of the keyboard echoing off the walls, punching up my anger.

I stalk forward, more jealous of anyone or anything than I've ever been in my life. It's a fire blazing through me, consuming me, hazing the edges of my vision. Cora is mine.

"What the hell do you think you're doing?"

She turns to me then. "Excuse me?"

"You go off and kiss some other guy—"

"Slow up. I did not go off and kiss anyone. He kissed me. On the cheek. And what do you care, anyway?"

"What do I care? What do I care?" I couldn't give three shits that I'm shouting. "Last night!"

"What about it?"

She's doing this on purpose, purposefully trying to get me to say what I can't say. "You know what!"

"No. I don't. I don't know what or why or anything about what's got you so pissed off."

"Yes, you do. Stop messing with me."

"I'm not messing with you. You made it very clear that last night was it for you. You don't want anything more and that's fine. But you can't come at me now like some jealous boyfriend, demanding answers to questions you don't have the right to."

My hands fist. "Jealous boyfriend?" I need to punch something. I look around, but there's nothing. "Jealous boyfriend?"

She turns back to her computer. "You're repeating yourself."

"What the actual fuck, Cora?"

Rolling her eyes, she glares up at me. "What do you want from me?"

"What do I want? What—"

"Did you hit your head? Is that why you keep repeating everything?"

"I did not hit my head."

"Then either shut up and help me or say something that makes sense. I've got work to do."

I growl—actually growl in frustration. I'm so in over my

head with her it isn't even funny. I'm drowning and she won't throw me a fucking rope. "You can't go around letting other guys kiss you."

"Whatever." She goes back to what she was doing.

I grab the arms of her chair and swing her around to look at me. "I mean it, Cora. Knock that shit off."

"Or what?"

Gripping her face, I smash my mouth to hers. She pushes at me. I give it everything I've got. Pain shoots up my groin, making me sick to my stomach. Releasing her, I grab my dick and drop.

She stands over me. "If you ever come at me like that again I'll grind your nuts to dust with my boot heel. You got it?"

I can't breathe, let alone answer her fucking question.

"Are you okay?"

"No," I wheeze.

"I'm sorry, but you have to admit you had that coming."

She's right. I did have that coming, and now that it's here —and I'm barely managing to hold down the vomit—I see where everything went wrong. I see what an idiot I've been. Cora didn't want or need me in her life, but she let me in anyway. That's no small thing, and yet I treated it as if it was. I roll onto my back and stare up at the ceiling. Cora leans over me, reluctant concern in her vivid blue eyes. I did this to her, to us. I got what I wanted and then for some reason decided I didn't deserve it. I jerked her forward, pushed her back, then tried to pull her to me all over again. She was right to drop me like this.

I put my forearm over my face, cutting off the sight of her. I can't look at her right now. Looking at her means looking at what an asshole I've been. Savannah was right.

About everything. I'd tell Cora to knee me again because I deserve it, but I don't think I could survive it.

"Do you need a doctor?" I can hear the worry in her voice.

So all that not caring one way or the other about me—about us—was partly for show. Or at the very least to show me what I should've seen all along. Funny how a swift knee to the crotch clears the head.

"No." I snake my other hand out and wrap it around her ankle. I need to make sure she doesn't go anywhere. I need her right here for what I have to say because if I don't say it, if I don't act in this moment of clarity, I could lose her. If I haven't already.

"I'm sorry," I say, still a little out of breath and queasy. "I shouldn't have grabbed you and kissed you like that." I move my arm to my forehead so I can look up at her again.

I shouldn't have done that because all the words are backing up in my brain while I just stare at her, taking in how incredibly beautiful she is. Our gazes lock. Hers is very direct, but there's something close there too and it gives me the encouragement I need to press on.

"I really am sorry." My voice cracks on the last word like I'm going through puberty. I'm sorry about so many things with her.

She kneels down on the floor next to me. "Okay."

"I'm an idiot."

"Yes. You are." But she's smiling.

"I don't deserve you."

"No. You don't."

"You shouldn't kiss me right now."

"No." She leans close so that our mouths are nearly touching. "I shouldn't."

"I lo—"

She cuts me off with a kiss. I don't know if I'm relieved or disappointed. I was going to say three words I've never said to anyone ever. Maybe she didn't want to hear them. I don't know. All I know is that she's kissing me and I'm kissing her.

"Oh, good. All back to normal." I didn't hear Savannah open the door.

Cora must not have either, because she's up and off me like I'm on fire.

"Mostly." I say, stacking my hands under my head. "I'm still waiting for the feeling to come back into my crotch."

Savannah gives Cora two thumbs up. "I knew there was something I liked about you."

"He had it coming," Cora says, a corner of her mouth kicked up.

"Don't I know it." She winks at Cora. "I'm taking off for the night. Will you guys lock up when you're done . . . recovering?" She starts to leave, then turns back. "Oh, your dad called," she tells me. "He said to tell you that he wants to see the both of you tomorrow morning first thing."

"Thanks, Savannah."

She closes the door, leaving me alone with Cora again.

"Why did you cut me off earlier?" I ask, against my better judgment, referring to my almost declaration. I'm really not sure I want to know the answer.

She sits back down at her desk again. "Because it's not true."

I prop myself up on my hands. "But it is true."

"No, it's not."

"Yes, it is." I slowly make my way to a standing position.

"There are two times a guy will say he loves you and won't really mean it—before, during, or after sex and when he thinks he's going to lose you."

"That's four times, and who in the hell told you that bullshit?"

"Beau."

"Well, he's wrong."

"No, he's exactly right. I didn't believe him, but it's true. I'm pretty sure you were this close"—she holds her thumb and forefinger a hair's breadth apart—"to asking me to marry you."

She's starting to piss me off. "I was not."

"Yeah. You were. Look, just because we got naked and did stuff doesn't mean I want or expect anything from you." She gives her computer the attention she's supposed to be giving me.

I gape at her, my mouth hanging open. When she says stuff like that it makes me want her more than anything in the whole world. And it's not because of what Beau said. It's because she's so far and away different from anyone I've ever met. Every time she throws me a curve ball I fall for her a little more.

"You probably have a hard on right now because I'm not falling at your feet," she says.

Damn it. I might have the beginnings of a hard-on. "How can anyone get wood after you kick them in the nuts and piss them off every chance you get?" I stomp over to my desk and sit down. Something occurs to me. "Did you kiss me because you wanted to or because you wanted to shut me up?"

"Both."

"Aha! I knew it. You want me as bad as I want you." If that were a real thing we'd be rolling around on the floor right now.

"What I want is for you to figure out what you want."

"I want you to stop letting other guys kiss you." And for

her to be half as crazy about me as I am about her. "Who the hell was that, anyway?"

"Dylan Newman. Beau's friend and the guy who was going out with Cassandra shortly before she was killed."

"And you hugged him? He's a suspect."

"He's no more a suspect than you. What happened with Zelda?"

"Nothing and something."

She finally gives me eye contact. "What does that mean?"

"I was supposed to tell you about it on our date tonight."

"We're not going on a date until you figure out what you want."

"I know what I want."

"You think you know what you want, but you really don't."

"Stop saying that. I know what I want and what I want is you right here, right now on top of this desk. I want you to wrap your legs around me and scream my name when you come."

She laughs. "Not going to happen."

"What can I do to make you believe me?"

"I don't know. Probably nothing."

I can tell she's done talking about what's going on between us. I'm not done, but I let it go and ask her about what Dylan told her. If we're talking about the case, we're on even ground. It's when we veer off into the uncharted territory of what's between us that we seem to falter. Maybe it's one of those things that just is and the more you think about it or talk about it the more impossible it seems.

I wasn't fucking around about loving her. I fell hard for her the second I laid eyes on her. Every minute since has been like riding an amusement-park ride I can't get off even if I wanted to. One thing's clear—I'm so much deeper into this than she is and it pulls at me. How in the hell am I going to get her to fall in love with me? Because if I can't accomplish that, I'm looking at a life without her, and that is not an option.

23

CORA

I couldn't hear Leo say those three words because I might believe them. If I believed them then I'd buy into the whole idea of "us." And if I bought into the idea, then I'd have to look at my own very illogical feelings and how they've grown wildly out of control. It was easier when this was just going to be a summer fling, an experiment living in a world I've never walked in. Leo seemed like the perfect person to go there with. He's experienced, he's leaving in the fall, he seems more than willing, and most of all he's sexier than hell.

I have to shut this whole thing down before one of us says or does something we can't take back or ignore. The other side of the issue is that Beau was right. Leo suddenly found his supposed feelings when faced with the prospect of me walking away. So what happens if I really do break things off? I was half joking about him asking me to marry him. That's not the way I want things to happen. I don't want things between us to be anything but easy and natural. I have enough strained obligatory relationships in my life to add one more.

So where do we go from here?

I'm dying to know what sex feels like and most especially what sex with Leo would feel like. The small taste I've gotten has left me wanting more. A lot more. Leo still seems like the perfect candidate to help me accomplish my goal. He's leaving at the end of the summer to go back to school. He's incredibly skilled and if how he's looking at me right now is any indication, he's also very willing. The way my body reacts to that look makes it obvious that I find him incredibly attractive.

So. There's all that and half the summer left to go. Maybe if we agree to keep it just about the physical this could work. I should be able to convince him. He always seemed like the type of guy who appreciates no-strings-attached sex. I'll lay down the ground rules and he can either accept them or not. Either way, I'll know where we stand with each other and it will all be very much under control.

But first I need to find out who the officer was who answered Cassandra's call. He or she might know something about the man who I now suspect not only harassed Cassandra, but also may have killed her.

I fill Leo in on my chat with Dylan over burritos at Taco Mia—which is just dinner, not a date.

Leo wipes his mouth. "This should've come up during the investigation and trial. You don't have anything in your files about a police report?"

"No. Nothing. Can you check with your friend at the DA's office and see if they ever came across one?"

"Sure." He points to the half burrito on my plate. "You going to finish that?"

"You can have it."

He scoops it up and takes a big bite. The movements of

his mouth mesmerize me as he chews. Suddenly I'm thinking of other things that mouth is skilled at. I shift in my seat and redirect my gaze, which snags on a familiar face ordering at the counter.

"Isn't that one of the cops who showed up when my apartment got broken into? I wonder if they got any leads that would help find out who broke in."

Leo glances around until he spots the officer. "Looks like him. Must be his beat. That reminds me." He turns back toward me. "I was followed to Zelda's house. The guy didn't even try to hide it. Black Mustang with heavily tinted windows and no license plates. He took off before I could get any kind of description."

"We must be onto something to stir up all of this attention. Do you think he knew you were going to see Zelda?"

"No idea, but he wanted me to see him. He wanted me to know he was onto us." He leans across the table. "I think he's worried, and if he's worried it's because we're onto something. We just have to figure out what."

A shudder runs through me. I never thought for a moment my investigating would bring the killer out of the shadows. He was always this faceless, nameless unknown, the answer to all of my prayers, and the key to get Beau out of prison. We must be close to a break if he's willing to take these kinds of risks.

Leo puts a hand on my arm. "It's going to be okay. We're going to figure this out."

I'm not as certain as he is. I know what that bastard did to Cassandra. I see it when I close my eyes at night. I nod anyway.

"There's something else I need to tell you," he says. "Zelda's gone. I have a lead on where she might be living, but she was hard to find when she had a home. Now that she's in the wind it's going to be even harder to locate her. But don't worry. I found her once. I can find her again."

"I feel like we're further away from solving this than ever. The more we discover, the more there is to be discovered."

"My dad's meeting with Damien LeFeaux tomorrow. With any luck we'll catch a break there."

"I hope so." I can't remember a time in the past five and a half years when I ever felt more overwhelmed with the task of freeing my brother. "I think I'll go see Beau tomorrow. It's been too long since I've seen him."

"That's a good idea. I'll go with you."

"About our earlier conversation . . ."

"Yeah?"

"I have a proposition for you."

He puts his folded arms on the table and leans in. "What kind of proposition?"

"I was thinking since you'll be going back to L.A. in the fall that we should keep things casual between us. Nothing to keep us from going our separate ways when you leave."

"No strings."

"Right. We seem to have a lot of chemistry between us. I was thinking we could keep things going the way they are. You know, just fun."

"Cora. Are you saying you want to have uncommitted sex with me?"

"Yes."

"So in this non-commitment would we get to go out with other people?"

"Well, no. While we're, you know, we're not doing it with anyone else."

"Not even with that Dylan guy who was all over you?"

"He was not all over me. Besides, Dylan's like a brother to me and I'm nothing more than Beau's little sister to him."

"Let me get this straight. You want to have committed non-commitment sex with me until the end of the summer."

"Right."

"I can't do it."

Is he joking? "Why not? All you have is casual sex. This wouldn't be any different."

"Except that it is. And thanks for calling me a man-whore."

"I'm not judging. In fact, I like that you've had a lot of experience, since I don't really have any."

"So you want to use me for sex?"

"Well . . . yeah."

He stares at me for a moment. I wish I knew what was going on inside his head. I didn't think he'd get insulted over me pointing out the fact that he's slept with a lot of women. He always seemed pretty open about that.

"Okay, I'll do it. On one condition—you can't fall in love with me."

"What? Why would I fall in love with you?"

He shrugs. "It happens." His phone rings. He glances at the display, his brows bunching together, and hits the accept key. "Hello?" His body language changes, going from curiously annoyed with me to alert. "I'm so glad you called, Zelda."

I jerk upright in my seat. Finally something is going our way.

"I'm sorry to hear that," he tells her. "Yeah, I can meet you anywhere you want. Twenty minutes? See you there." He ends the call. "She wants to meet at that new coffee shop on Baker."

We jump in the car and hightail it across town. Leo parks with less than a minute to spare. Through the window

I can see that Zelda isn't here yet. We climb out of the car and go inside.

"Find a corner booth that's out of the way so she doesn't see you," Leo says. "There." He points to the far end of the café. "That one over there."

I slide in and try to make myself as inconspicuous as possible. Leo, on the other hand, chooses a spot where he can see and be seen. We don't have to wait long. Zelda comes in and looks around. Leo walks up to her. They exchange some words and then take a seat at a table by the window.

Zelda looks different than she did the last time I saw her. I might not have recognized her except for the small red birthmark on her cheek. She looks tired and sad until Leo works his charm on her, then she becomes all smiles and coy looks. I sure as hell hope he's able to get something out of her about her and Cassandra's old neighbor Mrs. Wheeler.

The waitress arrives at my table. I order a pot of Earl Grey and take out my cellphone to look busy. The conversation at Leo's table gets chummy. Twirling a strand of hair around one finger, Zelda narrows the distance between them across the table. Leo does the same. They look like a couple having an intimate discussion. They're more evenly matched than Leo and me. I can almost see them together. I slump in my seat and try not to let that thought get too far.

What Leo said back at the taco place about me not falling in love with him comes back to me. He shrugged it off like it happens to him all the time. I can see it. He's nice to look at, funny, sexy as hell, dependable, and easy to be around. I imagine a lot of girls have fallen for him. But he's also stubborn, immature, and arrogant. Those should be negative traits, and yet mixed in with the rest they work. At least for me. And for Zelda too, by the looks of it.

I'm not jealous. I'm not. Leo's free with his affection and charm. His personality more than his looks make it hard to resist him. When he turns those chocolate eyes on you you're the only girl in the room. It's just the way he is. I wouldn't change him for anything, and yet . . . uhh. I want him all to myself. It's going to be difficult to say goodbye to him at the end of the summer.

24

LEO

I'm trying really hard to focus on getting Zelda to tell me about Mrs. Wheeler, but Cora is sitting across the room in my line of sight right over Zelda's left shoulder. I can't believe Cora sexually propositioned me. And I can't believe I almost didn't take her up on it. She's more than a quick summer fling to me. What am I to her other than a means to gain some sexual experience? If I give her what she wants, then what? Where does that leave me?

Because if I sleep with her I know it's going to mean more to me than it means to her. And if I don't she'll eventually meet someone else and they might not make her first time everything it should be. She should be loved and cherished and cared for and have orgasms that shock her. She should be with someone who will take care of her and be there for the hard stuff. Not someone who will leave her.

But what choice do I have? I want her past August. She apparently wants me only for the interim. There is no place for me in her life unless she makes a place. Or I somehow make it hard for her to live without me. If I make the sex so good she won't be able to live without it or me. Three hours away isn't that far. People make cross-country relationships work all the time.

I smile at Zelda, pushing back all those thoughts. There's another way I can make myself necessary to Cora—help her free her brother.

I leaf through the notebook I brought with me, looking for the entry about Mrs. Wheeler. It holds all the notes I've taken on Beau's case and supports my story of a student studying a local case. Zelda's curious about it. I catch her trying to read it upside down.

I start with easy get-to-know-you questions. I'm good at getting women to feel at ease with me. Before I know it Zelda's opening up about a lot of other things.

"I didn't believe Beau could've done it at first. I mean, what was done to her was so brutal." Looking away, she sips at her coffee. "But the evidence was overwhelming."

"The case file is one of the thickest I've ever seen. I've been going over some of the witness testimony, including yours. I'm sorry you had to go through that and I'm sorry you lost your friend."

"Thanks. I still can't believe she's gone."

"How long did you know each other?"

"A couple of years. When the apartment across the hall from me came available I called Cassandra right away. I knew she wanted to move close to campus. She wanted to be on her own, have the whole college experience, even if she was only moving across town. Her parents were very strict. I think she also wanted to get out from under that."

"She liked having her own place?"

"Oh, yes. She even got a cat." Her brow creases. "I wonder what ever happened to him. Maybe her parents took him in."

"Going over the case, I noticed your downstairs neighbor"—I flip through my notebook for show—"Edith Wheeler didn't testify in the trial. I tried to track her down, but I couldn't find anything on her."

"Oh, gosh. She probably died. I mean, she was old back then."

"I couldn't find any record of her death. I'm trying to put together as complete a profile as possible. You wouldn't know how I could maybe find her, would you?"

She bunches up her forehead. "She had a cousin who used to visit."

"She passed a few years ago."

"Oh. I'm sorry to hear that. Did you try her husband's niece? She used to work at an old-folks' home up north somewhere. Mrs. Wheeler was always joking about how if she ever went up there they'd probably roll her into a snow-drift and forget about her until spring. She liked the beach. I couldn't see her moving to a landlocked state, but you never know."

"Do you remember the niece's name?"

"Gosh." She rubs her forehead. "I want to say it's some-thing like Roberta or Robin. She had a different last name too. I think it started with a D, but I'm not sure. It's been so long since I've seen Mrs. Wheeler. I moved out right after Cassandra's death. I couldn't stand to live there anymore."

She's given us the first real lead on Mrs. Wheeler. I want to split and go check it out, but that would totally blow my cover. Instead, I ask her more questions about the case. Who knows? Something else might pop. She's the closest person to Cassandra that we've been able to talk to and she was a key witness in the trial.

"Did you know Damien LeFeaux?" I ask. "He claimed to have seen Beau leave Cassandra's apartment right after the murder."

"No. I saw him for the first time at the trial. There was something not quite right about his testimony though."

"In what way?"

"He said that he walked down Fletcher toward Seventh and turned right on Wardlow and that's when he saw Beau. Fletcher dead-ends into Wardlow. He couldn't have walked down Fletcher from that direction. Unless he meant that he walked away from Seventh Street and turned left onto Wardlow.

"It was obvious that he was a drug user. I imagine he just got confused. I don't know. No one mentioned anything about it during the trial—not even Beau's defense attorney."

"You're sure that's what he said?"

"Yeah. I lived there for over a year. They didn't bring Fletcher through until about two years ago, so unless he time traveled . . ."

"That's a big discrepancy."

"That's what I thought. But then they had Beau's DNA and him admitting to the police that he was there that night, so I didn't say anything. I figured it didn't matter if Beau really did it."

"You really think he killed Cassandra?"

She grows thoughtful. I expected her to answer right away. Her hesitation makes me think the trial wasn't the slam-dunk everyone thought it was.

"I didn't at first. Or at least I didn't want to. I knew how much they loved each other, but then they broke up and everything was so strange after that. When they arrested him I just couldn't see it. I mean, what happened to her was so . . . brutal." Her eyes fill with tears. "I knew Beau. He had to have had a major psychotic break to do something like that. It was just so sick." I hand her a napkin and she dabs at her eyes. "She suffered so much."

She starts bawling then. I glance across the room at Cora. She motions for me to reach out and take Zelda's hand. I do, muttering apologies and words of sympathy. After a few moments Zelda gets herself together enough to speak again.

"No," she answers. "I don't think Beau could've done that to Cassandra."

We talk a little more, but I don't learn anything else new from her. That info about LeFeaux's testimony could be the break we need with my dad going out to visit him tomorrow. Any leverage we can get we can use to discredit him. I've got to double-check the trial transcript against a map of the neighborhood just to be sure. I don't want Dad going in there with incorrect information.

I walk Zelda to her car. "Thanks for meeting me. You've been a big help."

"It was nice to talk about it with someone. Most people just want to sensationalize the gruesome parts. Cassandra was my friend. She deserves more than to be reduced to a notorious headline."

Nodding, I take out my wallet and hand her two twenties. "I know you're going through a tough time."

She hesitates, then accepts it. "Thanks. Normally, I wouldn't take the help, but . . ."

"We all need help every now and then. You helped me."

As I watch her drive away, Cora joins me. "I saw that. That was very nice of you."

I shrug.

"Did she tell you anything useful?"

"And then some. We need to go back to the office. I want to check on something Zelda said about the trial and I think I might know where Mrs. Wheeler is."

"What did she tell you?"

"I'll fill you in on the way."

We climb into the car and take off. There's a buzz running through me, making my skin itch. This is it. I can feel it. This is the lead we've been looking for. I can tell Cora feels it too. She's animated in a way I've never seen her, gesturing with her hands and moving nonstop. I'm glad I got to be the one to give her this moment.

We finally arrive at the office. It's dark, darker than normal. I look up at the sky, wondering if the clouds are covering the moon, and realize that the lights in the parking lot are all out.

Cora must've noticed that something was off too, because she doesn't move to the stairs right away like she usually would. She stands by the open car door, her head cocked to one side like she's listening. I'm listening too and scanning the building and the empty parking lot. Nothing moves. Our gazes catch across the top of the car. I put my finger to my lips. She nods and reaches into the car, shutting the interior light off. I wish I'd thought to do that.

I pull the gun Dad gave me from between the seats and motion for Cora to stay where she is. Creeping toward the stairs, I listen hard for any odd noises. A hand grips the waistband of my jeans and I nearly jump. Damn Cora didn't stay put. I glare at her. She glares back. I should've known she wouldn't listen. I motion for her to stay quiet. She rolls her eyes at me like "no duh." Damn stubborn woman.

We edge up the stairs, careful not to step on the one board we know always creaks. I stay low as we reach the top. Cora does the same. The walkway is empty. And dark. The lights are off up here too. Unless there's a power outage in the area, something's definitely wrong.

Cora tugs on my waistband and whispers, "Should we call the police?"

"And tell them what?" I whisper back. "The power's out?"

"You think it's just an outage?"

No. "Probably."

We creep along the walkway, past the front window of the agency. The blinds are drawn over the blackened window. The only sound comes from the occasional car passing by. It's too late for anyone to still be working in any of the other offices. Most likely we're on our own here. I'm starting to think Cora's idea about calling the cops might be a good one. We reach the door to the agency and pause. It doesn't look disturbed in any way, and yet . . . I push on it and it swings open. Just like at Cora's house.

Cora jerks me back. I stumble into her, knocking her down. She's still got ahold of my pants. I pinwheel my arms, but it's not enough, and I go down too, landing on top of her. She makes the sickest noise I've ever heard—a grunt mixed with the rush of air leaving her body and a crack that sounds like a broken bone. She pushes at me. I roll off and look down at her. Her hands go to her throat. In the dimness I can see the panic in her eyes as she tries to catch her breath. Just then there's a loud swooshing sound. Light flickers in the open doorway, but it's not the right kind of light.

Fire.

I scoop her up and run down the stairs. Bending, I lay her down in the grass. I take my phone out to call 911.

KABOOM.

The building explodes behind me, knocking me on top of Cora. Fiery debris rains down around us. There's a burning on my back. I roll to put it out. When I'm sure I'm not on fire anymore I go to Cora. She's trying to reach her pants leg. I pat her leg, dousing the ember. Running my hands over her, I check to make sure she's not on fire anywhere else.

"Are you all right?" I ask her.

"No." She winces as she tries to sit up. "You landed on me. Twice."

"Did you break anything?"

"I didn't." She points to my hand that's resting on her thigh. "But I think you might have."

I look down. The middle finger of my left hand is twisted, pointing in the wrong direction. My head swivels. The next thing I know I'm falling, then black.

25

CORA

"Leo?"

I push at him until I finally roll him off me. Which isn't easy. He's a big guy. Oh, thank God. He's still breathing. I can't believe he fell on me three times tonight. And not in a good way. I glance up at the office building. It's fully engulfed. Flames shoot out of the agency's door and window. If Leo hadn't picked me up and gotten us out of there, we'd be toast right now.

I pat his cheek. "Leo?"

He's out cold. Could he be more seriously hurt than his finger? I run my hands over him, checking for any obvious signs of injury. His head, his arms, his chest, his thighs—

"A little higher and more to the middle," he mumbles.

"Idiot." I laugh in relief at his perverted joke. "Are you okay? Are you hurt anywhere?"

"Just my pride for passing out. And the finger. It burns like a son of a bitch." He eases up to his elbows and gets his first look at the building. "Holy shit. That could've been us."

"I know. You saved us."

"Focus on that and not the part where I blacked out like a wuss."

"Are you sure you're okay?"

"I'm fine. What about you? You scared the shit out of me up there."

"As long as you don't fall on me again, I'll be fine."

Sirens wail in the distance.

"Did you call them?" he asks.

"No. Did you?"

"No."

"Maybe a passerby called."

"Maybe."

"That fire was deliberately set." I shiver at the thought that someone could do something like that.

He scoots closer and puts his arm around me. "Yup."

"Most people would've walked inside right away. We might've been inside when the fire started if you hadn't been so cautious."

"Probably."

"This is more than breaking and entering. It's attempted murder."

"Maybe." He examines his finger. "Nasty. Thank God I'm right-handed."

"You're being very blasé about this."

"Not really." He stands, brushes himself off, then holds his good hand out to me to help me up. "I'm thinking this is more of a message. And a way to get rid of evidence." He brushes the hair out of my eye. "Your box was in there with everything you have on your brother's case."

"And all of our new notes and info."

"I'm sorry, Cora."

"Don't be."

"But this'll set us back."

"Not really. I made copies of everything. Just in case. I have them stashed somewhere safe."

"Damn, you're clever. More clever than the asshole who set that fire gave you credit for."

"I also have electronic copies of the notes we made. I backed up my backup. Beau is too important to me not to."

"My dad will be impressed. Hell, I'm impressed." He puts his arms around me. "You're pretty damn impressive, Bluebird."

"So are you. Not counting the fainting."

"I didn't faint. I passed out."

"Same thing."

"My finger fucking hurts. Look at it."

He shows it to me. It's already swelling. We need to get him to a doctor. The fire trucks round the corner, their lights slashing red across Leo's face.

I reach up, put a hand to his cheek, and kiss him. "Thanks for getting us out of there. I'm sorry about your dad's office. And your finger."

"I need to call him. He's going to be pissed. This place was his life."

"I bet he'll just be glad you're okay."

While we wait for Mr. Nash we watch the firefighters do their job. Whatever the office building is made of doesn't have a chance against the flames. Before we know it the scene gets out of control. More fire trucks arrive. The police close the street down. News helicopters circle overhead. A crowd gathers. I try to get Leo to have one of the paramedics look at his finger, but he refuses.

"Your dad will have to get here on foot," I say. "They've blocked the street in both directions."

"Uh-huh." He's not paying any attention to me or to

what's happening with the fire. He's too busy checking out the crowd that's gathered.

"Who are you looking for?"

"The guy who set the fire."

I glance around at the people standing around. Could Cassandra's killer be here, watching? I move in to Leo, needing his warmth, his strength. Out of instinct or habit he draws me closer to him, even though his attention is definitely elsewhere.

"You really think he's here?" I ask.

"On TV they say the perp sometimes stakes out the crime scene or goes to the victim's funeral. He wants to see the chaos he's caused. He wants to relive the moment, relish in the notoriety of his crime. He wants to watch the fire burn. It gives him satisfaction. It's a part of the allegory. Almost like reliving the crime all over again. He's here. I can feel it."

"Where?" I can barely get the word out.

"I don't know, but he's here."

"Son of a bitch!" I jump at the sound of Mr. Nash's voice behind us. "What happened?"

Leo tells him about the break-in and our narrow escape.

"Are you kids all right?" Mr. Nash asks.

"Yeah," Leo answers.

"No." I lift Leo's arm to show Mr. Nash the bent finger. Leo tries to pull it away.

"What the hell?" Mr. Nash grabs Leo's wrist, turning his hand in the flashing emergency lights. "You need to get to a doctor."

"It doesn't hurt . . . much."

"Leo's car's blocked in by the fire trucks," I tell him. "I've been trying to get him to have the paramedics look at it."

"Take my car." Mr. Nash gives me his keys. I give him

mine. "It's parked around the corner on Third. I'll stay here and talk to the police, see if I can't get them to tell me anything." Mr. Nash heads for an officer who looks like he's in charge.

I can tell Leo wants to protest, but I grip his arm and tow him toward the car. I can't believe someone blew up the agency office. We have to be getting close for him to do something so desperate. Thank goodness I'm militant about my backup and he didn't succeed in destroying my files on Beau's case. Something nags at me as we squeeze through the crowd. There's something familiar about this scene, reminding me of the scene in front of Cassandra's house after her body was discovered—the chaos, the crowd, the emergency vehicles.

Out of the corner of my eye I catch a familiar face, gazing up at the burning building. I change direction, causing Leo to stumble to make the adjustment.

"Dylan?"

He blinks, clearly surprised to see me. "I heard about the explosion on the news." Grabbing me, he wraps me in a hard hug. "I'm so glad you're okay. I was worried when they said it was the agency's building."

I'm too stunned to do anything but let him hold me.

Behind me I can practically feel Leo's irritation. "Hey, get off her."

Dylan lets me go and looks past me to Leo. "Who are you?"

"Her boyfriend."

"Her—" Dylan starts.

"He's something, but not my boyfriend. Dylan Newman, Leo Nash. Leo, Dylan. Leo's dad owns the agency. He's helping me with Beau's case for the summer."

The guys shake hands, sizing each other up. If Leo was

suspicious of Dylan before, that's nothing compared to how he's eyeing my brother's friend right now.

"I'm sorry about your dad's agency," Dylan says, glancing up at the fully engulfed building.

"You really just came down here to see about Cora?"

Dylan's gaze swings back to Leo. He doesn't seem to like Leo any more than Leo likes him. "What business is it of yours?"

"Are you sure you didn't just come down here to check out your handiwork?" Leo jabs a thumb toward the fire.

"What? You think I set that fire?"

"No," I tell Dylan. "We don't. Thanks for coming down to check on me. We've got to go." I put my arm through Leo's and drag him toward the car. "I'll call you later."

"The hell you will," Leo mumbles, giving Dylan a backward glare.

"Not this crap again."

"Come on. He's a suspect, Cora. And he's got the Forbidden Little Sister thing for you, whether you want to admit it or not."

"What? That's not a thing."

"Ah, yeah, it is. He's already ticked the Best Friend's Girl thing off his list. You're next."

"No way. Even if I thought for a moment he had feelings for me he wouldn't get far. I don't think of him that way."

"I bet Cassandra said the same thing at one point and he ended up banging her."

I jerk to a halt. "He did not bang Cassandra. They just went out a few times."

"Right. I've seen pictures of Cassandra. She was beautiful. There's no way he didn't try to get with her."

"He might've tried, but that doesn't mean he succeeded."

"Zelda didn't say it in so many words, but the gist I got

was that ol' Dylan back there slept over. A lot." He makes air quotes around slept over.

"No."

"You might think you know Dylan, but I know guys. And guys like sex. They especially like sex with hot chicks. You and Cassandra are definitely hot. I'm telling you he wants you."

"You're imagining things. He's never made a single move toward me."

"He's working up to it with all that fake worry and touching. Lots of hugs and kisses. I'd put money on him making a move the next time you see him. If not, then he for sure will the very next time he sees you. You can also expect a phone call from him tomorrow."

"Are you sure the pain hasn't addled your brain?"

"My brain's not addled." We arrive at his dad's car. He hits the unlock button on the remote and hands me the keys. "And we're going to work out what exactly that something I am to you is."

He climbs in the car, leaving me to sputter expletives at no one.

26

LEO

My finger was only dislocated, no broken bones or torn tendons. The doctor said I was lucky. Right now the only thing I feel lucky about is that the pain meds haven't worn off all the way yet and Cora is lying next to me in bed. She's draped across my chest, one of her legs hooks over mine, and her arm is banded around me. I can't move. I don't care. She's warm and good-smelling, with all of her soft parts pressed against me. She rejected my delirious half-pain, half-pain-meds attempt at seduction last night. I would've been shit anyway, so she saved me the humiliation.

This morning is a whole other story. There's a throbbing more incessant than in my finger. She shifts, grazing her thigh across my rock-hard dick. I don't know if it's pleasure or pain or some perverse in-between that makes me want to roll her over, part her legs, and drive into her. Or at least play with her a little. I smooth my good hand up her thigh, raising her nightgown. Her skin is soft. I could touch her all day. The edge of her panties is little barrier. I slip a finger under, then another, circling around the edge of the fabric to where she's hot and . . . wet. Holy shit. Sliding a finger into her, I stroke through her slickness.

She stirs. This time I know rubbing her leg across my dick is anything but accidental.

"You're sure you're up for this?" she asks, her voice still heavy with sleep. "Your finger."

"Right now I can't feel anything except what I'm doing to you and what you're doing to me." I turn us so I can look down at her. "Are you up for this?"

She widens her legs, giving me better access. "Mmm, I'm getting there."

Staring down into her amazing blue eyes, I can't believe what a lucky bastard I am. She's warm and willing, and in this moment . . . mine. But she's made it clear that I'll get only a few of these moments and that's it. There is nothing for us beyond this summer.

I kiss her, not giving a shit that my mouth reeks of morning breath or that my body probably stinks just as bad after running down the stairs carrying her. I want her. I want her to want me. Most of all I want her to want a future with me beyond September, beyond Beau's case. I put everything I've got into making love to her. I use all of my tricks. She's panting, practically begging me for release, but I won't give it to her. I can feel her annoyance building right along with her need.

She sits up so I can pull her plain cotton nightgown over her head. It floats down onto the bed next to us. She's naked, looking up at me like I'm everything she needs. But I know I'm not. I can make her come a thousand times in a thousand ways and it won't change a damn thing between us.

She fists the front of my T-shirt and drags me down on top of her. I'm so fucking hard for her I can hardly breathe. The scent of her arousal permeates the air around us. I take her in with each inhale. She's inside me the way my body demands to be inside her, to join with hers. I know what she likes now. I know how to make her beg. I try to make her as hot for me as I am for her, but no matter what I do to her I know she never will be.

She's close. So damn close. Her head falls back, her lips part. She's half moaning, half panting, and she's so goddamned beautiful it makes the backs of my eyes sting. I push her over the edge with my mouth, just the way she likes it. I watch in amazement as her orgasm slams into her. Her whole body goes taut. She grips the sheets, twisting them as she cries out. I pump my dick once, twice. It takes nothing for me to come with her, spilling onto her stomach on a barely suppressed growl.

I'm empty afterward. In every way. I leave her to get a washcloth to clean her up. I can feel her confusion. She expected to lose her virginity. I expected to take it. I told her I would. When it came down to it I just couldn't.

I can't take what's not mine. She's not mine.

I don't look at her as I clean her off. I don't entirely understand the way I feel. She's going to have questions I have no answers for. The one thing I know for sure is that it has nothing to do with finally getting to have sex with her or making her a trophy like Savannah accused me of. I could have her. In ten or so minutes I could push her back onto the bed again, get her hot for me, and push inside her the way my body cries out to do whenever I'm with her.

It has nothing to do with me being freaked out about being her first. I'm not weirded out by her virginity and it doesn't add a sick twist to my desire for her either. It's a factor in that I want her first time to be something she looks back on with good memories and no regrets. It's a part of her, the way her blue eyes and her chewed-down pinkie nails are.

I need something from her that I can't express. Until I figure out exactly what that is or if it's even possible I can't have sex with her the way she wants me to. And that realization scares the shit out of me because I think I might need her to love me the way I love her. No. It's more than that. I think I might need her to marry me.

God, I'm such a girl.

If I told my friends any of this shit they'd give me never-ending crap about it. And if I told Cora . . . Hell. I can't tell Cora. She'd run so far and fast from me that I'd never recover. She may have already ruined me for anyone else. If she left now, that would be some shit I'd never get over.

I rinse the cloth out in the sink and throw it in the laundry room next to the other jizz-soaked washcloth. At this rate I'll have to buy Mike a whole package of new wash-cloths. When I get back to the bedroom, Cora is sitting up in bed, talking on the phone. She pulled her nightgown back on. Her knees are drawn up to her chest underneath the gown and she hugs them, staring out the window at the ocean. She doesn't acknowledge me or even turn to look at me as I pull my boxers on.

"No," Cora says into the phone. "I can't." There's a pause. She rocks back and forth. "I don't think that's a good idea. Yeah, I'll let you know if I change my mind, but I doubt I will. I just don't think of you that way."

That son of a bitch Dylan. I knew he'd call her.

She finishes the call and tosses her phone on the bed. "That was Dylan. But then you probably already know that." She looks at me then, and there's something I've never seen before in her eyes—insecurity. "Did I do something wrong?"

"You turned that asshole down, so no."

"I mean here." She gestures at the bed. "I saw the box of condoms in your bag. Did you have them that first night?"

How do I answer her? I lied to her then. Do I lie to her now too? How many times can I lie before that's all that's left between us?

"Yes."

"Why did you tell me you didn't have any that first time?"

I shrug, not because I'm trying to be flippant, but because she's opening up a conversation I want no part of.

"Why don't you want to have sex with me?"

I can tell my reluctance to go all the way with her and my lying and avoidance hurt her. What do I say that won't either creep her out or scare her away?

"We have sex." My voice comes out as a hoarse whisper.

"We get each other off."

"There's more to sex than penetration." I can't believe my response is to give her a fucking sex-ed lesson she doesn't want or need.

"Why won't you have sex with me the way I want to have sex with you?"

I crack a teasing smile when there's nothing funny here. "How do you want to have sex with me?"

"I want you to stick your dick in me like I know you want to but for some reason won't. Why not? And by the way, you were right about Dylan. He asked me out. I bet if I went out with him he'd fuck me."

"Is that what you want, to be fucked and thrown away? You don't value yourself enough to be more than a quick fuck?" I'm motherfucking Dr. Phil now, talking about feelings and shit. I should be getting my first period any day.

"Why won't you answer my question? Do you have a problem with me being a virgin?"

"No."

Glaring up at me, she hugs her knees. That white cotton nightgown is having a strange effect on me. There's nothing special about it. In fact it's kind of plain, but it's doing my head in. I picture her wearing it with a white veil, holding a bouquet of flowers. She's walking down the aisle toward me. Then it's our wedding night and I'm taking it off her like I did just a few moments ago, only this time I don't freak out. She's my wife and it feels right, like coming home. I slide into her. She welcomes me. She's not wearing the look she's got now that tells me I'm a big giant asshole.

"I don't believe you," she says. "Have you ever been with a virgin?"

"That's not what this is about."

"Then what is it about?"

"I'm going to take a shower, then I want to check the map against what Damien LeFeaux said in his testimony during the trial before we meet with my dad. He's got that meeting with LeFeaux this afternoon." I head for the bathroom.

"My virginity freaks you out."

"Your virginity doesn't freak me out. Would you let it go, already?" I slam the bathroom door on her reply.

It would almost be better if I had some kind of hang-up about virgins. I'd be less of a head case if that was what's going on here. Maybe then I'd recognize myself. Because this Leo—the one who can't bring himself to open a box of condoms when he's got a hot, willing woman in his bed—is not someone I know. I'm not sure he's someone I want to know. That guy is a loser, holding out for something he's never going to have with Cora.

27

CORA

I don't understand Leo. He's not behaving the way I expected him to. The only explanation is that my virginity weirds him out. He certainly seems to like touching me and doing things to me and with me, but he won't screw me. It's starting to feel like I'm wearing a scarlet V on my chest. I'm impenetrable, like some kind of unsexy superhero. I'm coated in penis repellant. My own kind of invisible super power that no one wants.

Of all the guys for this to be a problem for, I never would've guessed it would be a problem for Leo. I figured he'd have a whole bedpost notched with virgin conquests. I'm starting to think I'm his first virgin and he doesn't know what to do with that. I should read up on it. I bet there's a protocol or treatment for this sort of thing.

The shower goes on in the bathroom. I grab my phone and do some Google-fu. Huh. Apparently Parthenophobia is the mortal fear of virgins. Symptoms of Parthenophobia include heavy breathing, profuse sweating, nausea, vomiting, an inability to speak, cotton mouth, and a feeling of paralysis. He definitely didn't seem to have any of those. So if it's not a clinical thing requiring a doctor it must just be only a slight hang-up. If he legitimately had this fear, then he certainly wouldn't have been able to get me and himself off.

Maybe he just needs someone to help him work through it. I grab Leo's box of condoms, open it, and take one out. Then I take a second one out ... just in case. I test the bathroom doorknob. It turns easily, so I enter and close the door quietly behind me. I slip out of my panties and drag my nightgown over my head. Taking a deep breath, I tell myself that I'm doing this for him. The truth is I'm doing it for me.

The crazy thing is, the more he refuses to have penetrative sex with me, the more I want it. It's starting to be all I think about. And it's not just sex in general. It's sex with Leo. Period. End of story. I want him to be my first time. It's more than his skill, which is fucking amazing. Not that I have anything to compare it with. I just really like the things he does to me and how he makes me feel when he's doing them —like I'm the most beautiful, sexiest woman he's ever been with. Like he can't believe he's with me.

I like the things we've done together and I want more. So much more. I want him to fulfill the wicked promise in his eyes when he's got me naked and is going crazy on me. I want what I've only read about in books and seen in movies. I want a connection with someone I trust and care about who cares about me.

I don't think about any of that as I open the shower door and step inside. I'm scared and excited all at the same time, gripping the condoms, one in each hand.

Leo braces himself on the tiled wall, his head bent, letting the water run down his back. I carefully set the condoms on the shampoo shelf and slip my arms around him.

He starts, nearly hitting his head on the shower nozzle. "What are you doing?"

His question is full of knowledge and uncertainty. He knows what I'm doing, but he's not sure he should allow it . . . however much he wants to. And as I slide my hands down his body, I feel how very much he wants to. I stroke him how he showed me, how he likes it. He lowers his head again and lets me. The slick feel of my breasts against his skin makes my nipples hard. I move back and forth, grazing them across his back. It feels so good. Touching him feels good. He's hard in my hands and getting harder.

"Faster," he murmurs. "Harder . . . Yeah, like that." He breaths through his nose, his body is almost as rigid as his dick.

"I want you, Leo," I whisper. "I want you inside me."

I can't believe how bold I've become. I reach for a condom, knocking one of them off the shelf. I tear the other open with my teeth.

His head jerks up at the sound. "What are you doing?"

"No more talking."

"Cora." There's something in his voice that's not quite surprise, as though he sees that what's between us is inevitable.

He turns suddenly and I'm in his arms, pressed between the shower wall and his body. His mouth takes mine in a kiss that's desperate and punishing. He's mad and glad and hornier than hell. He wants me. I can feel it in the way both he and his body respond to me. I hardly have to make an effort and he's all over me. His hand is on my breast, doing wicked things. He pulls and twists, but it's gentle and makes me wet. His fingers slide through the slickness. I know now —thanks to him—what my body is seeking, what's building inside me. I give over to it.

He replaces his hand with his mouth on my breast and holy fucking God, stars explode behind my eyelids.

I grip the wrist of the hand that's between my legs and show him what I want, quickening his strokes. "Faster," I gasp. I'm getting so close.

He mutters something I can't make out.

I'm all sensation now. Everything he does adds another layer of pleasure until I think I can't take it anymore and then BAM. I bite his shoulder to keep from crying out. He holds me through it. He tells me I'm beautiful and kisses me, smoothing the wet stands of hair back from my face. I can feel how much he cares about me in the gentle way he helps steady me. I hadn't realized that I'd all but climbed him.

"You're really good at that," I tell him.

"You make me want to be better."

"I don't think you could get any better."

"Sounds like a challenge," he says against my neck, where he's doing something with his teeth and tongue that makes my knees nearly give out.

His penis is hard against my belly. I slide my hand up and down its length. I want it where his hand just was. I want him to thrust all the way into me, pinning me to the shower wall. I want him to lose his mind, driving into me over and over. I want to scream out his name while he's inside me and hear his heavy grunt when he comes.

I try to do to him what he did to me, trailing a line of kisses under his jaw to his ear. My hands are full of him. I have one hand on his ass and one hand wrapped around his dick. I have him just where I want him.

"Fuck me, Leo," I whisper next to his ear.

A shudder runs through him.

"Come inside me."

His only response is a low moan and his hand sliding

between my legs. He doesn't play fair. Too soon he's got me panting and I lose the rhythm of my strokes on his dick. I'm not going to let him make me come again without being inside me.

The condom. Damn it. I dropped it somewhere behind him. I'm not thinking about anything but that condom and getting it on him. I lean past him, making him move to the side. I bend over to find it.

"Holy fuck."

I look up at him over my shoulder. His eyes are glued to my ass. I renew my effort to find the condom. He grips my waist from behind. His cock slides against my butt cheeks. I have a split second of uncertainty and then he slips a finger into my pussy from the back and another one from the front. I'm suddenly full of him in a most unexpected way. He curls his body over mine. I put a hand on the wall to steady myself against the twin thrusts of his fingers.

He knows how to touch. In no time at all I'm close to coming, but I won't do it like this. I won't let him get away with chickening out again. I bite the inside of my cheek. The metallic taste of blood fills my mouth. Behind me, Leo's movements are hurried. He hooks his finger in such a way that every time it brushes over some undiscovered spot inside me it makes me whimper.

I start to rise, but he reaches around and tweaks my nipple. That's all it takes. I can't hold back. My orgasm barrels through me. Behind me, Leo thrusts between my cheeks and his hand. He holds me to him as he, too, climaxes, that deep growl reverberating off the tiled walls as his hot cum shoots onto my back.

Goddamn it. I pound my fist against the tile. Not again.

Wrapping me in his arms, he rights us. He holds me tight against him, my back to his front. He presses his lips to my shoulder and murmurs something against my skin. His touch is tender and gentle as he moves us into the spray of the shower, letting the water run between us as he rinses away the only evidence of our coupling. He turns me and kisses me, cupping my face in his hands. And then he reaches for the soap. Covering me in lather, he washes me, taking his time with the parts of my body he especially likes. I do the same to him, luxuriating in all of the ways his body is different from mine. The hard planes of his stomach, the coarseness of the hair on his legs, the way his muscles bunch and flex when I hit an especially sensitive spot, and the way his penis reacts to what I'm doing.

Before I know it, he's got me plastered against the shower wall, his hands and mouth doing wicked things to me. He hooks my leg over his shoulder and uses his mouth on me. I didn't think I could come again, but I should know him better than that by now. When I can finally stand without falling over, I go down on my knees in front of him. He tries to wave me off, but I ignore him and take him into my mouth. He coaxes and teaches me how to do it the way he likes. Slapping his palm to the wall to steady himself, he comes in my mouth, gently massaging the back of my head in encouragement.

Somehow this act feels more intimate than anything else we've done. I feel like we've reached some kind of compromise with it. This is the only line we'll cross. I won't push for more.

Not yet.

28

LEO

We're supposed to leave to meet my dad in ten minutes. It's barely enough time for Cora to fire up Mike's desktop, access her cloud drop box, and print out the part of LeFeaux's testimony where he talks about Cassandra's neighborhood. We compare it to a Google image we find that was taken about six months after the murder and months before they brought the street through. It's not much. Hell, it's a shot so long we'll be lucky if LeFeaux doesn't laugh my dad out of the place. On the other hand, after reading LeFeaux's testimony he doesn't strike me as an exceptionally smart guy. I'm putting my money on this plan working.

I pop another prescription pain pill when Cora's not looking. Our shower sexcapades did me in. I took the splint off to take a shower not expecting Cora to join me. If she finds out how bad it fucking hurts right now she'd feel guilty. The last thing I want her to feel about what we did in the shower is remorse. She seems to have accepted the boundaries I set. And if the shy, wicked smiles she keeps sending my way are any indication I left her satisfied, wanting more. Hell, I can hardly stop grinning like an idiot even with the pain.

We meet up with my dad at a coffee shop down the street from the office. He wanted us to meet him at the house, but there was no way in hell I wanted her to go through with my mom what she went through the last time they met. That shit was seriously fucked up. I don't know how Cora lives with that kind of judgment from people who don't know anything about her except that her relative was convicted of a heinous crime. I'm going to have to find a way to straighten things out with my mom about Cora.

Right now my dad is walking through the door with my old laptop under his arm and a frown so deep it nearly drags on the floor. What the hell happened now?

He slides into the booth across from us and passes me the laptop. "Call your mother."

"Any news on the fire?" Cora asks.

"They're sure it's arson. I'm going to be up to my eyeballs in insurance forms for the next twenty years."

No surprise there. "Do they have any idea who did it?"

"The power outage caused the security cameras to go down too." Dad's frown deepens. "Whoever did it knew what they were doing."

"I'm so sorry," Cora says. "This . . . all of this is because of me and Beau's case."

Dad puts a hand up to stop her before I can. "None of this is your fault. I don't blame you any more than I blame Leo. Now tell me what you've been working on."

The waitress appears at the table and takes our orders. As soon as she's gone I fill my dad in on the things we've learned, including the inconsistency in LeFeaux's testimony. I show him the print outs we brought.

"Nice work," he tells us both, then to Cora, "I'm

impressed that you thought to back up your files. You've got the instincts of a great detective. If I had the budget I'd hire you on at the agency in a minute. If there's an agency at all by the time the insurance company gets finished."

Cora looks like she's going to apologize again, so I put my hand on her knee and change the subject. "We also might have a lead on the downstairs neighbor, Mrs. Wheeler. If we can find her it just might be the piece we need to blow this whole case wide open."

"You guys make a great team," Dad says.

He glances back and forth between us, no doubt taking in how close we sit and how my arm turns out toward Cora under the table. It's probably obvious from where he's sitting that my hand isn't in my lap. We haven't discussed what's going on between Cora and me other than him telling me to stay away from her. If he only knew the dynamic between us, he'd laugh his ass off. I'm the one likely to get hurt here, not Cora.

"Thanks." Threading her fingers through mine, Cora looks up at me. "I think we make a great team too."

"Well. I'd better go. I'll call you when I get done with Mr. LeFeaux." Dad slides out of the booth. "Don't forget to call your mother."

We watch him walk out. He didn't even touch the coffee he ordered.

Cora squeezes my hand. "Do you want some privacy?"

She's not dumb. She knows the phone call to my mom likely won't go well. I don't blame her for not wanting to sit next to me while I defend her for something that's not her fault.

"I'll call her later." I set the laptop on the table and turn it on. "First I want to see if we can find out any info on Mrs. Wheeler's niece."

It takes a while to get the old beast up and working and connected to the café's Internet. I log on to one of the genealogical websites the agency uses to track people's relatives. I looked mostly on Mrs. Wheeler's side of the family, not expecting that her long deceased husband's family might step in and take care of her.

The waitress comes by to give us a third refill right about the time I'm ready to give up. There are no Robins or Robertas with a last name that starts with a D on Mr. Wheeler's side of the family.

"What about this one?" Cora points to a box on the screen with the name Alice Denise Rodriguez. "It's the only name that's vaguely close and has the right letters in it."

I click on the box. Alice Denise Rodriguez is on the old side for a niece. She could be a younger cousin. I put her name into People Locator, a program we use to get people's addresses. It's surprisingly easy to find people these days. Too easy.

There are twenty people in the U.S. named Alice Denise Rodriguez. We sort through them, setting aside the ones who are too old, too young or dead. When we're done we're left with no names to work with.

I sit back in my seat, frustrated. "Damn it. I thought for sure Zelda's info was good."

"I've learned not to get my hopes up." I hate the dejection in her voice.

And I hate that I'm the one failing her. Sitting forward, I click out of that program and try another and another. No luck. Then a thought strikes. What if Alice Denise Rodriguez isn't in the U.S.? I switch programs again. Her last name is Spanish, so I try People Finder in Mexico. We get thirteen hits. Lucky thirteen. We weed through them until we're left with one name. I check the birthdate. It's a match.

All the hair on my arms stand up. Cora leans so far over me I can barely type. She must feel it too. That low buzz at the back of my head that tells me we could be onto something here.

Alice Denise Rodriguez lives in Ensenada. Just two hours away.

"This might not lead to anything," I say, trying not to get her hopes up as high as mine. "We should call and see what's what."

Cora nods. She's vibrating in her seat as she pulls her cell out and hands it to me. "Call."

I open a new window and Google how to call internationally. Before I know it I'm calling Alice Denise Rodriguez in Mexico.

She answers after the second ring. "Hola?"

Shit. I didn't figure on her speaking Spanish. I know enough to order a burrito and that's about it.

"Hola," I say in my crappy Spanish accent. "Habla Ingles?"

"Yes," she says with barely an accent.

I introduce myself as a private investigator looking for Edith Wheeler. I give her some bullshit excuse about old Edith being owed some money by the insurance company I work for.

"Do you know how I can reach Mrs. Wheeler?"

"Yes. She's in an elderly care center here in Ensenada. I have power of attorney over her affairs. She's quite infirm."

I turn to Cora and nod. She grips my arm, her eyes wide. We fucking found Mrs. Wheeler.

"I need to verify she's alive and your power of attorney before I can release the funds," I tell Denise. "I'm in San Diego. I can be there around three. Will that work?"

"How much money are we talking about?"

"A little over twenty grand. I also have some papers that'll need to be signed. Where should I meet you?"

She rattles off the address of the care center. As soon as I disconnect the call Cora screams and launches herself at me, planting a big kiss on my lips. I can't believe it. I can't believe we found her.

"I can't believe it," Cora says, reiterating what I was thinking. "This could be it. This could be the thing that frees Beau."

I don't want to bring her down with the possibility that Mrs. Wheeler could be in a coma or in some other way unable to speak. And even if she can it doesn't mean she'll be able to tell us anything useful. But I don't say any of that to Cora because she's looking at me like I'm a big fucking hero, with something I've never seen before in her expression—hope.

"It could," I say instead, bringing her in close. "It very well could."

29

CORA

I'm really not trying to get my hopes up, but finding Mrs. Wheeler is the single best lead I've ever had in Beau's case. She could free him. The thought of Beau free is almost too much. My brain can't process it. I've never allowed myself to imagine it. How could I, when the possibility has always been so completely impossible? I bet my parents never envisioned it either. Why would they, when they believed in his guilt from the start? I try to picture their faces when I tell them Beau is going to be freed, that he didn't kill Cassandra, and that their complete lack of faith in him made them no better than a stranger.

I wonder if my dad will even be sober enough to fully comprehend how badly they fucked up. Or if my mom will pretend she believed in him the whole entire time. She'll twist the past five and a half years in some way so she comes out the victim in the story.

How will Beau feel to finally be free? What will he want to do first? What will he need? I can't wait to be standing there when he walks out of that hellhole. I can't wait to hug him and have him smell like him instead of a stranger. I can't wait for his hair to grow back out and not to have to constantly worry that he'll be beaten or killed. I can't wait to have him home.

Leo and I cross the border into Mexico. It's been a long time since I've been here or anywhere. I had to dig out my passport for the return trip back to the United States. I flip it open and look at my picture. My mom took me to have my hair done like it was some kind of fashion photo session. She made Beau wear a tie for his picture. That winter we went to Italy as a family. The next winter Cassandra was dead, Beau was on trial for her murder, and my dad moved out.

What a difference a year makes.

Leo follows the directions Siri gives him. We're going to arrive well before the time Leo told Mrs. Wheeler's niece we'd be there.

"Why did you tell Alice we'd be there at three?" I ask Leo. "We're going to get there at least an hour before that."

"I didn't want her there when we talk to Mrs. Wheeler. I wasn't exactly honest with her about the reason for our visit." He winks at me.

"True."

"I also don't want to take the chance that she won't let us talk to Mrs. Wheeler. She might not want to get involved."

"Also true."

We grow quiet again. Leo squeezes my hand in his lap. He must sense my nervous excitement. I haven't been still since the moment Alice confirmed that Mrs. Wheeler is still alive. We ride the rest of the way in silence except for every now and then when I have to translate something for him. My Spanish is much better than his.

We pull up to the care facility and park. Before hitting the road we stopped off at Jamie's house and recovered the backup copy of my binder that has all of the profiles of everyone involved in the murder investigation. I brought it to help jog Mrs. Wheeler's memory. There's no telling what her mental state is and I might need to remind her who Cassandra was to her.

I tell the woman at the front desk that we're relatives of Mrs. Wheeler's. She takes us through a winding maze of hallways until we're standing before room number 232. Mrs. Wheeler's room. We're so close.

The woman tells me in Spanish that Mrs. Wheeler is having a good day. Thank goodness for that. Although I'm not sure how good her good days are. The woman leaves us to enter the room on our own.

Mrs. Wheeler lies in her bed, looking out the window. She doesn't seem to realize we're here. I hardly recognize her. She's so much older and more shrunken than the last time I saw her.

"Mrs. Wheeler?"

She turns her face toward us. "Yes?"

Her response encourages me. "Hi. My name is Cora Hollis and this is Leo Nash. I was friends with Cassandra, your upstairs neighbor when you lived in San Diego."

She blinks at me. I'm not sure she understands me. I repeat myself in Spanish.

"My Spanish isn't that good. English, please. Come closer so I can see you."

We move to her bedside. She presses a button on the remote for her bed and raises herself into a sitting position.

"Do you remember when you lived in San Diego? You had an upstairs neighbor named Cassandra Williams?" I ask.

Her gaze is unfocused on mine. I try again. "She lived upstairs from you. She was murdered."

"Oh, yes." She does some slow blinking, then her eyes go wide. "Yes. So terrible."

"Would you mind if we ask you a few questions about what happened to Cassandra?" Leo asks.

"I suppose not. Who are you again?"

"Leo Nash and Cora Hollis. Cora knew Cassandra," Leo says. "Is it okay if we ask you a few questions about what happened to her?"

She nods. Leo's worked his magic again. She's more with it than I could've hoped. There doesn't seem to be anything wrong with her at all, other than being bedridden.

I inch a little closer to her. "Did you see anyone enter or leave Cassandra's apartment the day of her murder?"

"Just the delivery man like I told the officer."

I ask, What delivery man? at the same time Leo asks, What officer?

I cast Leo an annoyed glance. He puts his palms up, letting me know it's all mine. I'm annoyed because his question was better than mine.

"You were questioned by a police officer about Cassandra's murder?"

"Yes. He spent most of that afternoon with me, asking over and over about the delivery man."

"Can you tell me who the officer was who spoke to you?"

She lowers her brows. "I don't remember his name."

"If you saw his picture do you think you'd recognize him?" Leo asks, opening my binder.

I'm too grateful he thought of something I didn't to be mad at him for butting in again.

Mrs. Wheeler glances down at the binder. "Maybe."

I turn the page and Cassandra's pretty face is smiling back at us.

"Oh," Mrs. Wheeler breathes. "She was so beautiful, wasn't she?"

"Yes, she was."

"Wait a minute." She puts a hand out to stop me from turning the page. "Hollis. Are you related to Beau Hollis?"

"Yes, ma'am. I'm his sister."

She pushes at the binder. "I can't help you."

"Please. Please help me find the officer who spoke to you that day. My brother's life is on the line here."

"That's of his own doing, not mine. No. Take that thing away and leave. I don't want anything to do with that monster."

Leo takes the binder, snapping it closed. "You don't have to help us."

What the hell is he doing?

"I just hope you can live with the fact that you refused to help free an innocent man." He turns and walks toward the door.

I gape at him, unable to believe what he's doing. He's blowing this whole thing.

He's got a hand on the door handle when Mrs. Wheeler finally finds her voice. "What do you mean 'innocent'? A jury convicted him."

"A jury convicted Maurice Battle too." Leo turns, but stays next to the door. "Mr. Battle sat in prison for thirty-nine years for a crime he didn't commit before our agency took on his case and found someone like you who helped prove his innocence. Wait. No. Not like you. You won't help us." He puts his back to us again like he's going to leave.

"Is that what you do?" she asks. "Free innocent people?"

"It's one of the things we do."

"And you think the boy—her brother—who was

convicted of Cassandra's murder is innocent like that other man?"

He faces us again. "Without a doubt. We just need the proof, and I think you have it."

She looks up at me. I can't breathe. I grip the railing of her bed, willing her with everything in me to agree to help us. She's our only real hope. Every other lead we've had so far isn't enough to bring before a judge to reopen Beau's case.

"Please," I beg. "Five and a half years. That's two thousand and eighty-nine days—including today—he's sat in prison for a murder he didn't commit. He'll never get those days back, but you can help us give him the rest of his life back." I don't even care that I'm crying. I'd get on my knees if it would get this woman to help us.

"Two thousand eighty-nine days," she whispers.

"Please."

She holds her hand out toward Leo. It shakes. "Bring that book back here."

Leo returns to her bedside and opens the binder again, laying it on her lap. He slips his hand into mine. When I look at him I see tears in his eyes. He wipes mine away with the backs of his fingers.

Mrs. Wheeler turns the pages. I watch her face for any reaction, any sign of recognition. If we can find that officer, we can find out why he didn't report what Mrs. Wheeler saw. She's the only one who can put someone other than my brother at Cassandra's apartment on the day of her death— a deliveryman. Her missing statement could be the something we need to take to a judge.

If we can get Damien LeFeaux to admit he lied about seeing my brother that day the DA's case takes another hit.

There would be no witness putting Beau there at the time of Cassandra's death.

We also need to find this deliveryman. He could be a potential witness or even the killer himself. This small, frail woman has done more in the past five minutes than I've been able to do in more than five years.

She turns the pages, taking her time, examining each photo as though memorizing it. I can't move. I keep waiting for her to point to a page and shout, "This guy! This is the one!" But she keeps turning the pages slowly, methodically. I don't look away from her. I don't want to miss the moment she blows the whole case wide open.

And then she gets to the last page.

Her watery brown gaze rises to mine. "I didn't see him."

30

LEO

Cora walks out. I'd go after her, but Mrs. Wheeler is looking up at me like she might cry. I don't think I've got the words to reassure her. I can see how badly she wants to help, how much I made her want to help with my bullshit speech about freeing Beau. I pat her pale, wrinkly hand and mumble something about how grateful we are that she tried.

"Do you think she'll be okay?" Mrs. Wheeler asks.

"Yeah." Eventually. Possibly.

She leafs backward through the binder as slowly as she did the first time she looked through it. I study the pages with her. Now that Cora's not in the room there's really nothing else to look at. She pauses on a page with a newspaper clipping about the murder Cora printed out from the Internet. I recognize the front of Cassandra's apartment building cordoned off with police tape. There are a number of uniformed and plainclothes officers in the photo. A crowd has gathered. But none of that is the center of the photo or the accompanying article.

Two officers wrap up Beau, who is struggling to get past

them. I almost don't recognize him. His hair is longer, sure, but that's not why. There's something fundamentally different about him from the man I met several weeks ago. He's rougher, harder, and a lot less sure of himself now. I try to imagine what happened to Beau happening to me. If someone murdered Cora in the cruelest, most brutal way imaginable and then I was convicted for it . . . I don't know how he wakes up every day carrying that. How has he not gone insane missing her?

Mrs. Wheeler struggles for a closer look at the photo. I hold it up for her.

"Do you see something?"

She points to a drawer in the tray table. "Get my magnifying glass."

I find it and hand it to her. I adjust the binder to the right height for her.

She peers through the magnifying glass. "I should've done this sooner." She gestures upward. "Turn on the overhead light."

I do as she asks. A part of me wants to go get Cora, but I don't want to get her hopes up like she did last time.

"Is there another picture like this?" Mrs. Wheeler asks.

I flip through the binder. "Here."

This one is a different angle from the street, looking up. The door to Cassandra's apartment is open. A bunch of people stand around. I never realized how many people showed up at crime scenes. There are reporters, too, like the one who took the photo we're looking at.

Mrs. Wheeler runs her magnifying glass over it, then looks up at me. "Are there any more?"

I find the third and what I know to be the last photo from that day. She does her magnifying-glass thing again, this time slower, and it's like my heartbeat has slowed too.

She stops moving and holds the glass over one spot in the pic. My arms are killing me, holding the binder all this time, but I don't care.

She slides a finger between the paper and the glass. "There. Do you see that?" She leans back so I can have a look.

I'm not sure what she's talking about. "The guy in the blue shirt?"

"No. The one in front of him with his face turned away. All the pictures of him are like that. I wasn't sure because he does a real good job of blending in and hiding most of his face, but I'd recognize that ugly tie anywhere." She taps the page with her finger. "That's the detective who interviewed me."

"Detective? You said it was an officer who interviewed you."

"Same thing, different clothes."

"I'm not sure they'd see it that way. And he doesn't appear anywhere else in the book?" I flip back to the pages with the detectives who were involved with the case. "Are you sure it's not one of these guys?"

"It's not one of those guys."

I take out my cellphone thinking I can do a search, but I forgot I'm in Mexico and my cell service doesn't translate.

We have an almost match. Maybe if I jogged her memory a little it might help.

"What else do you remember about him besides his tie?"

We chat a little more, but she's not able to give me anything else on the detective, so I change tactics.

"What company was the deliveryman from?" I ask. "Was it UPS, FedEx, the U.S. Postal Service . . . ?"

She shakes her head. "No. It was that one with the arm-in-arm logo. Always reminded me of snakes."

"Postal Pronto?"

"That's the one."

"Do you remember approximately what time he made his delivery?"

"Around four o'clock. Which was weird because usually they delivered to our complex around seven. I remember it being four because my favorite talk show came on. I guess that's why I only saw him leave."

"Wait a minute. You didn't see him arrive with the package, you only saw him leaving?"

"Yes."

"So he could've been there for hours before that. I know it's been a long time, but do you remember what time you woke up that day?"

"Probably the same as every day. I liked to watch the local news before Good Morning America starts at seven."

"So you woke up around six a.m. What time did you go to bed the night before?"

"Early. I'm usually asleep by nine."

I sort it out in my head. Beau said he arrived at Cassandra's at about ten after Mrs. Wheeler was asleep, so she wouldn't have seen him. He left just after one in the morning. Some time after one a.m. the delivery guy got there and then he left around four the next day, according to Mrs. Wheeler. LeFeaux said he saw Beau leaving Cassandra's apartment around two, but his testimony is bullshit, so I can't count that.

"Do you know if he delivered to only Cassandra's apartment or to any of the other tenants too?" I ask.

"My window rattled just the slightest whenever she closed her front door. That day it rattled and then the man came down the stairs. I figured I missed his arrival. It happens. I get caught up in my shows sometimes. I couldn't ever hear when the door opened, just when it closed."

"And you told all of this to the detective with the ugly tie?"

"Yes. All of it."

"What else did you tell him?"

"He asked me a lot about what the man looked like—height, build, hair color, that sort of thing."

I tap open the notes app on my phone. "How tall would you say he was?"

She looks me over. "About your height, I'd say. It's hard to tell from the angle of my bed."

"About six-two. How was he built? Was he fat, skinny, muscular?"

"About like you except he had a little more around the middle, but that might've been because his uniform was a little small for him."

If he stole a uniform to get into and out of Cassandra's apartment it wouldn't be a surprise it didn't fit him.

"What color was his hair? Was he black, white, Aslan . . ."

"White with brown hair. He wore sunglasses, so I couldn't see his eyes. And he had a tattoo."

"Where? What was the tattoo of?"

"I could only see the last half of it. The sleeve of his shirt covered a good part of it. It came to a point at the bottom."

"Like a triangle?"

"More like a shield." She closes her eyes for a moment. "I'm guessing that because of the shape, and it was gold with lines and words."

"Which arm was it on?"

"The side that was closest to me—his left upper arm."

"Could you draw it if we had paper?"

"There's some in the drawer there."

I find a pad and pen and hand it to her. She sketches for a few minutes, then hands me the pad back.

"It does look like a shield. You're pretty talented."

"I used to teach art."

"Is there anything else you can tell me about the detective? Did he have an accent? A habit, like clicking a pen over and over? Did he smoke? What were his teeth like? What kind of car did he drive?"

"No accent, but he did smoke . . . cigars, I think. No habits. I don't remember his teeth. His car . . . now, that's what's interesting. I didn't notice it at the time because I was so upset over poor Cassandra. It wasn't until later when I went over it again—as I like to do—that I noticed the duplicates."

She's been pretty lucid up until now, but I wonder if maybe she's getting tired.

"The duplicates?" I ask.

"In my book. It's right over there." She points to the dresser on the other side of the room. "There's no point in my keeping it anymore. No cars drive past my window. The third drawer."

Now I'm sure she's losing it. If she even had it in the first place. I open the third drawer as she directed. There are some clothes and a stack of spiral-bound notebooks.

I hold them up. "These?"

"Yes. Bring them here."

I do ask she asks.

She pulls out the second one from the top. "This'll be the one. What was the date Cassandra was killed?"

I give her the date and she flips through the pages.

She taps a line with her finger. "Right here is the day he came over to talk to me. 6TPW001." She turns back a couple pages. "Then see here it is again—6TPW001. There are so many on this day. The neighbors across the street had a lot of parties back then." She points it out a few more times. "Right here is the first time. A couple of months before the last time. All told, 6TPW001 is here twelve times."

"What is 6TP whatever it is?"

"A California license-plate number."

"Hold on. You're telling me you have his license-plate number?"

"I have just about every license-plate number parked on our street that I could see from my window." Her gaze goes to the window. "There are no cars now to keep track of." There's nothing on the other side except the blank brick wall of the building behind the care center.

31

CORA

I'm sitting outside in a little patio at the front of the care center. It's hotter than the surface of the sun, but I'm not bothered by it. I can't believe we came all this way for nothing. Now that my tears have all dried up, I want to scream in frustration. I thought for sure Mrs. Wheeler would be the answer to all my prayers. I'd held out too much hope. I should know better than that by now. Just when I gather the strength to pick myself up, life strolls by and kicks me in the teeth.

Out of the corner of my eye I catch Leo exiting the care center. He's probably looking for me.

I jog to catch up to him. "Hey."

"There you are." He takes me by the hand. "Come on. We gotta make this quick so we can get back to San Diego before dark." He tows me across the street to a little market.

"What are we doing here?"

"I'm getting Mrs. Wheeler a present. You won't fucking believe what she told me." He grabs a couple spiral note-books and heads to the cashier.

I help translate and then we're heading back to the care center.

"Why are we going back here?"

"It'll be quick. Wait here." He leaves me at the front desk and jogs down the hall. In a few minutes, he's jogging back.

"What are you doing?"

"Come and help me talk to the lady at the front desk."

"What is going on?"

"I'll explain everything in the car. Ask her if there's an empty room with a window that looks out on the street."

Giving him a What-the-fuck? look, I do as he asks. "She says there is one. She wants to know why we're asking. I'd like to know why too."

"Ask her if Mrs. Wheeler can have that room."

I relay the message. "She says it costs fifteen hundred pesos more a year than the rooms she's in now."

"How much is that American?"

I ask the lady and she taps on her computer. "She says it's a little over a hundred dollars, depending."

Leo pulls his wallet out and peels off three hundred-dollar bills. I can't help but gawk that he has that much on him.

He hands it to the lady. "Tell her that's the difference for two years and there's a little something there for her if she can have Mrs. Wheeler moved today and her bed set up near the window."

"What are you doing?"

"Repaying a favor."

"What did Mrs. Wheeler tell you after I left?"

"Will she move Mrs. Wheeler or not?"

I chat with the lady at the desk, who is so thrilled at her sudden windfall she picks up the phone and makes the arrangements. "She's having her moved right now."

Leo flashes a wicked smile. "Muchas gracias." He takes my hand again. "Let's go. We've got a lot of work to do."

We jump in the car. It's the most animated I've seen Leo, and that's saying something, since the guy is practically an anime cartoon. He tells me about Mrs. Wheeler's notebooks and the photos and a bunch of other stuff I can't believe. I was so sure this trip was a monumental waste of time.

As soon as we cross into the United States, Leo calls his dad who has some news of his own. Damien LeFeaux admitted to lying on the stand in exchange for having his outstanding grand theft warrants reduced to minimal charges and his DUI case dropped altogether. When faced with the proof of his lies, LeFeaux gave up everything. He agreed to recant his testimony if Mr. Nash can make it so he doesn't serve any extra time for lying on the witness stand.

Leo tells his dad what we learned from Mrs. Wheeler and how she's willing to testify to what she saw. Leo gives Mr. Nash the license-plate number of the detective who took her statement and then didn't add it to the case file. We also tell him about our suspicions that this detective may have harassed Cassandra before her death and he may be the real killer.

"If there's a cop behind this, then we're talking about a whole other level of danger here," Mr. Nash says. "You kids be careful. I've got a friend at the DMV who can run the plate, but I'm concerned if we do there could be some kind of alert set up by the owner of the car that lets him know if anyone runs it. I'm going to have to see how we can go about this in the safest way possible. He's already onto you guys. He knows you're getting close. If he suspects for one minute that you found Mrs. Wheeler . . . On second thought, I have a better idea. It's time to bring in the lawyers to see what they can do. You kids stay safe. I'll call you as soon as I know something." He hangs up.

"I can't believe it," I say. "I can't believe we're so close. I need to see Beau. I need to tell him what we've found out. I just can't believe it."

Leo chuckles and takes my hand. "It's too late to go out to the prison today and we're not on the list for tomorrow. You could call, but it'll probably be faster to send him a letter." He brings my hand up and kisses it. "I can't tell you what it does to me to see you smile like that."

I lay my head back on the seat rest and study his profile. Haloed by the low, late-afternoon sun, he's breathlessly handsome. I can't believe I'm sitting here with him. A few months ago I never would've imagined I'd be interested in someone like him, let alone have a relationship with him. I didn't think I needed anyone in my life. I had Beau and Jamie and a handful of work acquaintances. I had my case files and more than I wanted to handle with my parents.

I realize now that I had nothing, nothing to call mine. Everything I did, from the way I dressed to how I spent my time, revolved around getting Beau freed. I'm not sorry about it. At all. I wouldn't change a damn thing except to find Mr. Nash's agency sooner ... and Leo.

The summer's almost over. We're closer than I've ever been to accomplishing my goal. I can't help but look toward the future. My future. What will I do with myself if I'm not spending every waking moment on Beau's case? What am I going to do when Leo leaves for school? How can I go back to the way things were before I met him? I don't think I can be that person again. I didn't realize it then because I was so obsessed, but I was lonely. Instead of doing something about my loneliness, I dug myself deeper into Beau's case.

There's something solid and real between Leo and me. I

know there's a word for how I feel about him, but I can't bring myself to say it, let alone accept it. Not yet. I've come to depend on him in a way I can't depend on anyone else . . . even Beau. My brother's in a place both mentally and physically that's so far from where I am that I wonder if he'll ever find his way back. His words echo in my head about finding a life for myself. I'm close, so close, to finding that life for both of us.

Dad's right. If we're talking about a cop murdering Cassandra we're in way over our heads here. How am I going to protect Cora from a professional? I can't show it, but I'm scared shitless. This guy has gone to great lengths to stop our investigation. He's a murderer, for fuck's sake. If he finds out we're onto him, really onto him, there's no telling what he'll do. We're just going to have to lay low until Dad and his attorney friends can work their magic.

I think Mrs. Wheeler's notebook might have given us even more than I originally thought. The first time the license plate appears in Mrs. Wheeler's notebook could provide us with the date Cassandra initially called the police about the strange things happening around her apartment building. I don't think I was far off when I told Cora that I think this whole thing started with that call for help.

The cop who killed her must've been the one to respond to it. I'm guessing by his subsequent visits to her apartment that he gave Cassandra his business card to call him directly if there was any more trouble. Just like I called it—Hero Syndrome. The more problems Cassandra had, the more reasons she had to call him. He created her need for him to come to the rescue. According to Mrs. Wheeler's notebook, he created that need more than ten times in a two-month period. That's more than once a week.

Cassandra's phone records would show her calling the cop's number. That would've come out in the investigation. He had to have known that. How did he get around it? A burner phone, maybe? He could've written his burner cellphone number on his business card when he gave it to Cassandra. My private line. Special for only you. If you need me I'll be here in a flash. Call me. Anytime.

I can see it. He thought he was smart using the burner phone. He didn't count on Mrs. Wheeler's notebooks. She was smart not to tell him. It probably saved her life. She puts him at Cassandra's apartment too many times to excuse away. The unidentified hair in her bed must be from him. He lucked out there. They never ran it for a DNA match, but when they do it will put him in her bed. He could claim they had a romantic relationship. Who's alive to say they didn't?

It would cause a lot of problems for him though. Especially with the hidden witness interview. At the very least, it could create reasonable doubt for Beau. The cop is another potential suspect who was never interviewed. A suspect who tampered with the case. That alone could cast enough suspicion to reopen the case against Beau.

We've got all the pieces. We just need to reveal the final player.

We grab some food at a drive-through restaurant and head for my friend Mike's place. He was cool to let us stay here for as long as we need to. That need is greater than ever. With his state-of-the-art security system, it's the safest place we could be.

Cora's been very quiet since we talked to my dad. I wonder what she's thinking. I imagine a lot of the same things that have been going through my head. It's weird to be at a complete standstill. There's nothing to do but wait. Everyone's been found who needed to be found. We've pulled all the threads we can pull in the case. It's now up to my dad to do what he did for Maurice Battle—contact the legal group that works on cases like Beau's. It's now in the hands of lawyers.

It feels strange to me to be in waiting mode. I can't imagine what it must be like for Cora. I want to fast-forward to the day Beau gets released from prison, not just for Beau and Cora, but for me too. Because on the day he's free she'll be free too. And then maybe, just maybe, she'll give us a chance.

"How long did it take?" she asks, as we go through the front door of Mike's place.

I turn off, then reset the security system. "How long did what take?"

"To free Maurice Battle."

"Longer than you'd think. Too long. Nearly six months."

This information does nothing to cheer her. It does even less for me. I don't have six months with Cora. I don't even have one month.

"That's not fair." She's looking out the window when she says this.

"No. It's not fucking fair at all."

I want to go up behind her and put my arms around her, but I know if I do I won't be able to stop at just a simple hug. I need more from her than she's got to give. And I have nothing that she needs anymore. I can feel the lengthening between us. It started in Mrs. Wheeler's room. Maybe even before that. I don't know. All I know is that I'm desperately, hopelessly, in love with her. It hurts. No one tells you that.

In the movies it looks so easy. In two hours a couple meets, falls in love, encounters problems, someone makes a grand gesture, then BAM, happily ever after. I don't have a grand gesture. I don't have anything she wants or needs. The one thing I had to give her I've already given her—the leads and connections to free Beau. It's so fucked up that I—of all people—couldn't give her the only other thing she wanted —sex. What's wrong with me? Even now I want her so badly I practically vibrate with it. But I know if I touch her I'll only disappoint her. Again. It's all just so fucking fucked up.

"That's another one hundred and fifty-two days," she says.

She did the math. Of course she did. I don't know if it's a coping mechanism or an obsession. Either way, I feel the anguish and anger she'll endure in every single one of those days. And that's if we're lucky. It could take longer. It could not happen at all. What then? What if Beau is never freed?

"Two thousand two hundred and forty-one days alto-gether," she intones, like some fucking electronic clock.

I can barely see her through the rage that hits me out of no-fucking-where. "How many hours is that? How many minutes? Seconds? Nanoseconds?"

"Why are your mocking me?"

"I'm not mocking you. I want to know. I want to know how deep it goes. Come on. How many hours?"

"I don't know."

"Need a calculator?" I pull out my cellphone, punch up the calculator setting, and hold it out to her. "Go on."

"Why are you doing this?"

"I'll do it for you." I jab my finger at the buttons. "Two

thousand two hundred and forty-one times twenty-four. That's fifty-three thousand, seven hundred eighty-four hours." I hold it up for her to see. "That's sounds a lot worse than two thousand and some odd days, doesn't it?"

"Stop it."

I can't stop. "There are sixty minutes in an hour." I punch the clear button. "If we times twenty-four by sixty that's one thousand four hundred forty minutes in a day. Times that by your two thousand two hundred forty-one and it equals . . ." I'm out of control. I know I'm out of control, but I can't stop. "Holy fuck. Three million two hundred twenty-seven thousand and forty minutes."

"Stop."

"Three million is fucking dramatic, isn't it? You should count the motherfucking minutes, not the days. People will really feel sorry for you then."

"What is wrong with you?"

"Nothing. There's nothing wrong with me. What's wrong with you, Cora?"

"Why are you doing this?"

"I'm helping you. It's what I do. I help you. That's all I do, all I'm good for."

"I don't know what you want from me."

I stalk toward her. "Don't you?"

Watching me with wide eyes, she shakes her head.

"I want you to care about me half as much as you care about counting the days, Cora. I want to mean more to you than how much longer it's going to be before you can resume your life. I want you to resume your life right now, no waiting to see what happens with Beau. Because you know what? At some point counting the days has to end. You can't keep going on like this. If you won't do it for me, do it for yourself. Hell, do it for Beau. He practically begged you to so many times. And I know you'd do anything for him. Do this. Do this one thing. Have a life."

"I have a life."

"No. You don't."

"What do you know about having a life, having responsibilities? I'm all Beau has. I'm it. If I leave him, he's got no one."

"There are no absolutes here. You can have a life and still be a good sister."

"You want me to pick you over Beau."

"You can have us both."

"No, I can't! I can't move on like everyone else has and leave him behind. I won't do it. I'm all he's got." She defiantly swipes at a tear that dares to fall.

She's broken. I'm broken. I don't know what I'm doing here. I don't have a chance with her. I never did. But there's one undeniable fact that neither one of us can ignore.

"I love you," I say simply. "I'm not saying it because I'm losing you. I can't lose what I never had. I'm saying it because it's true."

She takes in a rough breath. She's a fighter, my Bluebird. A fighter right up until the end. And this is it. The end. The end of us and whatever we might have been. The end of her needing my help. And the end of me fighting an unwinnable battle.

I let her go and walk away.

33

CORA

He doesn't slam the bedroom door. No, he closes it softly. The sound of it is so quiet, nearly inaudible, but it echoes in my head like a gunshot, jolting my body as if I've been hit. His words rip through me, exposing the cracks in my defenses.

He doesn't love me. He can't. That's not what was supposed to happen here. He wasn't supposed to make me want things I can't have. He wasn't supposed to make me want to follow him and slam the door behind me and make him feel what he's making me feel right now. I choke back a sob. And he sure as hell wasn't supposed to lay down that ultimatum.

I can't abandon Beau now. There's too much on the line. I'm too close. I can almost see him the way he used to be. I can see the days he's been in prison falling off him like leaves on a tree, revealing the old Beau one by one. Two thousand and eighty-nine days, counting today. Leo mocked me for keeping track, but he doesn't understand. No one understands. No one but Beau. I count them because Beau does. It's the only thing we can still do together.

I discovered it early during one of my first visits with him at Chino Men's. He threw it out there—The Number. Sixty-three. He said, "I've been here for sixty-three days, but it feels like forever." He was right. It did feel like forever. It was forever. More than two thousand days later, I've learned the hard meaning of forever and what failure really is. Because I'm not just counting the days, I'm counting the ways I failed him. Every day a new way. I can't turn my back on him. And I can't move on until Beau can move on too.

I don't look at the bedroom door as I pass. I don't glance back at it when I go in to feed and take care of Oliver. If I see it I'll want to go through it, and I don't know what I'll find on the other side. More than that, I don't know what I'll do if I cross over the threshold. I might decide to be selfish and choose him over Beau. If I go after him I might give up on someone who everyone has given up on and left behind. I can't do that. I can't look at that door.

Oliver lives in a cat's paradise here and I live in a perverted sort of hell. He looks at me just like he always does, with a mixture of tolerance and loathing. He hasn't been the same since Cassandra died. None of us have. Does she know? Can she see what we've all become? What would she say?

I'm not just fighting for Beau. I'm fighting for Cassandra too. She's been gone more days than Beau's been in prison. I can't give Cassandra her life back. I can only give her justice. And take care of Oliver as best as he'll let me.

I put a hand out to pet him. He doesn't move away, so I touch him lightly, stroking from his head to his tail. He head-butts my wrist. I pet him again. We do this two more times and then he walks away. He'll only let me in so far and not an inch further. I get the parallels between us. The irony isn't lost on me.

I leave Oliver and go into the spare bedroom. This time last night I climbed into bed next to Leo. Tonight I'll sleep alone. It's better I make the transition sooner rather than later. Before I get used to it and can't sleep without him.

I tell myself this and other lies over and over for the next couple hours. It's because the sheets still smell like him. I'm not used to sleeping in such a large bed. This isn't my house. I'm not used to the sounds it makes. The bed's colder because we're closer to the ocean. I'm anxious about Beau's case. I'm lost because there's nothing to do but wait.

I wake up in the morning rusty-eyed, with a headache. The sun is barely over the horizon. I throw on a sweatshirt and go in search of something hot to drink to soothe my aching throat. There's a box of doughnuts on the counter and a take-out coffee cup. Leo must've gotten up early too. I lean over the cup and inhale. Earl Grey. Damn his thoughtfulness.

"You're up."

He looks as bad as I feel. I can only imagine what I look like.

"Thanks for the tea. You didn't have to."

"Habit, I guess." He shrugs and takes a sip from the cup in his hand. "My dad called. He has some news for us. He's on his way over."

"Okay."

There's a knock at the door. Leo goes to answer it. I don't know what to do with myself. This is so much more awkward than I imagined it would be. I want to say something to Leo, but there's nothing really to say.

Mr. Nash comes in looking like he had almost the same night we did. The look on his face when his gaze swings to mine makes my stomach do a painful swoop. "You're going to want to sit down for this."

"What's wrong?" I ask. "What happened? Is Beau okay?"

Leo pulls out a stool for me. He doesn't put his hand in mine like he usually would to reassure me. Instead, he moves to the other side of the counter and leans against it.

"It's not about Beau," Mr. Nash says. "It's about Mrs. Wheeler."

Leo comes off the counter. "What about her?"

"Someone broke into the retirement home she lives in last night. The guy knew exactly which room was hers. He used a pillow to try to kill her. She managed to get to her call button and the nursing staff came in and interrupted the attack."

"Oh, my God," I gasp. "Is she okay?"

"Fortunately, she was moved to another room earlier that day. The woman in her old bed has some bruising, but she'll be fine."

Because of Leo. He had her moved to a room with a window. She could've been hurt or worse.

"He followed us," Leo says. "He saw exactly which room we went into. Son of a bitch."

"It's not your fault, Son. This guy's a pro."

"Did they catch him?" I ask.

"No. He got away. But they got his license plate."

"Let me guess," Leo says. "California license plate number 6TPW001."

Mr. Nash nods. "The very one."

I leap off the stool. "Who owns that car?" I have to know his name.

"Detective Paul Winfro." Mr. Nash sets a file on the counter and opens it.

Leo and I both lean in for a closer look. Our gazes collide.

"Oh, my God," I breathe.

"He's one of the officers who showed up when your apartment got broken into."

"And at Taco Mia."

"And I bet that license plate goes to the black Mustang that followed me to Zelda's house. He's been fucking with us this whole time."

"As far as I know he hasn't crossed the border back into the states. Border Patrol has his info. If he tries to get back into the country he'll be arrested on the spot." Mr. Nash looks at his watch. "I've got an appointment in an hour with the Project Freedom attorneys to see if they'll take on your brother's case. I think with this new information combined with Mrs. Wheeler's testimony we'll have enough to bring Beau's case to a judge for review. In the meantime, you two stay together and stay safe. I'll let you know as soon as I hear anything."

"Thank you."

I'm too stunned to move. I can only stare at the photo of the man who killed Cassandra and destroyed my brother's life. He doesn't look like a monster. There's no obvious sign of what he's capable of. I can see why Cassandra trusted him and why he didn't send up any red flags for anyone who knew him.

Leo comes back from walking his dad to the door. "You okay?"

"Yes. And no. I don't know what I am."

He picks up the photo. "He looks so normal. But then they say that about most killers."

"You saved Mrs. Wheeler."

He lifts a shoulder.

"You did. Getting her that room to make her happy saved her. You're a hero."

"I'm not a fucking hero."

"You are."

He makes a face and sets the photo on the counter. "How does it feel to have a name and a face for your nightmare?"

"I'm still trying to figure that out." I drop back onto the stool. I don't know what I expected to feel, but this empty kind of numb nothing isn't it. I should be angry or sad or, I don't know . . . Anything except this hollowness. Where's the hate? I thought I'd at least feel hatred toward the man who destroyed so many lives.

"Maybe it will come to you later. I'm glad you finally know who was behind all this and that Beau will likely get his day in court. You've worked really hard. It's nice that it's paid off for both of you. Congratulations."

"Thanks." I guess. I can't even drum up any happiness.

"I'm going to take a quick shower."

"Yeah, okay." I take a sip of tea and turn the photo toward me. I can't stop staring at that face. I don't know what I expect it to tell me.

Why? I just want to know why? Why did he kill Cassandra? What did she do to deserve the cruel, inhumane things he did to her? How could he live with himself after doing that to her? And that poor woman in Mrs. Wheeler's room. If Leo hadn't moved her I don't know that she could've fought him off the way the other woman did. Leo saved her life. He doesn't think of himself as a hero, but he is.

I wouldn't have thought he was capable of it when I first met him. I really didn't think much of him at all other than his being the owner's son. He's so much more than the lazy skater dude I first took him for. So much more.

34

LEO

I'm dying. I have to be. There's no way anyone could survive this. Except Cora. She seems to be totally fine.

That's not true. She looks like hell. Beautiful to me still, but she looks like she didn't get any more sleep than I did.

And she cried. Her eyes are red-rimmed and swollen. It guts me to see her like that. I wanted so badly to put my arms around her and hold her. But if I touch her I know I'll only end up dropping to my knees and begging her to love me back. Pathetic. I'm fucking pathetic. I can't believe I held it together as long as I did. I couldn't wait for my dad to leave so I could get the hell out of there. Being near her and not touching her, holding her, kissing her, fucking hurts.

I put on some swim trunks and find a beach towel. It's still summer and I haven't been to the beach once. Maybe a swim will help put things in some kind of perspective. Or at least give me something else to think about.

I find Cora sitting on the stool in the kitchen, staring at the photo my dad brought. How long has she been sitting there like that? She looks almost as miserable as I am. I fight the urge to go to her. Instead, I stay on the other side of the room, out of reach.

"I'm going for a swim," I tell her.

She glances up. Her eyes take on that look and it's not fucking fair. She doesn't get to look at me like she wants me when I know she doesn't.

"Wait," she says. "I'll go with you."

"I don't think that's a good idea."

"Why not?"

"Stop fucking with me."

"I'm not." She looks hurt. I tell myself I don't care.

"I'll be right out there." I hold up my cell. "Call me if anything happens."

I go out the back door and jog down to the water. I don't stop, dropping my towel-wrapped phone on the sand, and run right into the water. It's colder than I expected, making me lose my breath. I swim until my heart is pounding and I'm almost too tired to drag myself out of the water. When I do, I find Cora standing next to my towel, her arms wrapped around her.

The breeze lifts the black and neon-blue strands of her hair. Her bare feet are dug into the sand so far it looks like she doesn't have any. She stares at me, daring me. Her eyes are brighter in the late-afternoon sun. I'm out of breath from more than my swim. I stop when she's still out of reach. Everything about her is defiant, from her gaze to her stance to the tilt of her head.

"I love you too."

Her words are a sucker punch to the gut. I now get what she was saying that day in our office when I first tried to tell her I love her. The falseness of it is insulting. It hurts more than if she hadn't said anything at all.

"You're only saying that because you're losing me."

Me throwing her words back at her surprises her. I remember that feeling too, being shocked into examining everything about yourself. Are the feelings even real or am I saying them only because I'm afraid, and does my being afraid make them real? It's a puzzle I turned over and over in my head until I wasn't sure of anything at all. The arrogance gets swept away and you're left feeling more uncertain and vulnerable than at any other moment in your life.

And then when you realize you mean it, that you're in love, well, then it's too late. There's no fucking going back from that or the realization that you're in it alone.

"Don't deny it," I tell her. "Don't fucking lie to me."

"I'm not."

"Stop it, Cora."

She takes a step toward me, making me move back. She tries again. I back away again.

"Listen to me, Leo. I didn't get it. I didn't."

"And you suddenly do now?"

"Yes."

"I don't believe you. What about Beau?"

Her gaze shifts away.

"So you're telling me this as what? A parting gift? No, thanks." I storm past her, scooping up my towel on my way back to the house.

My phone rings. It's my dad.

"Hello?"

"They got him!" He's out of breath and excited. "They got him trying to get back across the border."

I stop just inside the back door of the house. "And they arrested him?"

"The Mexican police have him, but yes, he's been arrested."

Cora touches my arm, making me turn. "They got Winfro?"

Looking down at her hand on me, I nod. I didn't know a touch so soft could be so excruciating. I shift, causing her hand to slide away.

"They got him," I tell her.

Her hands go to her mouth. Above them, her eyes are big and watery.

"Tell Cora I have some more good news. I'm on my way over now. You guys did it. You did it." He ends the call.

"He's on his way over. He says he has more news."

"Oh, my God. I can't believe it. I can't believe they got him. I just can't believe it."

"I'm gonna take a quick shower before my dad gets here." I start forward, then turn back. "I'm glad they got him."

"Thanks. For everything. I couldn't have done it without you."

I nod and turn away. I can hardly look at her anymore, let alone be in the same room with her.

The shower does nothing to change my mood. My dad's already there when I come out. He's sitting on the couch in the living room with Cora. The bright orange sun hangs high over the water, the brightness of it nearly blinding. I drop down into a chair on the other side of the room from Cora. My dad takes notice and looks like he's going to say something, then shakes his head. I try not to look as miserable as I feel.

"What's your news?" I ask him.

"As you know, I had an appointment with the Freedom Project people. I brought them your notes and those photos you sent me of Mrs. Wheeler's notebook. They're taking

Beau's case. While I was there they had a conference call with a retired judge they've worked with before to get his take on it. Nothing's for sure, but they're pretty confident they can get his conviction overturned. It'll take some time. The wheels of justice move at the speed of frozen molasses.

"You kids did amazing work on this case. Seriously, some of the best investigative work I've ever seen. Leo knows he's got a place at the agency if he wants one. Although I'm pretty sure that's not where his heart lies. As for you, Cora, I'd like to offer you a job. From the first moment I met you, you've constantly surprised and amazed me. You're a natural at this. One of the best I've ever seen. I know guys who are twice your age and half as skilled. What do you say?"

Cora's mouth opens and closes. She looks to me and I nod in encouragement. My dad's right. She is a natural. She'd be a great asset to the agency.

"Can I think about it?" she asks.

"Sure. It'll take some time to get a new office set up. Let me know when you decide." Dad stands to go.

"Thank you." Cora leaps up and throws her arms around Dad. "For everything. You've given me so much more than I can ever repay. Thank you for taking a chance on me. And Beau. If he were here, he'd shake your hand." She releases him and wipes away a tear. "Thank you."

Dad clears his throat. "You're welcome."

I walk him to the door.

"You okay?" he asks.

"No, but I'll live."

"I take it things didn't work out between the two of you."

"Something like that."

"I'm sorry. She's . . . one of a kind. I liked the way she didn't put up with your bullshit."

"I did too."

I close the door after him. There's only one more goodbye to make. And it's the hardest I'll ever have to endure. How do you say goodbye to someone who changed your life? How do you go and leave a piece of yourself behind?

35

CORA

When I first started visiting Beau I never thought I'd get used to the procedures you have to go through to enter a prison. Now they're almost routine. What's not routine is the jolt I get when I first see him. Time and repetition have not dulled that moment. It's a shock every time. It's no different this time, except the tears burning the backs of my eyes. We're soldiers in the same war. I want to run to him and hit him hard, throwing my arms around him.

Instead, I walk sedately across the room and sit down across the table from him. I don't comment on the fresh stitches above his left eye or the cuts on his knuckles.

"Hi," I say in my most cheerful voice. "How are you?"

"Better than you." He leans across the table, a line of worry between his brows. "What's wrong?"

"Nothing." I'm smiling, but a tear leaks out. "Everything's great. You won't believe what's happened."

"Did someone die?"

"No." I sniff and wipe at my face. "Your case is being reopened. A judge agreed to hear the new evidence. The lawyers of the Freedom Project say there's a really good chance you'll be exonerated."

"Are you serious?"

"It'll take some time, but you could be free by Christmas." I'm crying so hard now, it's a wonder he can understand me at all.

He sits back in his chair and stares off at nothing. He doesn't speak for so long I think that maybe he didn't understand me.

"Did you hear what I said?"

He nods. "I just don't believe it."

"It's true."

"But it's not for sure."

"No, it's not for sure."

I tell him how Damien LeFeaux recanted his testimony. I tell him about Mrs. Wheeler and her notebooks. I tell him about the hair found in Cassandra's bed that's a match to Paul Winfro. I tell him about Winfro and about how he's going on trial for attempted murder in Mexico. I tell him about how impressed the people at the Freedom Project were with how easy we've made their job.

I don't tell him about Leo and me. I don't tell him about Dylan and Cassandra. I don't tell him that our dad's in the hospital for alcohol poisoning . . . again. I don't tell him what our mom said when I told her Beau could be freed. And I don't tell him that it was Winfro seeing Beau leave Cassandra's apartment that night that drove him to rape and murder her, because in Winfro's mind they were a couple and she cheated on him with Beau.

When I'm done speaking I see something in my brother that I haven't seen since before Cassandra died—hope. I want to start crying all over again. The rush of relief is so great I nearly sag from it. We're in the home stretch.

He doesn't speak for a long time. There's so much to absorb. I lived it and I still get overwhelmed when I think about it all.

"I don't—" His voice cracks. He puts his face in his hands and takes a deep, shaky breath. When he lowers them his eyes are red from unshed tears. "I don't know what to say."

"Oh, Beau. I wanted this for you for so long. I'm just so sorry it's taken almost six years."

"Sorry? Jesus, Cora. What do you have to be sorry about?"

More than I have words for. There's so much more that needs to be fixed.

"Thank you for not listening to me when I told you to fuck off and stop investigating. Thank you for being the only person"—he digs the heels of his hands into his eyes and takes a breath—"who believed in me."

I want to reach across the table and take his hand. More than that I want to hold him and tell him everything's going to be okay.

He rubs his eyes. When his hands fall away I can see that his eyelashes are clumped and wet. "Are you going to get a life now?"

"I have a life."

"Bullshit."

"I'm fine. Don't worry about me."

"What happened with Leo?"

I rub my lips together and look away.

"Ah, shit, Cora. Really? You fucked that up because of me, didn't you?"

"It's fucked up, but not because of you."

"I liked him for you. He seemed like the kind of guy who would call you on your shit."

I nod. "He did that." Too well.

"So what happened?"

"I don't know."

"Bullshit."

"Okay, I know. I fucked it up."

"Because of me."

I don't meet his gaze.

"Goddamn it, Cora. You gotta stop this shit. Get a life. You've put yours off for too long because of me. Go get him back or else I'm not going to talk to you when I get out."

I jerk my head up. "That's the first time I've ever heard you say that. You finally believe you're going to get out of here."

"It only took two thousand one hundred and—"

"Fifty-three days," I finish for him.

He stares at me in disbelief. "Fuck me, Cora. You may as well be doing time in the cell next to me."

I feel almost as though I have.

"That's it." He gets up from the table. "Don't visit me. Don't write me. Don't talk to me until you get your shit together. I have enough to deal with in here without being responsible for fucking up your life too. You're not putting that on me." He storms out without a backward glance.

I can't move. He's never spoken to me like that before.

A guard approaches the table. "Time to go."

"Right. Okay."

I get up and go through the routine of getting out of this hellhole. The drive through the desert is a blur. I don't remember the songs that played on the radio. I take the wrong freeway and keep going. I'm going to get my life back.

I hate my criminal law professor. I should be at a party with my roommate, getting shitfaced. Instead, I'm working on some bullshit side project that gets me an in with him but doesn't do shit for my grade. The doorbell rings. Finally. I swear. For as many times as we order pizza from this place, they never seem to get it here while it's still hot.

I swing the door open, my hand on my ass ready to pull my wallet out, and freeze.

"Hi." Cora. On my doorstep. "Can I come in?" She shifts from foot to foot, her gaze sweeping the interior of my apartment.

"Ahh, yeah. Sure." I hold the door open for her. "Is something wrong?"

"No." She walks past me and her scent hits me with memories.

I close the door and point to the couch. "Have a seat."

"Thanks."

"Do you want something to drink?"

"No, thanks."

We're so fucking polite.

We sit in awkward silence. It's been sixty-three days since I've seen her. You'd think her impact on me would've been lessened by them, but no. I'm just as fucked where she's concerned as the day I watched her drive away from Mike's house.

"I saw Beau today."

"Yeah? How's he doing?"

"Good. I told him the good news."

"He must be relieved."

"Yeah, he is."

"I'm glad. I hope everything works out with the hearing."

"Me too."

"Why are you here?" I think I have the right to ask that after everything.

She rubs her palms on her jeans. "I came to tell you that you were right."

"About what?"

"Me. Us. Everything."

What does she expect me to say? There is no "us" for me to be right about.

I jab a thumb over my shoulder. "I have a project due Monday."

"Right. Sorry. I'll get to the point."

She digs her palms into her thighs. I notice all of her fingernails are bitten down to nothing. The makeup around her eyes is smudged and missing in places. There's a tear in her shirt. She's lost weight. And her hair, always so perfect before, is black before the blue starts. But there's not a woman in the world who compares to her.

She turns her body fully toward me. "What I said to you that day on the beach. It's true. It's more true now than it was then. Everything with Beau isn't settled. The hearing might not go his way. I'm going to take a chance here because if I don't he might never speak to me again."

"Is that why you're here, because he made you come?"

She shakes her head. "No. Beau's never been able to make me do anything. Pisses him off."

"I know the feeling," I mumble.

"Anyway, he said something that was a lot like something you said and it got me thinking. About life and about how I've been doing time like him except on the outside. And I realized that even when he gets out I'll still think of reasons why I can't move on until he does. It could be forever, maybe. Or not at all, if the judge decides there's not enough evidence to free him.

"I looked into the future and it scared the shit out of me. I can't go on like I have been. And I especially can't go on without you. Because I love you and I want you in my life. I want you to be sitting next to me, holding my hand, when the judge delivers his decision. And I want to go home with you and deal with whatever that decision is. So I'm here asking if you still feel the same about me and if you're willing to walk through the uncertainty with me."

My body moves before my brain tells it to. I'm kneeling in front of her, taking her hands in mine. They feel small and strange and familiar all at the same time. She's crying when I kiss her. I can't believe I went so long without touching her and kissing her.

"I love you," she whispers against my mouth.

"Oh, God. I love you too, Bluebird."

EPILOGUE

Beau

I forgot how stiff shirt collars feel and how dress pants ride up and crush your nuts. I yank on my collar for the trillionth time and glance over my shoulder at Cora. She's sitting next to Leo on the hard-assed bench two rows back. He's holding both of her hands in his. I'm glad she finally moved on and got a fucking life. Half of rotting in prison was me wanting to pound the walls and half was me worrying that my screwed-up life somehow screwed hers up too.

My new attorney leans in and whispers something to me. I can't hear anything she says. If I close my eyes I wouldn't even be able to say what she looks like. All of my focus is on the judge. He's glancing through some papers, riffling through them casually, like he's reading a fucking novel on the beach. Everyone in the room is on pins and needles, and it's a regular afternoon for him.

He picks up the gavel and bangs it. He blathers on about the justice system and the balances of justice and some other bullshit I couldn't care less about. One of the takeaways from my justice-system experience is that judges love to hear the sound of their own voices. They love to expound on the greatness of our country's justice system.

They haven't been bent over and fucked in the ass by it.

If they had, they might not think it was so fantastic.

I realize he's addressing me, so I sit up in my seat. I'm playing a role like everyone else in the room. I have to look honest while everyone in the room judges my sincerity. I have to look contrite while everyone tries to figure out if I'm really guilty or not. I have to look worthy while everyone decides if I'm worthwhile.

"Mr. Hollis. I sincerely regret the way in which your case was handled. I hope you find meaning in your experiences and are able to create a life of profound goodness and honor. It is my pleasure to reverse the verdict set down by this court. Mr. Hollis, you are a free man. God bless you. And God bless the United States of America." He bangs the gavel. "We're dismissed."

The courtroom erupts. There's so much noise. My attorney is saying something about filing this and that. I turn in my seat and find Cora. Her face is streaked with tears. She holds a hand out to me.

I'm free.

After two thousand, two hundred seventy-one days, I'm free.

THANK YOU FOR READING VINDICATE! The next book in the RECOVERED INNOCENCE series is ATONE.

★ Nominated in 2017 for the Romance Writers of America Rita® award★

➤CLICK HERE TO READ ATONE

If you enjoyed VINDICATE, please consider leaving a review on your favorite book site. Reviews help readers find books!

➤VINDICATE (RECOVERED INNOCENCE novel)

➤GOODREADS

Join my VIP Facebook group Babes with Books for exclusive sneak peeks at my upcoming books & other, members only, perks:

➤www.facebook.com/groups/BabesWithBooksReaderGroup

Sign up to receive my newsletter for new release alerts, exclusive bonus content, and giveaways!

➤**www.bethyarnall.com/newsletter**

Turn the page to read an excerpt from **ATONE** now!

EXCERPT FROM ATONE

I walked out of the California Institute for Men in Chino, California two thousand, two hundred and seventy one days—nearly six years—after I walked in. I was finally free.

Free.

I don't have the same definition that most people have for that word. While I'm no longer serving a life sentence for a crime I didn't commit, I'm far from free. The repercussions of my incarceration blasted every area of my life, pitting or obliterating everything in sight. There isn't a single thing left unscarred. I don't have a home. I don't have friends. I don't have a job or any qualifications to get one. I don't have any money. I don't have the same family I had on the day of my conviction.

And I don't have Cassandra.

There's a big gaping hole in me where she once lived. Of all of the things that were taken from me she's the one thing I can never get back. I left her sleepy, naked, and sated in her bed six years ago, stealing out of her apartment with other things on my mind, unimportant things. I had an early day the next morning and needed to get home. I bent down, kissed her forehead, told her I loved her, and left.

I never saw her again.

She was brutally raped and murdered that night.

I haven't been able to take a full breath since. Not because of my subsequent arrest and conviction for her murder. That was nothing. Well, not *nothing*. It's definitely something. But it's not why I can't pull in enough air. There's a hole in my chest she used to fill. There's too much space and I can't imagine or even remember what it felt like to be whole. I've been walking around with this big, sucking chest wound since the night she died.

I'm raw yet scarred over. Little things scratch at me, reopening the wound so it never truly heals. A song. The scent of jasmine. A movie. A joke. Her name. I haven't been able to say her name out loud since I screamed it outside her apartment when her body was found and the place crawled with law enforcement personnel.

I see her everywhere. I get a glimpse of her at least once a day. Every time I turn my head I have to remind myself it's not her. It will never be her. I won't get to hold her hand, have her lay her head on my chest the way she used to or make love to her ever again. I can't call her and tell her about the stupid things that happened to me that day. She won't ever tilt her head up with the look in her eyes that was only for me. I haven't laughed in so long I'm not sure if I remember how.

My sister, Cora, thinks I should see someone, a grief councilor. I don't want to. My grief is all I have left of Cassandra. Cora doesn't understand that. No one does. I can't explain it. There are no words for what it feels like to carry it everywhere. I'm pretty sure it's the only thing holding me together. I walk around, going through the day-to-day of living, relying on those feelings to get me through. What would I have without them? Who would I be? I'm not the same man who left Cassandra's apartment that night. I'll never be him again. I shouldn't be him. I sure as shit shouldn't want to be him.

And yet...

Sometimes I wonder what it's like to be *normal*. What would happen if I took off this mantel of grief and laid it down? Would I stop seeing Cassandra everywhere? Would the smell of a common flower stop reminding me of her unique scent? Would I forget what she sounded like, her laugh, and how she felt under me? Would I lose her all over again this time forever?

The air outside of prison not only smells different, it *feels* different. I'm not used to anything resembling normal life. I'm still on prison schedule despite having been out a couple of months now. My only rebellion is letting my hair and beard grow. I don't know who that man in the mirror is. He's rougher, harder than he was six years ago. He has scars and crude tattoos jabbed into his skin by makeshift prison tattoo guns. He looks like he doesn't give a fuck about anyone or anything.

That couldn't be further from the truth.

Cora arranged for me to come to work with her. I think she's hoping it will give me something to aspire to. I'm lost. I don't recognize anyone or anything. I don't know who or what I want to be. There was a time when everything I wanted to do and be was lined up in my head just waiting for me to tick them off like a fucking checklist. Go to college. Check. Get a good paying job. Check. Marry Cassandra. Check. Buy a house. Check. Start a family. Check. Grow old with Cassandra. Check.

None of those boxes will ever be crossed off.

I have to create a new list. But where do I start? I'm twenty-four years old. I should be halfway through my checklist by now. Cora tells me I can do or be anything I want. She pushes community and technical college catalogs at me, trying to get me interested in something. At night I lay awake and attempt to imagine my life a year from now. All I see is me *still* lying on Cora's couch, *still* struggling to figure my shit out. I'm frustrating her and myself. Maybe this Take Your Brother to Work Day will give me some kind of direction even if it only helps me realize what I *don't* want to do.

I wait outside for Cora, sipping a cup of strong black coffee. I got the taste for it in prison. Before that I never touched the stuff. Cora bought me a coffee maker even though she doesn't drink it. She's been good to me. Too good. Better than I deserve. She's the reason I'm leaning against her car on a foggy San Diego morning, waiting for her instead of sitting in a prison cell wondering *why me*. She was the only person who believed in my innocence. The only one. Not even our parents—who should've stuck by me no matter what—considered for a moment that I could be innocent.

I don't know who that says more about—them or me. Cora says them, but I'm not so sure. My conviction destroyed my parents individually and as a couple. I haven't seen either one of them since shortly after being assigned a prison uniform. At first Cora made excuses for them when she visited, and then she stopped mentioning them altogether. We're supposed to have a family reunion this Sunday. Cora arranged it. She's the only reason I agreed to go. I'd do anything for her. She's more than proven she'd do anything for me. She's done *everything* for me.

Cora backs out the front door of her garage apartment,

her arms full. I jog up the walk and relieve her of the files she's carrying. She locks the door and turns to me, a big smile on her face. It gets me every time. A combination of joy and surprise like she can't believe I'm really there. I can't believe it either. I hope I never get used to this feeling or that smile. I hope she doesn't either.

I follow her down the walk to her car and put her files in the trunk. I stand just in time to see the car keys flying at my face and catch them before they smack into my nose.

"You have to practice sometime," she says. "Drive us to work."

I haven't driven in six years. My license expired while I was in prison. My parents sold my car.

"Are you sure?"

She opens the passenger door and climbs in with a wink. I let out a frosty breath in the cool morning air. This is one more thing I have to relearn in my life *outside*. I slide into the driver's seat and adjust it for my bigger body and longer legs.

"The mirrors too," Cora reminds me.

It's like I'm taking Driver's Ed all over again with my little sister as my teacher. I hope driving isn't as hard as riding a bike. That shit took me too many tries to get right. I'm wobbly like a kid riding without training wheels for the first time. Bike riding is a fucked up metaphor for my life now. Everything is an uphill struggle and scary as fuck. I suck so bad at it I wonder sometimes if I shouldn't just commit a crime for real this time so I can go back to the predictability and reliability of prison life. I won't, but the thought is scarily tempting sometimes.

You wouldn't think being free would be so hard.

I do as Cora instructs and start the car. She coaches me the whole way. I'm relieved when we arrive safely. Driving is a hell of a lot easier than riding a bike. We get out of the car and head into the offices of Nash Security and Investigation. I owe Cora and everyone in this place *everything*. If Mr. Nash and his son, Leo, hadn't agreed to help Cora find the bastard who killed Cassandra and worked to set me free, I'd still be sitting in a cell. How do you repay someone who rescued you from hell and gave you your life back?

I juggle Cora's files that I retrieved from the trunk, open the door for her, and follow her inside. The receptionist, Savannah, looks up at Cora, then does a double take when she spies me trailing behind my sister. Her first, fleeting glance is full of female appreciation that quickly morphs into avid curiosity tinged with fear. She doesn't want to be attracted to an ex-con, but I'd put money on her panties being soaked at the thought of fucking me. I'm a walking, talking good girl's bad boy dream. I'm the guy she bangs once or twice on the quiet just so she can brag about it later to her friends.

I grin at Savannah, following it with a wink and lick of the lips. She gasps and presses her hands to her chest, her cheeks bloom red. If we were alone I bet I could take her right there on top of her desk. Wouldn't even have to pull her panties all the way down, just push up her skirt and pull them aside. She'd shower after, feeling dirty, later she'd jack off reliving it. I'm not even slightest bit tempted by her or any other woman I've met since I got out. Another way my life's fucked up.

I set Cora's files down where she directs me. Her office is small with two desks in the middle facing each other. It's an odd arrangement, but Cora likes it this way I guess.

She gestures to the desk opposite hers. "Have a seat." She sifts through her pile of files until she finds what she's looking for, then pulls it out and comes around to where I'm sitting. "I thought maybe I'd start you off with some simple searches." She twitches the mouse, bringing the computer screen to life. "These are the search sites we use."

Clicking on the top three bookmarked sites, she brings them up, explaining how they use them and what info they can provide. She has me do some easy searches, then leaves me on my own. I don't suck at it. I'm actually quite good. And I like the work. I'm half way through the searches Cora wanted me to do when Savannah sticks her head in the door.

"Your ten o'clock is here," she tells Cora, her gaze darts to me then back to Cora.

"Thanks, Savannah. Want to sit in?" Cora asks me. "Take a break from the computer?"

"Sure." I stand and stretch.

Savannah jumps and squeaks, then disappears from the doorway.

Cora's mouth bends into a frown. "I don't know what's wrong with her lately."

"Don't you?"

"I'll talk to her."

"Leave it."

I follow Cora into the reception area. Savannah blocks whoever it is she's talking to so I can't see who it is, but whoever they are they're small, much smaller than Savannah's five-nine frame. Savannah shifts, revealing a pastel confection of a young woman about Cora's age.

All lace and silk, she's sweet looking in her soft colors like she just walked out of a Sunday church service. But the look in her eyes is wary...guarded...jaded, reminding me of angry, hard prison stares. This chick's seen some shit. More than that, she's experienced some shit, has maybe even done some shit. She's a survivor. This I understand. I recognize her in the same way I recognize the new man that stares back at me in the mirror.

Her costume is nearly perfect. I bet if I sniffed her she'd smell like baby powder and lemons. I edge closer to her. She catches me with a sudden flick of a glance, freezing me where I stand. Everything about her shouts *back the fuck off*. It only makes me want to draw closer. Who is she? Who or what made her this way? And why does she look at me like she knows who I am? Not the TV news segment me, but the real me, the Beau deep, down inside.

For the first time since I got out of prison I don't feel alone. There really are others out there like me. One of them is standing mere feet in front of me, regarding me with the same guarded, expectant look I'm wearing.

And she's *beautiful*.

WANT TO READ MORE?

➤One-click ATONE Now➤

★ Nominated in 2017 for the Romance Writers of America Rita® award★

If you loved VINDICATE, you'll love the sexy, funny, award nominated DANGEROUS LINES series. Someone is stalking Miyuki Price-Jones and it's up to former Navy SEAL, Lucas Vega, to protect her.

➤One-click LOST Now➤

Looking for something lighter and funny? Check out THE MISADVENTURES OF MAGGIE MAE series, starting with WAKE UP, MAGGIE, available now! Maggie has to keep her very inappropriate thoughts to herself about the FBI Special Agent assigned to protect her from a murderer.

➤One-click WAKE UP, MAGGIE Now➤

For Hannah Beth, who left us too soon
And as always, for my husband, Mr. Y, for buying into and
supporting every single one of my crazy Lucy-and-Ethel schemes
. . . including the one where I thought I could write a book

ALSO BY BETH YARNALL

Dangerous Lines

Lost

Saved

Fake

Real

Urge

Rare

Betray

Recovered Innocence

Vindicate

Atone

Reclaim

The Misadventures of Maggie Mae

Wake Up, Maggie

You're Mine, Maggie

Find Me, Maggie

Azalea March Mysteries

Killing It In Vegas

Beth Writing as Betty Paper

Crazy On You

Captive

Tinsel

Piano Lessons

BETH'S BOOKS FOR WRITERS

Crafting Unputdownable Fiction series

Going Deep Into Deep Point of View

Making Description Work Hard For You

Some Like It Hot: Writing Sex and Romance

ABOUT THE AUTHOR

USA Today best selling author and Rita® finalist, Beth Yarnall, writes mysteries, romantic suspense, and the occasional hilarious tweet. She lives in Southern California with her husband, two sons, and their rescue dogs where she is hard at work on her next novel. For more information about Beth and her novels please visit her website- www.beth-yarnall.com

f facebook.com/bethyarnallauthor

a amazon.com/author/bethyarnall

BB bookbub.com/authors/beth-yarnall